D0290121

ALL
OUT

Books edited by Saundra Mitchell
available from Inkyard Press and HarperCollins

All Out: The No-Longer-Secret Stories of Queer Teens throughout the Ages

Defy the Dark

Out Now: Queer We Go Again!

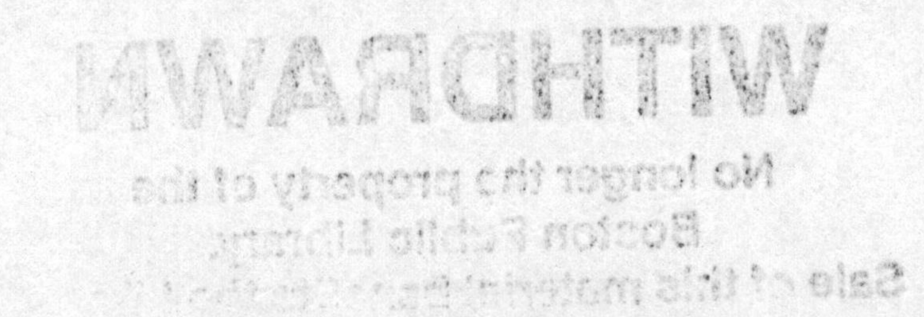

ALL OUT

EDITED BY
SAUNDRA MITCHELL

ANNA-MARIE McLEMORE
NATALIE C. PARKER
NILAH MAGRUDER
MACKENZI LEE
ROBIN TALLEY
MALINDA LO
DAHLIA ADLER
KATE SCELSA
ELLIOT WAKE
SCOTT TRACEY
TESS SHARPE
ALEX SANCHEZ
KODY KEPLINGER
SARA FARIZAN
TESSA GRATTON
SHAUN DAVID HUTCHINSON
TEHLOR KAY MEJIA

ISBN-13: 978-1-335-14681-6

All Out: The No-Longer-Secret Stories of Queer Teens throughout the Ages

This edition published by arrangement with Harlequin Books S.A.

For questions and comments about the quality of this book, please contact us at CustomerService@Harlequin.com.

Inkyard Press
22 Adelaide St. West, 40th Floor
Toronto, Ontario M5H 4E3, Canada
www.InkyardPress.com

Printed in U.S.A.

CONTENTS

For Jim McCarthy.

Thank you for trusting me with your baby.

ROJA

BY
ANNA-MARIE MCLEMORE

El Bajío, México, 1870

They all gave him different names. The authorities, who had been trying for months to catch him, called him El Lobo. The Wolf. *La Légion* called him *Le Loup.*

His mother, back in Alsace, had christened him with a girl's name, though he had since forgiven her for that. It was a name he had trusted me with but that I knew never to speak. The sound of it was too much a reminder of when he'd been too young to fight the hands trying to turn him into a proper *demoiselle,* forbidding him from running outside because young ladies should not do that. His heart had been a boy's heart, throwing itself against his rib cage with each set of white gloves for mass.

I called him his true name, Léon, the one he'd chosen himself. None of this was strange to me, a boy deciding his own name. The only strange thing was the fact that he knew mine.

No one outside our village called me or anyone else in my family by our real names. They worried that letting our names onto their tongues would leave them sick. The rumors said our hearts were dangerous as a coral snake's bite. They carried the whisper that the women in my family could murder with nothing but our rage. They pointed to our hair, red as our skin was brown, and insisted el Diablo himself had dyed it with the juice of devil's berries, to mark us as his.

Abuela had told me our rage was a thing we must tame. Though everyone else feared that our rage might kill them, the lives it more often took were ours. Poison slipped from our hearts and into our blood, she said. The venom spread to our fingers and the ends of our hair.

But even she found a little joy in it. She flaunted it. So we would have enough to eat, she taught me to crush red dye from the beetles that infested the nopales. They were pests, ravaging the cactus pads, but if caught they made a stain so deep red we could sell it. My grandmother even tied tiny woven baskets to the nopales, luring the insects to make nests.

That only added to the rumors. Las Rojas, the grandmother and granddaughter whose hearts blazed so red it showed in their hair, and who made the same color and sold it with stained fingertips. We heard whispers as we passed churches, families drawing back from us, afraid we could kill them with a glare.

Now, as I stood in front of Deputy Oropeza's polished desk, I wished all the stories were true.

"You want El Lobo released?" Oropeza rested his boots on the smooth-finished wood.

The toes of his boots, long and pointed as a snake's tongue, narrowed and curved up toward his shins. They had become the fashion of rich men, who now wore them not only for celebrations but in the streets, the forks nipping at anyone who got in their way.

"Tell me you've come here as a joke," he said. "Tell me one of my friends sent you to see if I would be taken in. Was it Calvo?"

His hand flashed through the air. I flinched, thinking he might strike me. But he was halting me from speaking.

"No, don't tell me," he said. "It was Acevedo, wasn't it?" He clapped his hands. "I swear on the gospel, that man stops breathing if he isn't trying to trick someone."

If Oropeza attended church, if he worshipped anyone but himself, he'd know better than to swear on la Biblia. But I kept silent.

"How much did he pay you to do this?" Oropeza's boots thudded on the tile floor. "Because I'll double it if you help me play my own little trick on him."

The rage in me shuddered and trembled. It felt like it was flickering off my eyelashes.

"No one sent me," I said.

The richest men in El Bajío couldn't have paid me to be here. But I had begged every official who would see me.

Most I found by stopping them in the street. The ones who listened bowed their heads to tell me there was nothing they could do, not for any Frenchman, least of all El Lobo.

The ones who didn't want to hear me—Senator Ariel, Governor Quintanar—shoved me to make me move. They backed away from me like I was crafted out of mud, as though if they came too close I might dirty them.

I was not a girl who could ask for things. I was not powder and perfume and lace-trimmed fans. The kind of women who could wheedle favors from wealthy men wore dresses in the purples and deep pinks of cactus fruit. They wore silk and velvet ribbons tied as necklaces. The owners of blue agave farms sent them sapphire and emerald rings.

They were not girls in plain huipils.

But Deputy Oropeza had agreed to see me. Hope had bloomed in the dark space beneath my heart. Yes, he wore the pointed boots of rich men, but he hadn't gotten into the same competitions the others had, driving one another to have boots made with toes as long as I was tall. Maybe there was reason in him.

"Please," I said now.

The war had ended. But the hills still lay scorched and barren, and Léon had been captured as an enemy Frenchman. Un francés. And now a blindfold and a bullet waited for him at dusk.

"He didn't even want to fight with them," I said. "He deserted."

The things Léon had seen had driven him to betray his own country. I hated *la Légion* for what they had done to Léon. He hated them for letting their soldiers loose on this land. They raided villages, throwing women down on the earth floors of their homes, killing the men and keeping locks of their hair as trophies.

And those were only the things he had been willing to tell me, as though I myself had not known families killed or scarred by the French uniform. But he didn't see the brown of my skin and consider me less than he was. He did not see the red of my hair and decide I was wicked. He saw me as something soft, a girl he did not want to plague with nightmares.

By the time Léon deserted, he had grown to hate not only *la Légion* but his own country, for starting this war in the name of unsettled debts, and for doing it while los Estados Unidos were too deep in their own civil war to intervene. So Léon had done the small but devastating things that earned him the name *Le Loup*. At night, he strolled into French camps wearing his stolen uniform. The blue coat with gold-fringed epaulettes. The red pants that tapered to cuffs at the ankles. The stiff yellow collar that rubbed against his neck when he nodded at the watchmen as though he belonged there.

He stole guns, throwing them into rivers. He set horses

loose, driving them toward villages too poor to buy them. He pilfered maps and parchments, leaving them burning for the men to find. The rumors said he'd even called wolves from the hills, scattering the camps. But when I'd asked him about that, he only smiled.

Now the memory of Léon's smile stung so hard I looked for the cut of it on my skin.

"He was working against them," I told Oropeza.

Oropeza looked out through the silk curtains and onto the rows of curling grapevines.

"Then he is a traitor," Oropeza said. "He is not even loyal to his own country. What would make you think he would be loyal to you?"

He turned his gaze to the square of tile where I stood in my huipil. In that moment, I saw myself as Oropeza must have seen me.

Men like Oropeza would never consider me worth looking at. I was short, wide hipped, a girl from the villages. I had only ever been told I was pretty by my abuela.

And Léon. My lobo.

Oropeza laughed. "The little campesina thinks el francés loves her?"

Campesina. I knew what that word meant to him, how he wielded it as both insult and fact. It was a word men like Oropeza kept ready on their tongues, a way to show their judgment both of where I had come from and the shape of my body. To them, my height and form marked me. A peasant's shape, men like Oropeza called it, a shape made for work close to the ground.

"All he told you was lies," Oropeza said. "He might have thought you were a little bit interesting." He gestured at my hair. "A distraction."

The salt of my own tears stung.

"One day you will thank me for what I've saved you from," Oropeza said.

I set my back teeth together. He considered me and everyone like me a child. Men like him thought they had more of God in their hearts than we did, as though they held it in the lightness of their skin, or, for a few of them, in their eyes as blue as the seas their ancestors had crossed to claim this land.

Oropeza lurched forward, clutching his chest as though it had cramped. And then his stomach, as though he'd had a portion of bad wine.

I stepped back.

The venom in me, carried in my family's blood, was spilling out. It had built in me, spun and strengthened by my rage. Then it had flowed into the air between me and Oropeza until he was sick with it.

This was the poison of Las Rojas, the venom our rage could become.

I kept myself back, pressing my tongue behind my teeth to stop myself.

I could not let the poison in my blood make Oropeza sick. If he'd heard the stories about my family and realized they were more truth than superstition, he would have me dragged into the street and killed as a bruja.

One of Oropeza's men showed me out. My steps led me over the polished tile, and then out into Oropeza's front gardens.

Léon had stayed for me. He had kept himself here, caught between *la Légion* he'd deserted and this country that considered him an enemy. And he'd been taken for it.

He'd never had the stomach for *la Légion*. He'd told me the night I found him, once I'd given him enough water for him to speak and he'd come out of the fever enough to make sense with his words.

He'd only joined because it had given him a way out of

Alsace. He'd been told that *la Légion* would never check on the name he'd been born with, the name that would give away more than he ever wanted anyone to know of the body he kept beneath his clothes. The chest he bound down. The shoulders and back he worked hard enough that they could take as much weight as any other man's.

And *la Légion* hadn't checked. They did not want to know. They preferred their *légionnaires* forget who they'd been.

He could take the fighting, and even the beatings they gave *les légionnaires* to harden their spirits. But he could not stand how his *régiment* let the men work out their rage on village women. How they killed brothers or husbands who protested.

Léon had spoken up enough that they considered it rebellion. So each night they beat him in a way they called *les couleurs*. Blood on one cheek, bruises on the other, the pale, untouched stripe of his nose and lips between. The colors of the French flag, meant to put the allegiance back in him.

The night I found Léon, he'd worn those colors. It was the first time he'd tried running, and they'd caught him. So they'd tied him to one of the acacia trees that bloomed yellow each spring. His back against the thin trunk. His wrists and ankles bound behind it so he could not stand. All he could do was kneel.

They had told him that they may or may not come back for him, and if they did, it would be because they were curious if the wolves had eaten him.

That night, una vieja from our village had sent me into the woods. She asked me to bring her an oyamel branch from the fir tree she always held a little of as she prayed. I only noticed Léon because, at the sound of brush crackling under my feet, he lifted his head. His forehead shone with sweat. And through his fever, the thing I would later come to know as his charm seemed a kind of delirium, a madness. He'd mumbled a few words in French before saying, "If I'd known a beautiful woman would be calling on me, I would have made myself presentable."

I unbound him and brought him home not because I was kind. I brought him home, holding him up as his eyes opened and shut, because if it had not been for the mercy of the other families in our village, my abuela would not have had a proper burial. I could not have done it myself. My heart was so weighted with losing her I was sure it would pull me into whatever hollow in the ground I made for her.

So I brought home this tall, underfed boy with hair so blond the moon made it look white. I boiled water and made pozole, to show God I was grateful, and that there was mercy left in me.

But there was no mercy in men like Oropeza, and Ariel, and Quintanar.

I had failed Léon. I had lost him. And now, at dusk, when a shot rang through the air, I screamed into the sound.

I screamed into the wind bringing me the rattling laugh of the men who killed Léon. I sobbed into the silhouettes of mesquite and acacia, and into the darkening blue of the sky.

Still screaming, I crossed myself, saying a prayer for the soul of Léon Bellamy.

Léon, the boy who made me laugh when he tripped over rolling his *r*'s. Léon, who had startled the village with his eyes, so pale gray that at night they looked silver, and his hair, light as bleached linen. Léon, who had won them over with his wonder about armadillos, how the animal rolled itself into a ball of plate armor.

Léon, the boy who had put his mouth to my ear and told me the brown of my skin made him think of wild deer roaming the woods where he was born.

Even in this moment, opening under me like a break in the

earth, Abuela would have told me to find some small thing to thank God for. There was one, just one, I could get my fingers around.

No one, not *la Légion,* not Oropeza, ever knew Léon as anything but a boy. They did not know that his mother had christened him with a girl's name. They did not know that he had joined *la Légion* less out of patriotism and more for the chance to live as who he was. If they had, Oropeza would have thrown it at me, mocked me for it. He would have made clear what he thought of us, Léon living among the other soldiers with his bound-down chest, me lifting my chin in the street as though I were the equal of the powder-pale women in their escaramuza dresses.

But even this small mercy broke in me. All of it broke.

First I had lost my grandmother, made sick from her rage over what this war had taken. She always warned me not to let my rage kill me, but in the end her own had spread its venom through her.

They said this war was over, even as women wept over their stoves and into their sewing. Even now when an Alsatian boy had just been blindfolded and shot.

My rage felt so hot it would singe away my smallest veins. There were so many empty places where everything I had lost once fit. Now there were only the dustless, unfaded patches where all I loved had been.

There was nothing left. Yes, there were the women who had loved me and my abuela; my abuela had fed them when they were sick and prayed over them when they bore children. There were even the ones who had taken to Léon like he was a stray. But now they only reminded me of those empty places.

I found the few clothes of my grandfather's that Abuela had kept, the ones he'd left behind. He had dared to hit her once, and her rage had struck him back so quickly, felling him, he called her a witch, yelling, "Bruja," as he fled our village.

I hemmed his trousers with quick, rough stitches. I stuffed his boots with scrap cloth so they would fit. I had the small, wide feet of my grandmother, the edges rough from years of running without shoes.

Like a silent prayer, I gave her my gratitude. Abuela had wanted me to play outside barefoot as much as I could stand, so that if ever I could not afford shoes, my feet could go without them. Now I understood what my grandmother had wanted, for me to keep my heart soft but the edges of me hard enough to survive the world as it was.

My grandfather's poncho, I plunged into red dye, the rough agave taking it fast.

At night, the color wouldn't show. But I would feel it against my skin.

I would not let this rage kill me. By using it, I would drive it from my body. I would turn it against the last man who would not save Léon. The man, who, by dawn, would be robbed of his finest things.

Oropeza's guards, I took first.

I neared the hacienda with my head lowered. My hat hid the red of my hair. The brim shaded my face. I left the guards no chance to wonder if I was some messenger boy bearing midnight news, or whether they should draw their brass-throated pistols. I let my rage stream into them. I let it become liquid and alive.

They fell, one gripping his side, another holding his chest as though the venom clutched his heart.

Anything I could carry, I stole. Fine cigars. Money and papers from the desk drawers. Jewels that had once belonged to Oropeza's wife; Abuela was sure he had killed her with his cold heart as well as we could with our poison.

I slipped through the house, the moon casting clean squares of light through the vestíbulo windows. The strap of my woven bag cut into my shoulder, heavy with all I had taken.

The rustling of grape leaves outside and the tangle of voices stilled me.

Oropeza and his friends stumbled drunk through the dark grapevines. Calvo and Acevedo and other men with more power than sense and more money than mercy.

They laughed. They swapped echoes of the same questions.

"How much are los franceses giving you for the traitor?" Calvo asked.

"How did you even manage this?" Acevedo asked. "I thought the only Frenchmen you knew were the ones you'd had shot."

"Why didn't I think of this?" another man asked.

"Because you're not as smart as I am," Oropeza said.

A question had just formed in me when I saw the figure held between them, being shoved forward and made to walk. Blindfolded, his wrists bound behind his back.

Because he could not see, he stumbled, drawing their laughter. The long points of their boots needled his shins.

They were forcing him toward the road that ran behind Oropeza's estate.

My gasp was sharp as the first breath waking from a nightmare, the moment of wondering if, as in those dreams, my fingers were made of lightning or the sky was truly a wide blue blanket woven by my abuela's hands.

Léon.

They hadn't let the firing squad take him.

Hope bubbled up under my rage, but with it my anger thickened.

They hadn't killed him, not yet. Instead, Oropeza was trading him to the country that now considered him an enemy.

Trading him for money, for favors, for the currencies of men who owned so much ground but never bent down enough to touch it.

He was surrendering El Lobo to the country that called him *Le Loup,* the country Oropeza declared his enemy but still bargained with in secret.

My hope lifted my rage higher, driving it into a swirling cloud that flew out the windows and rushed at the men. It caught them, striking them down like el Espíritu Santo had slain them.

But this was not God's work. This was not the Holy Spirit filling these men. This was the work of una Roja. A poison girl, veiled in men's clothing.

The men fell to the ground, holding their throats and chests and sides. The richest ones, the ones whose boots had the longest tapered points, twisted to keep from stabbing themselves with their own shoes. Oropeza jerked as though demons poured through him. My vengeance, a vengeance I shared with my grandmother and all Las Rojas, was toxic as thorn apple and lantana. It was poison as strong as moonflower and oleander.

I threw open the glass-inlaid doors to the back gardens. I stepped between writhing men and grabbed Léon's arm, pulling him with me. I caught the smell of his hair. Even now, it held the scent I'd come to think of as the countryside in Alsace. Dust and rain on hills. Fields covered in the blue of flax flowers and the gold brush of oats. He'd brought it with him on his skin. And when he told me the brown of my naked back reminded him of the deer that roamed that land, he gave me a place in his country.

Even through my rage and my fear, my lips felt hot with wanting to touch his skin. They trembled with wanting to give him my name.

Oropeza gazed up at me. His face showed no recognition, only the fear that I was a boy born of robbers and devils.

Through the open doors, Oropeza yelled into the house for his servants. He called them stupid and slow. He called them fools.

They ran across the tile. But when they saw the scene, when they saw the writhing men, and me, and the blindfolded man I had stolen from their patrono, they sank to the floor. They clutched their stomachs as though they, too, had been poisoned.

My breath stilled with worry that I had made them ill, that my venom was in them even though I had no rage for them.

But they caught my eyes, and smiled.

They twisted as though I was striking them down, so they could not be blamed for letting me rob Oropeza.

They had heard the stories. Las Rojas. They noticed the wisp of hair falling from my grandfather's hat and onto my neck. They saw me as the poison girl I was, a daughter made of venom, even as I hid in my grandfather's clothes.

I held on to Léon, leading him around the stricken men.

Oropeza and his friends would not die, not tonight. But they would thrash on the tile and the dirt until I was too far for my anger to touch them.

"Who are you?" Léon asked. His breath sounded short more from trying to press down his fear than from how fast I made him walk.

I cut the rope off his wrists and pulled off his blindfold and kissed him as fast as if I had more hands than my own. I didn't care if the act would reveal me. My rage kept these men down like a blanket over a fire.

Léon's lips recognized mine. He kissed me harder, setting his hands on my waist to hold me up.

"Go," I whispered, my mouth feathering against his jawline.

Now he smelled like sweat, and the bitter almost-rust tang that I swore was the last trace of his fear. But under these things I found the smell I remembered. The warmth of flax and oats, things his family had grown for so long his skin carried the scent across the ocean.

"You have to run," I said, my forehead against his cheek.

"I'm not going anywhere," he said. His breathing came hard. I could feel his heartbeat in his skin. "Not unless I'm going with you."

I pulled away so we could see each other as much as the dark let us.

"They took you because you stayed for me," I said, still keeping my voice to a whisper. "I am poison. Don't you see that?"

Léon set his hand against my cheek.

"Emilia," he said, quiet as a breath. He meant it for no one but me.

The wind hid the strain of his breathing. The far lamp of the moon turned the gray of his eyes to iron. The sound of my name made me feel like the cloth on my body was blazing to red, my hair a cape as bright as marigolds.

"You are here and I am alive." Now his accent turned sharp, not his practiced Spanish. "So tell me what makes you poison."

He put his hand on the back of my neck and kissed me, this boy who wanted to belong to the girl I was, brown and small and poisonous.

To the men, we might have looked like two boys, one pressing his mouth to the other's. Tonight, we would pull off our shirts and trousers for each other. Léon would be a boy, no matter the shape of his chest beneath his shirts. And I would let my hair fall from my grandfather's hat and be the girl I had always been to him. For Léon, I would put on my best enagua just so he could push the soft cotton of the tiered skirt up my thighs. I would let my breasts lay against his skin. I would kiss where the rope had cut into his wrists and the cloth into his temples.

I wanted to protect his body as though it were mine.

But my own, I wanted these men to see it, and remember. I wanted them to know that I was my abuela's granddaughter, that I carried the blood of poison girls.

The men still lay on the floor, gripping their chests and ribs.

I lifted my red poncho and my shirt, and I showed the men my breasts.

The moon lit the rounded shapes. It lit the fear on the men's faces, the horror on Oropeza's.

I gave them only that one second, just enough to let them wonder in the morning if they had imagined it, and then I let my shirt fall.

I reached for Léon. But it was not the men he was watching, or even me. He stood in the moon silver on the vestíbulo floor, looking out toward the hills. He lifted his face to the sky, breathing like he was taking a drink of the night itself.

And the wolves came. They came with their claws ticking against the ground and their muzzles stained with the blood of their last prey. They came with coats the same red gold as the hills they had run down from. They came with their backs streaked dark as the ink of the night sky.

I drew back from them, the wolves now crouching at the edges of Oropeza's property. Then I caught Léon's smile, slight but intent, telling me we had nothing to fear from them.

Léon took my hand, and we ran down the steps, the wolves filling the space behind us. They stood as guards, moving toward Oropeza's men only when the men moved to pursue us. When the men lifted their heads to watch us run, the wolves showed their teeth. When they shouted curses at us, the wolves growled and snapped.

That was how Léon and I left them, both of us showing hearts so fierce these men considered them knives. We fled from the feigned cries of the men and women who worked for Oropeza but who loved us for defying him. We fled from the howls of men who wailed more for their pride than their bodies. We left them with the salt-sting memory of us, a brazen girl, and a boy with a heart so fearless wolves were his guardian saints.

Many stories found us after that night. Some said the French soldier known as El Lobo had called down from the hills a thousand wolves who not only scattered the men but ravaged Oropeza's grapevines. Others said a girl known only as La Roja poisoned them all with her wicked heart, hiding the red of her hair so they would have no warning.

Some said El Lobo and La Roja were enemies, rivals, the girl capturing the French soldier just so she could have the pleasure of killing him herself. Others said La Roja stole El Lobo, only to fall in love with him the moment she first touched him.

When we hear word that every rich man who witnessed that night has died, I will tell the rest of the story. I will say what we have done since that night. What haciendas Léon has called wolves to destroy. What merciless hearts I have poisoned with the rage in my own. All that La Roja, the girl with the red hair and the red cape, and El Lobo, the boy as feared as wolves, have done.

But this is the part I will tell now. We rode off on Oropeza's finest Andalusians, the wolves' call at our backs. We vanished into the midnight trees faster than first light could reach us. We lived. We survived to whisper our names to each other even if we could not yet confess them to anyone else.

★★★★★

AUTHOR'S NOTE

I grew up loving fairy tales. But as a Latina, I didn't look much like the girls I saw in storybooks. Later, realizing I was queer, the loves I saw portrayed in those fairy tales felt even further away.

When I went looking to reclaim a fairy tale in a historical context, I could think of few better starting places than Leonarda Emilia. An outlaw in early 1870s Mexico, Leonarda had a short but infamous career that began when officials executed the French soldier she'd fallen in love with. Known to history as la Carambada, Leonarda wore men's clothing, but became notorious for revealing her breasts to the powerful men she'd just robbed as she rode off.

Léon is a tribute to the many assigned-female-at-birth soldiers who have fought in wars throughout history; though in most cases history doesn't give enough context for us to know what these soldiers might have claimed as their gender identity, Léon is imagined here as a transgender character. As this story's interpretation of the Wolf, he, along with Emilia's

Red, are meant to embody the spirit of la Carambada. With much respect to the historical Leonarda, this story takes liberties in the spirit of reclaiming a well-loved fairy tale for the communities I'm proud to call mine.

For their thoughts, advice, and guidance, I owe much gratitude to Elliot Wake, Jayne Walters, Mackenzi Lee, Tehlor Kay Mejia, the trans boy I'm lucky to call my husband, and of course, editor Saundra Mitchell. Thank you for helping this story navigate the path between history and fairy tale.

THE SWEET TRADE

BY
NATALIE C. PARKER

Virginia Colony, 1717

Clara Elizabeth Byrd had been married twice by the age of sixteen and she had decided she had no taste for it.

Her first husband, Mr. John du Pont, being of Huguenot lineage with an estate on the James River, had been a kind man. Though nearly twenty years her senior, he had not laughed when Clara suggested he might make her a wedding gift of a sloop. Instead, he asked in what color he should commission the sails be dyed. Clara imagined that they'd have made good companions for one another had he not swallowed a chicken bone and died before the cake had been cut.

It was a tragic affair, resulting in Clara's return to her family home farther down the river. The sloop came, too, in accordance with Mr. du Pont's presumed final wishes. Clara was incandescently thankful. Never mind that she had not yet learned to sail it. She had read every novel on the subject and was certain she could manage without too much trouble.

Before she had occasion to try, her father selected a second husband for her. Mr. Frederick Earwood, as if the name weren't bad enough, was a quiet young man with no humor about him. Upon learning of his betrothed's sloop, he sat back in his chair, studied one corner of the ceiling so intently it seemed he'd quite forgotten there were others in the room and then said in a careful monotone, "We shall take the ship with us if only to dismantle it and use its parts for firewood this winter."

In that moment Clara determined her second husband would be her last. She devised a plan, requesting to be wed in the Lower River Chapel on the bank of the James. From there, they would retreat to Mr. Earwood's holdings near the Carolina border. Her sloop would be moored by the dock awaiting its miserable journey inland.

Which, of course, it would never take.

In all the tales of adventure Clara had ever heard, it was never young girls who were daring. It was always boys running off to rescue a friend or fetch much-needed medicine or stumble into good fortune. Clara knew girls would be daring if given half the chance. And she intended to take that chance, right from under the pale nose of Mr. Earwood.

And so it was that Clara Elizabeth Byrd took a second husband in order to have her first adventure.

She spent the weeks leading up to the wedding putting her scholarly knowledge to practice, sailing the sloop a little farther each day. She loved it every bit as much as she expected. The sun on her face and the wind in her hair, the horizon glinting with promise. She was meant for a life in full view of the sky.

Soon, the wedding was upon her. The vows were necessary, and so, unfortunately, was the moment Mr. Earwood was given permission to kiss the bride. Mr. Earwood leaned close, his lips puckered as delicately as a doll's. Clara feigned a girlish giggle, neatly pressing her own lips to his cheek.

Though it displeased Mr. Earwood, the congregation applauded her charmingly modest sensibilities. No one raised an eyebrow when she begged for a few moments alone after the ceremony. And while the rest of the party processed toward the town green for cake and feasting, Clara raced to the river and climbed aboard her sloop, where she'd stored everything she would need to make her journey: a few precious coins, clothing, some food, a fishing pole and even a sword from her grandfather's trunk.

The sun was just passing into the west as she raised the main sail and jib. The air was sharp with the last chill of winter, the trees eager to send green shoots into the Virginia sky. A thin sweat coated Clara's brow as she worked to unknot the ropes that kept her little boat tethered to the dock. If anyone saw, she would surely be stopped and dragged back to the side of an irritable Mr. Earwood.

The skirts of her black silk gown were twisted around her ankles in the narrow spaces. She'd have preferred to wear her new green mantua gown for the occasion; its open cut would've made maneuvering around the ship much easier. But both her maid and her father had been horrified at the idea of a bride wearing such an unlucky color, so she'd relented rather than give herself away. Now she moved slower than she desired on account of not wanting to trip and fall headfirst into the water.

Finally, with a ferocious shove, her little sloop drifted away from the dock and into the steady current of the river. Though the sloop was a modest size for traveling the James, twelve feet from prow to stern and four feet across, it would be noticeable due to the brilliant yellow of its sails. Mr. du Pont's generosity was both a boon and a curse, and since she could not obscure the color of the sails, Clara needed to disguise herself to avoid discovery.

Stowed on the boat was a set of boy's clothing, stolen a piece at a time from her own father's laundry, which she would don as soon as it was safe to do so. For now, she slapped one of her father's old cocked hats on her head and kept her body hidden in the belly of the hull, emerging only to adjust the boom when the wind shifted.

She sailed thus, lying flat on her back with her eyes trained on the gentle billowing of her yellow-dyed sails, until the sunlight sliced orange and pink across the sky. The air began to get cooler, the sky above darker and all of a sudden Clara felt a chill of fear. She was alone as she had never been. Alone with precious few possessions and no notion of where to take them except away from Mr. Earwood and the promise of a landlocked life.

It was then that she heard it: sudden splashing in the river and shouts in the distance. Her pulse quickened and the chill she'd felt only seconds before was replaced by a fresh sheen of sweat. She lay on the bottom of her boat with ears pricked and eyes open wide, hoping the sounds would pass her by. But instead of moving off, the splashing grew nearer, the shouting louder.

When her boat rocked sharply to one side, it was all Clara could do to keep from crying out in surprise. She bit the inside of her cheek and waited for the rocking to subside.

Nothing followed. Her boat resumed its course, floating smoothly downstream. Had she bumped a stone? Had some large catfish mistaken her for food?

"You there! Boatman!" The shout carried across the river to Clara's ears.

The shock of it caused her to bite too hard on her cheek. She tasted blood.

"Good sir! Pause and speak with us!"

If she lay in the bottom of her boat, they might assume it

was adrift and come out to retrieve it for themselves. If she answered, they might know her for a girl and still come out.

Though her hands shook, she knew she must move. Lifting only her head, she spied two figures pacing her on shore. They were smartly dressed and bore expressions of determination and mild panic. The one in front was tall; his stride was commanding and bold. The one behind had a flower pinned to his brocade waistcoat and ran twice as fast to keep apace with his friend. Here the banks of the river were peppered with long stretches of tall, marshy grasses several feet deep. The two men had to run farther up the hillside in order to see the river where she sailed.

Clara pitched her voice low. "Good day to you, sirs!"

With a pinch of panic, Clara noticed how the man behind seemed to pause midstride, as though aware that something was amiss. The other plowed on, shouting, "Have you seen a girl? She came this way! Did she cross the river? A girl!"

For just a second Clara's mind reeled. These men would know her for the runaway she was and force her to return to the dreadful life she'd only just escaped. She would be married and her sloop dismantled by sundown. But her sense returned nearly as quickly as it had fled. They sought a girl from their side of the river. She was not the delinquent they pursued.

Clara thought of the splashing and suspected it had been no catfish that had nudged her hull. She placed a steadying hand on the boom as the wind shifted. The sloop rocked in response. Lowering her chin and keeping her voice deep, she responded, "I'm afraid I haven't seen her. There's been nothing but sunlight on the water with me this day."

The taller man nodded his thanks and bolted back up the gentle hill to the pine woods above. The shorter man didn't follow immediately, but studied her for a long moment. It was too far for her to see clearly, but Clara was sure she could see some hint of malice in the slope of his shoulders.

Finally, both men were gone from sight. Clara adjusted the boom and carefully climbed to the starboard side of her little boat. Keeping her hat firmly atop her head, she peered over the lip of the hull and directly into the wide brown eyes of a girl.

She clung to the side of the ship like a barnacle, her face barely above the water as the boat swept her along. Her hair streamed behind her, and her lips were drawn tight across chattering teeth. Clara could see that she wore a gown as yellow as the sails above, which was probably trying mightily to drag her down.

Without a word, Clara removed her hat, then reached down with both hands to pull the girl aboard. The boat heaved and cold water sloshed over the side, but soon the girl was huddled beneath the jib, safely onboard.

Clara tightened the sail at once. The wind was in their favor and moved them swiftly downstream, away from any who might still be searching for a runaway girl or two.

"I'm Pearl," said the girl. She'd found the last glimmer of sunset and sat inside it. The light made her brown hair burn and her eyes glassy and deep. "Thank you."

"I'm Clara. You're welcome."

"I suppose you'd like to know who those men were?" Pearl asked, and without waiting for an answer, she plowed on. "The one who shouted was my brother, William, and I do feel badly for deceiving him. He's never been cruel to me, at least, not intentionally. The other was Mr. Michael Pitts, my husband-to-be, and I don't feel badly for him in the slightest. Mealy, indecisive and selfish. Took me to wife out of 'the kindness of his heart.' Pah! Well, I left him out of the meanness of mine."

Clara had not intended to inquire, but she was glad Pearl spoke so freely. "You ran away from your wedding day?"

Pearl raised her chin, defiance shining in her eyes. "I did."

It occurred to Clara that Pearl's dress was yellow. Not blue to signify years of faithful love, not pink to announce her purity, but yellow, the color of pagans and the wildest of flowers. This was a girl she knew already, even as she knew her not at all.

"Me, too," Clara answered, fluffing the skirts of her own black dress. "And I am sorry for the disappointment my father will feel, but I am full of too much life for Mr. Earwood. I'd have driven him to an early grave."

Pearl laughed. "Pitts and Earwood. They should be friends."

"After this, perhaps they will be!"

Pearl's smile softened. "I know we certainly shall be."

Something in the curl of Pearl's voice called a corresponding curl in Clara's breath. She did not respond and the two girls drifted in silence while the sun slowly drained from the sky. Clara sighted a particularly reedy section on the opposite side of the river from where Pearl had just fled and nosed the sloop inside it for extra coverage. It would be a cold night on the sloop, but it was still too dangerous to camp on shore. They would have to make do with what little heat her lanterns could provide.

But Pearl would need more than that.

The girl made no complaint, but she shivered in her layers of wet dress. She would make herself ill sleeping in such a state.

"Here," Clara said, offering her single change of boy's clothing. "Put these on."

Pearl accepted them gratefully, cold fingers brushing Clara's as she took them from her hands. Though they were surrounded by mere reeds instead of sturdy walls, Pearl quickly began the work of loosening her dress. Clara helped, tugging on cold, wet lacings until her own fingers burned.

The work was so familiar that it didn't occur to Clara that

Pearl was a near stranger until the dress slid from her shoulders, leaving only the shift behind. Then it wasn't only her fingers that burned, but her cheeks, her lips, her chest. She turned away to give Pearl her privacy and tend to the stirring in her lungs.

"I have bread and cheese," she said, rooting through the bag she'd stowed on the sloop ahead of time. "Jars of preserves and a few bottles of wine."

"You're my savior," Pearl said, voice muffled by cloth. "Let's start with the wine. Tonight's a celebration after all."

"You're right," Clara said, feeling the truth of it expand in her lungs. "We did it, Pearl. We left."

"And tomorrow's all about the life we choose."

The life we choose. The words were said with such anticipation that for a moment, Clara felt overwhelmed. She had spent so long trying to imagine herself inside a house she had no hand in creating, imagining the rooms and cabinets and nearest neighbors she might have as a married woman in a new town. Now there was no house, no town even, and the possibilities seemed as long and steady as the river rushing past.

The girls opened their wine and tore their bread and scooped generously of fig preserves. They drank until the bottle was gone and ate until the jar was empty, and then they lay on their backs on the flat nose of the sloop.

"What was your plan?" Clara asked. "Just…run?"

Pearl's laughter sounded like merry song of a wood thrush. "From start to finish. The thought came over me all of a sudden. I was standing there, at the entry of the church, staring down that short aisle to a long future with a man who was already calculating the value of our wedding gifts. And I tell you before I knew what I was about, I was running out the doors and down the road. So, yes, 'run' was my plan. And it worked, I'll remind you."

"Barely! And by luck alone!"

"What was your plan, then? More than run, I assume?" Pearl leaned up on her elbow to level Clara with a playful glare. "Did you steal this boat, Clara? You might've chosen something less conspicuous than a sloop with yellow sails."

It was Clara's turn to laugh, and she felt self-conscious as she did. "It was mine, but seeing as I was married when I took it and all my belongings were also Mr. Earwood's, it's probable he thinks I stole it."

"You're an outlaw," Pearl teased.

"In good company," Clara teased back, noting the way Pearl's gaze slid to her lips and back again to her eyes. "And my plan was to take my sloop and ride the river to the open ocean. I've food and a fishing pole to keep me fed, a blade to keep me safe and skills to keep me afloat."

"And then what?" Pearl asked.

Clara was almost afraid to say it. For so long, she'd nurtured this secret desire knowing anyone who heard it would think her too childish for the world. The words had been so long held back that now they feared coming out. But in the flicker of lamplight, Pearl's smile was encouraging.

"Do you know of the Sweet Trade?" Clara asked, fiddling with the delicate lace on her stomacher.

Pearl's expression was skeptical. "Piracy? That's your plan? Become a pirate?"

"It is," Clara answered seriously. "All my life, people have told me what to do or taken what's mine. The same is true for you! We've been raised among pirates who call themselves gentlemen. And I'm ready to turn the tables. I'm ready to take what's mine and maybe a few things that aren't."

"That sounds like a lovely sort of justice." Pearl smiled as she leaned close, her breath sweet with figs, her lips stained purple with wine. "Perhaps I'll join you and we'll rule the Carolina seas together."

"I'd gladly take you amongst my crew."

"And I would gladly join it."

Clara felt warmth spreading through her cheeks. Pearl's smile was softer now, her brown hair falling around her face to curl at her chin near her lips. She looked perfectly unkempt and radiant. Clara had started this day evading a kiss she didn't want, but she would end it with one she did.

Clara leaned up, and Pearl leaned down. Their lips met, gently at first, then more urgently, one kiss diving into the next and the next like little waves until they parted to breathe. Clara rested in Pearl's arms, a sheet of brown hair covering them both.

"We shall be the most dreadful of pirates," Clara said, cupping Pearl's chin in her hand. "Because between us, we've left three husbands wanting."

Silence fell around the girls. Clara watched as Pearl drifted away from her, though her body remained so near she could feel its gentle heat. Finally, after several long moments, Pearl sat up and spoke again.

"It won't work," she said. "It's just a dream."

"This whole thing is a dream. But we've made it real," Clara protested.

"No, maybe if we were boys, this would work. But we're not. We're only girls, and this won't work." Tears shimmered in Pearl's eyes. She scooted away, huddling in her boy's clothing, her cheeks still flushed from the kiss. "We have to do something girls can do."

Clara knew that she hated everything Pearl had just said, but she had no solution for it. "Perhaps you're right," she said. "We should get some sleep."

The girls settled down to sleep with their eyes on the stars above and their ears full of crickets and owls and the soft shushing of the river. It all sounded like tomorrow and like the future and like a life they'd chosen. For better or worse.

The morning came with a cold drizzle and the sound of men's voices.

Clara awoke sharply. Her skin was damp and shivering cold, but her heart was thumping heat into her veins. She could feel Pearl beside her, hear the sound of her steady breathing. Still asleep.

Making as little noise as possible, Clara rolled to her side, placed a hand over Pearl's mouth and gently shook her awake. She startled, but seeing Clara's face, she settled again at once, nodding to show she understood.

All around, tall grasses shuffled in the early-morning breeze, providing them cover, but obscuring their view of the shore. The girls sat still in their bobbing boat, listening again for the sounds of men.

They came softly at first. Low, indistinguishable voices threading through the reeds. Not until they came a little closer was Clara able to determine that there were two of them. She raised two fingers and Pearl nodded, agreeing.

Two girls to two men. They were decent odds, but Clara felt a tremor threaten in her breast. She stilled it with a plan.

Leaning close to whisper in Pearl's ear, she said, "The plan is to run. I'll ready the boat. You get my sword and be ready to look fierce with it."

Pearl nodded, but asked, "Where's your sword?"

Clara pointed to the cloth bag she'd filled with everything she could think to need, including one of her grandfather's short swords. Now she wished she'd thought to grab a second.

The men's voices grew louder and the girls quieter. They pushed their wool blankets aside and slipped around the boat as seamlessly as water. Pearl sorted through the bag with care until she produced the sword, and Clara eased the boat out of its moorings with smooth, steady motions. Soon, the sloop was free, held in place only by the thicket of reeds they'd nested it in overnight. But it would go nowhere without lifting the sails to catch the breeze, and that was sure to draw the notice of these men.

Clara was deciding how best to execute their escape, when she heard a shout, "You there! Lad!"

Pearl stood at the stern of the sloop, her hair tied at the nape of her neck, one hand resting on the boom for balance, the sword in her other. She looked every bit a boy in her breeches and waistcoat.

Without wasting a second, Clara whistled and tossed her cocked hat to Pearl, who snatched it out of the air and pressed it on her head. Next, Clara scooped up the still-damp yellow dress and tucked it in the narrow hold of the sloop's nose. She finished just as the two men spotted them through the reeds and called out again, "We don't mean you no harm, lad. You can put the sword away."

The voice was terribly familiar. By the way Pearl's hand tightened on the hilt of her sword, she thought so, too.

"We're looking for a girl. Maybe you've seen her?"

Now Clara recognized the voice. It was that of the man who'd called out to her yesterday afternoon. Pearl's brother, William, which meant the shorter man standing to his side was Mr. Pitts.

Pearl made no move to answer. In response, her brother began to push through the reeds. "Lad?" he called, coming into full view. His eyes landed on the sails. Though still wrapped and bound, they were glaringly yellow.

Clara jumped to her feet and moved to Pearl's side. "Please

excuse my brother. He's not much for conversation so early in the morning. I'm afraid I'm the only girl we've seen."

Pearl's brother stopped, eyes settling on Clara's face. It was still dim, but he was near enough now to see her clearly. His dark brown eyes traveled from her to Pearl's tucked chin with a hint of suspicion.

"We're out for the crabs," Clara offered, attempting to draw his focus back to her. "We've got traps down the river. But best of luck finding your girl."

Now Mr. Pitts stood forward, his narrow nose reaching only to William's shoulder. He raked his eyes from one girl to the other, but it was the boat he settled on, studying it for a long minute.

"You were alone yesterday." Mr. Pitts's voice was as dense as his gut.

Pearl shrugged, careful to keep her head bent away from the bruising gaze of Mr. Pitts. "So I was."

Clara could hear the slight shudder in Pearl's breath, but Clara wasn't afraid. She smiled kindly at the men, then gave Pearl a shove. "The mainsail won't raise itself, Jack."

Pearl took the invitation, throwing herself at the mast though she didn't have a clue how to do as instructed. But it didn't matter. The men, convinced these two had nothing to offer them, moved along down the banks of the river.

Clara joined her friend at the mast, quickly loosing the riggings and raising the sail. Within minutes, they were back on the river, riding the wind away from trouble.

"Jack!" Clara crowed when she was sure they'd put enough distance between them and the men. "Do you know what this means?"

"That I owe you twice over?" Pearl's voice was drawn tight as the sail.

"Yes, but also, it means we don't have to be boys." Clara

danced to her friend's side to steal the hat from her head and place it on her own. "They only have to think we are and we can be whatever we desire."

A smile teased at Pearl's lips. Clara pressed her advantage.

"What do you say, Pearl? Come with me to Carolina. Join my crew. Be my pirate brother."

The sun slid glittering pink across the river, gilding the horizon in layers of light like silk. It looked like treasure.

Pearl's chin tipped down as she studied her boy's clothing. She smoothed one hand over the fabric of her waistcoat with an expression that settled somewhere between distress and wonder. Her silence felt heavy like the prelude to disappointment, and Clara felt an unexpected pang in her chest.

But then Pearl's hand was in Clara's, her eyes flashing like sunrise and steel swords and stolen kisses.

Clara held her breath until Pearl gave her answer.

"I say you'd better get used to calling me Jack."

★ ★ ★ ★ ★

AND THEY DON'T KISS AT THE END

BY
NILAH MAGRUDER

Maryland, 1976

She listened to the sizzle of the neon sign overhead and pulled her jacket tighter around her in the early-autumn chill. Her left shoulder was weighed down by the pair of roller skates her parents had bought her for Christmas, the pair she'd hinted and begged and cried for, a jaunty light brown with slick red wheels. She tilted her head and searched the street for an untidy mop of curly dark hair poised atop a skinny frame.

Because if she saw Vince Ramirez anywhere near the skate rink tonight, she was taking her tail straight home.

Dee's friends knew she brooked no nonsense. She wasn't about to let herself get caught in some black-teen *The Parent Trap* by nosy, overly concerned friends who thought they knew what she needed better than she did.

But Lori had promised her Vince wouldn't be there. Apparently he'd stopped coming to the rink just after she had. Maybe she was the only reason he came out skating at all, but she wasn't thinking about that. She was just keeping an eye on all the other kids laughing and running into the rink for Skateblast Saturday Fun Night.

So far, what Lori had told her looked to be true. The rink was safe. It was hers again.

She stood a little straighter. A shock of nerves ran through her when she saw Lori making her way up the street with MaryAnn and Roger behind her. But Vince wasn't with them.

"Sorry," said Lori with a big grin as she wrapped her arms around Dee's shoulders. "You been waiting long?"

Dee shrugged. "Not really."

"This fool," said MaryAnn, and she elbowed the tall boy leaning over her like a wilting willow, "changed his shirt about five times."

"Hey," said Roger, who was fingering the edges of his fro even as he spoke. "You said you like your man looking sharp."

The two began to bicker. Lori rolled her eyes and gave Dee a conspiratorial grin. Dee laughed, and the two of them headed arm in arm up to the counter to pay their admission. They were still early. The floor was only starting to fill up. In an hour it'd be full of gliding bodies, all a blur under the strobing, tinted lights.

Dee and Lori sat side by side on a bench. Dee pulled the red laces of her skates snug, flexed her ankles and toes and stood. Three weeks she had been avoiding the rink. She hadn't gone so long without skating since the previous summer when she'd caught bronchitis.

She stepped onto the slick surface with practiced ease, one foot and then a push with the other. She was a long way from the tiny girl she used to be who couldn't get onto the rink without clinging to the wall. She was already pacing ahead of Lori, Roger and MaryAnn, but she didn't look behind her. They'd catch up.

She let her momentum carry her into the bend at the end of the rink and then crossed the right foot over the left to glide through the turn. She'd missed this. Skating was so much easier than avoiding Vince. They didn't have any classes together, thank God, but he seemed to be everywhere anyway. She'd stopped going to the library, too, because she didn't want to take unnecessary chances. Which meant most days she got through school as quickly as possible and then booked it for the bus home.

But Vince was a good guy, a really good guy, so he wasn't trying too hard to seek her out. It was probably driving him nuts that he didn't know why she'd cut him off and wouldn't explain. She couldn't remember a single day since they'd met that they weren't talking in between classes or hanging out in the library at lunch or hanging out after school.

Her dad had asked last Sunday why he wasn't over watching *American Bandstand* with them, which she thought was the greatest injustice. He was always fussing about that walking-stick boy with the bad haircut hanging around their house like he didn't have anywhere better to be—and he was full of it, because a couple times Dee had run upstairs and caught them talking about basketball enthusiastically when she came back down. "Well, at least he's not over here eating all our food like usual," her dad had said, even though he was always the one who reminded mom to set an extra plate.

Lori and MaryAnn reached her at the far end of the rink. "Where's Rodge?" Dee asked, perhaps a little too quickly. She tried to look nonchalant, but Lori had already detected the small note of panic in her voice.

"Some of the guys showed up," said Lori, and made eyes at the lockers. They could plainly see Roger at the center of a group of boys, laughing and elbowing each other. Vince was still not present. "Girl, you should just move on," Lori continued. "Look, there's Tony. He's so tall and fine. Go see if he wants to skate with you."

"I don't want to skate with anybody," said Dee with a bright, overly sweet smile. "I got you guys."

MaryAnn laughed. "Uh-huh! That's not what you were saying a month ago. It was just Dee and Vince." She said it in a melodic, drawn-out way, brushing Dee's shoulder with her own, fluttering her eyelashes.

"Vince and Dee," Lori added from Dee's other side, mirroring MaryAnn and ignoring Dee's scoff. "I'm surprised you remember our names."

"I still don't get why you're mad at Vince," said MaryAnn. "What he do?"

Dee sighed, because she didn't know how to answer that. Because Vince hadn't done anything. And because MaryAnn was always one step behind, a little out of sync. She didn't have to explain these things to Lori. Somehow, Lori always just knew what the problem was without Dee having to tell her.

"It's not about what Vince did," said Lori. Dee could feel the playful smirk on her face. "It's about what Dee did."

MaryAnn leaned in. "What'd you do, Dee?"

"You didn't see them holding hands during the couples' skate?" said Lori. "They were skating all close and slow, the lights were dark and we were just watching, and then outta nowhere Dee just let go and took off in the middle of the song. You didn't see all that?"

"Nooo!" gasped MaryAnn. "You did that, Dee?"

"Man, shut up, Lori," said Dee, and she shot ahead of them. She could hear Lori and MaryAnn calling after her, but she rounded the next bend, zigzagged smoothly between other skaters and didn't look their way.

It reminded her of last time. She and Vince were in their own world, but she'd come out of it when she heard Lori and Roger's boys snickering behind them.

And yet, even now, she wondered why she had let go of

Vince's hand. Was she embarrassed? Was she not ready for what their friends would say about them? What they would *expect*? Was there even a way to prepare for any of that?

Dee met Vince Ramirez almost a year ago, when he showed up in her biology class at the beginning of the spring semester. Dee and her classmates had been curious about the Filipino kid starting classes in the middle of the year. But he'd found his stride and fit in seamlessly, and soon he became background like most of the boys in Dee's class.

A few weeks later, Vince showed up at Saturday Fun Night at the local rink. The DJ played hits by Donna Summer, James Brown, and Ecstasy, Passion & Pain, sodas were free with a slice of pizza, and Dee and her friends went practically every week. Roger invited him. They had become friends, because Roger was friends with everyone and it was only a matter of time.

"Hey, Dee, you met Vince?" said Roger. "He likes *Soul Train*, too!"

"So?" Dee laughed. "Everybody likes *Soul Train*."

But they talked. About the Bee Gees, Archie Bell & the Drells, and Chaka Khan. About *Soul Train* and *American Bandstand*. And that Monday, in biology, they kept talking. The following summer was a blur of poring over vinyls in the record store, riding their bikes to the library, the newsstand and the snowball stand next door. They chewed candy and popcorn while Dee told Vince about the novel she'd read that week and Vince showed off his stack of comics. And every Saturday night, there was skating.

Until three weeks ago, at least, when she'd let go of Vince's hand and left him on the rink floor like a jilted lover, which was ridiculous because they were only friends. But there had been laughter and whoops from several mouths as Dee skidded off the rink floor.

The sounds followed her like the bays of disgruntled spectators from the box seats, robbed of a show. An older, smarter girl would have been more inconspicuous, and then perhaps everything would be all right now. Dee could only wish to have that level of charm and sophistication.

She wished she could be like Elizabeth Bennet. Her English class read *Pride and Prejudice* last semester. She'd loved the book so much she'd bought her own secondhand copy that she'd found in the Salvation Army store. She told Vince all about it, about how headstrong and clever Lizzie Bennet was, but Vince didn't really care about old-timey English literature. Dee liked how independent and gracious Lizzie was. She liked the reserved and distinguished Mr. Darcy. She liked that their romance was driven by intellect, conversation and art.

She liked that there was no kissing.

She had never seen the appeal of kissing, not after Mary-Ann had kissed her first boyfriend at the end of sixth grade and told half the block about it, not when Dee had had her first kiss freshman year, at one of Nadia Boone's weekend basement parties full of beer and disco.

That had been a whole year before Vince moved to town. Kevin Campbell was sweet, but the kiss had been messy and wet and Dee had been very miserably aware of every second of it. It had gone on forever, and not in a good way.

Dee had giggled with Lori much too loudly about it not ten minutes later. She'd locked eyes with Kevin standing just a few feet away, realized he'd heard every word and she didn't even feel bad about it.

Boys had tried to kiss her after that. When they stopped her to chat in the halls, or leaned into her at parties, she always found some excuse to slide away and go hide between her girlfriends. None of them seemed to care that she'd laughed about kissing Kevin right in his face—not even Kevin. He'd even invited her to go to the carnival with him a few months later. They went together with their friends, watched other couples laughing hand in hand, arm in arm, and Dee had never felt so outside of her own skin.

Lori and MaryAnn were into trashy romance novels. They devoured them like penny candy. They'd loaned a couple to Dee but Dee always cringed when it got to the steamy parts—or worse, she laughed. Those moments always took her right out of the story—and considering they *were* the story, she got taken out pretty quick.

Was this what romance was supposed to be? Was this all there was? And if that was the case, why didn't Dee want the same kind of romance as Lori and MaryAnn—and pretty much every other girl she knew? They were seventeen and already MaryAnn and Lori seemed to know so much more about sex than she did.

One time MaryAnn had shown her and Lori a porno. They'd watched it at MaryAnn's house late one night while her mother was working at the hospital and her dad was passed out in the living room with a couple of beers and the news still playing. They'd watched it in MaryAnn's room with the volume turned low.

Lori and MaryAnn had giggled and laughed and gasped, while Dee squirmed. Halfway through she'd got up to go to the bathroom. Instead she'd sat down with MaryAnn's dad and watched *NBC's Saturday Night*.

She wondered if Lizzie Bennet would suffer through a porno. She couldn't imagine it. She also couldn't imagine Lizzie laughing about kissing Kevin Campbell (well, maybe she would) or leaving Vince Ramirez alone in the middle of the rink.

Lori had suggested that maybe Dee wasn't into guys. Lori wasn't, and sometimes she linked fingers with other girls at the rink. Dee didn't think it was about boys and girls. She didn't know how to explain that she preferred to have no preference at all, and so she said nothing.

"What's with you, Dee?" Beverly Henderson had once asked her. "Don't you like anybody?"

Sure, she did. Dee liked plenty of folks, but she knew that's not what Beverly was really asking. What was with her, dodging away from perfectly good boys in school hallways, grinning at them under the rink's colorful lights and then skating away? Teasing them with full lips and long legs when she could be kissing them? Dee grimaced at the very thought.

Later, she'd caught Beverly calling her a prude once in the east stairwell, but Dee didn't mind. Maybe that was what she was. She didn't know what else to call it. Maybe there was no word for the way she felt.

Sometimes Dee tried to force herself to get used to the idea. She'd picture herself fooling around with Vince, kissing, letting their hands roam over one another. And she didn't care. Weren't you supposed to care? Weren't you supposed to want it? Why have sex if you didn't want to?

It wasn't just about Vince—it wasn't really about him at all. It was about Dee. She was pretty sure she liked Vince—pretty sure she *really* liked him, but what did that mean?

Why had she let go of Vince's hand? Because she wasn't ready for whatever was coming next. Because what if he wanted more? And what if she wasn't interested in giving it? Because letting go of his hand had seemed like a better option than him letting go of hers—because that was what would happen. The future—*their* future—loomed in front of her like an insurmountable wall, and she wasn't sure there was any way over it.

As she made another lap, Dee looked across the rink to the low wall on the other side. Roger was off the floor again; a few more of his buddies had just arrived. She didn't recognize all of them, but she recognized the one with a mop of curly dark hair, slim legs in corduroy bell-bottoms and a sports jacket he could practically swim in.

He turned his head, and she felt it like a lightning strike when their eyes met. Lori and MaryAnn were at her side not five seconds later, and she had to commend their response time.

"He's not supposed to be here," said MaryAnn. "I told Rodge—"

But Roger looked just as surprised and embarrassed as her friends did now. "We didn't know, Dee," said Lori. "I swear!"

Dee leaned away, and with the scrape of wheel on wood, she left them behind.

She could leave. But she'd have to squeeze by Vince to do it. Then…she could wait, just until he hit the floor and then she'd skate off, grab her shoes and be out the door before he'd made his first lap.

But she had left him that way once already. Her palm tingled at the memory. She had a feeling taking off that way again would sever whatever connection they still had. She'd be turning her back on the past year forever.

She wheeled toward the lockers. Vince was doing a poor attempt at pretending he was talking to his boys. He was still watching and saw the look she gave him. And then he was separating from his friends and hurrying to put on his skates.

Both her hands were tingling now. No, they were sweaty. Her body was warmed up from the lights and countless laps around the rink. "Jazzman" was blasting from the speakers, one of her favorite songs to skate to. As Vince crept up beside her, she used the familiar upbeat rhythm and Carole King's soulful voice to give her strength.

"Hey," said Vince, so quietly under the music that it was easy to miss. Dee said hi in return.

And then, silence...well, save the music from the speakers, and the sound of dozens of small plastic wheels turning around the polished hardwood floor, and laughter and chatter from every other person in the building. She had to say something, but every time she gathered up the words to speak, she felt the silence pressing closer and let the words go. The truth was, she just didn't know what to say.

"I should've said this sooner," said Vince suddenly. "I just didn't know how, and I didn't think you'd want to talk to me. But I'm sorry."

"For what?"

"For, you know, last time. For taking your hand. I should've asked first, asked if...if you were okay with it."

Yeah, darn right you should've, thought Dee, but she felt a pang of guilt, as well. The truth was, she couldn't remember who'd grabbed whose hand first. And she couldn't remember not enjoying it. "Well, it wasn't all you," she mumbled.

The song changed over to "Reasons" by Earth, Wind and Fire. They glided in silence. Dee listened to the rotation of their wheels on the polished wood surface, that soft, reassuring sound as she searched for words.

Before she found them, Vince said, "I read it."

Dee glanced at him. "You read what?"

"Pride and Prejudice."

Dee gaped. She nearly tripped and slowed to regain her balance. Vince slowed with her. He was looking at her with concern.

She looked back at him, wide-eyed. "You can read?"

Vince pushed her shoulder lightly. "Shut up." He shrugged. "We weren't hanging out, and I didn't have anything better to do."

"What'd you think?"

He shrugged again. "It was long. But I liked it."

"Who was your favorite character?" Dee was hoping he'd say Lizzie, Jane or Mr. Darcy.

Vince tilted his head. "I guess…that Bingley dude."

Dee's eyes widened. "Mr. Bingley?"

"Yeah. He was okay. I think I related to him most. How he knew he liked Jane, but was too polite and chickened out of telling her. And it took him twenty years to finally get around to it."

"It wasn't that long."

"Well, it felt like reading it took twenty years." At that, Dee pushed him away. He smiled and arched back toward her, and she found herself smiling, too. "What I mean is, I get how hard it is to tell someone what you're thinking. Especially when you like them. And sometimes you're so close, you assume they know what you're thinking, but it's not really fair… I mean, I'm kinda rambling, but—"

"No," said Dee quickly. "I get it."

She took in a deep breath and let it out again. She understood what he meant, not just for him, but for her, as well. She curled her fingers into her palms, readying her words like armor. Because what was she waiting for? She was no Mr. Bingley.

I am a twentieth-century black Lizzie Bennet. I like a boy. I like talking to him, I like his eyebrows, I like his laugh when I tease him, I like how he debates me on nineteenth-century heroines and twentieth-century superheroes, I like his secret sports conversations with my dad, I like how he focuses so hard when he dances even though he's not good at it, I like how he skates like he was born to do it. I like what I like and I don't like what I don't. I have nothing to apologize for.

"Kissing makes me laugh," said Dee quietly.

Vince turned sharply, peering at her through his long bangs. "Who've you been kissing?"

"No one. Just…the thought of it. It's just weird to me. All of it's weird to me, dating, and couples, and making out…" She rolled her hand and left it at that.

"Oh."

"I'm just a prude, I guess," said Dee.

"I've never called you a prude."

"No, but everybody else does."

As the song ended, the DJ seamlessly slid on another record. The lights dimmed low, way low, almost to full darkness but for the slowly turning tinted lights that passed over the floor and the walls. Dee held her breath against the flutter in her heart.

Couples' skate. Here they were again. Some skaters took this opportunity for a break, going to the restrooms, grabbing snacks from the bar. Other skaters found each other in the dark and linked hands.

Vince kept skating, and so did Dee.

"It's just, I don't know what it all means," said Dee. "I don't know why I feel this way, or if I'm gonna change—if I'm supposed to change, or—"

Vince laughed, and normally Dee would already be puffing herself up to give him an earful, but it just made her sad.

"I guess I'm being dumb," she said.

"Nah," said Vince. "I don't mean it like that. It's just skate night, Dee. We're just skating. I'm still trying to figure out things about myself, too. Who I am, who I want to be. But it's not gonna happen all at once."

"How do you know?" said Dee. "Maybe this is going to be the moment that the spotlights turn on and you have a big epiphany right here in the middle of the floor."

They fell silent. They looked around. But the lights stayed dim and the music kept playing, and they laughed.

"All I'm saying," said Vince, "is we don't need to have ourselves figured out in one night. You know?"

Dee's heart was fluttering again, but in a different way. She felt a warmth there that was spreading to her stomach and her limbs. She turned her head away a little, because she couldn't suppress the smile growing on her face and she didn't want Vince to see it, not quite yet. "Yeah. I know."

Dee dropped her hand by her side. She didn't want to wait to see if Vince would grab it. She didn't want to guess what he would think if she made him wait. So she turned up her palm.

And Vince's fingers grazed her skin, prodding and searching. Their fingers slid together slowly. They rolled along, their arms brushing, blue and purple lights casting an artificial twilight over skaters in like, or in love.

Lizzie Bennet would enjoy skating, Dee thought.

★ ★ ★ ★ ★

BURNT UMBER

BY
MACKENZI LEE

Amsterdam, 1638

Two weeks into the new year—the third of our apprenticeship—the master painter Cornelius van der Loos declares me the best of his students.

Though not for my skill behind the easel—I have yet to master shadows in the still lifes, so my light often seems to be coming from a cosmically improbable sun that has been spread across the sky like a pat of melted butter.

But I am the boy most accomplished at not becoming distracted by the first naked woman we draw. Which is something, I suppose.

It has been all *vanitases* and still lifes for us for years, though just before Nieuwjaarsdag we graduated to plaster casts of the human frame, so the appearance of the living versions in our studio seemed inevitable. But the first day that van der Loos plucks a round-hipped girl from De Wallen and perches her in the center of our circle atop a stool for us to sketch, the study for the other apprentices seems to be more about keeping themselves in control as van der Loos calls for her to change positions and she presents us with an arched back that make her breasts reach for the ceiling.

But for me, it's as easy as not going hard over the Delft candlesticks and Jakartan pomegranates we have been sketching since we were twelve.

Though if it were Joost Hendrickszoon reclining naked on a ragged sofa in front of me, a barely there whisper of silk draped over his most vulnerable bits—or, God help me, perhaps no silk at all—it would be me gasping down lungfuls of the frigid January air with my breeches tented, trying not to think about how desperately I would like to put my hands on some tackle that wasn't my own.

It's been a time since I spoke to Joost—though *spoke* seems too generous a term for the blushing conversations I occasionally stammered my way through with him after Sunday services. That hasn't stopped me from fantasizing about him without his clothes on when I am supposed to be staring at van der Loos's girls and sketching them in repose. His family put their money in Viceroy bulbs and when the tulip market shattered, he had to abandon his own apprenticeship with the faience maker and take up work with the dockhands who load the cargo onto the East India clipper ships.

I catch sight of him sometimes from afar, down at the docks, when van der Loos sends Augustus and me to fetch his imports for his *vanitases* and sacks of pigment powders, the sort than can be bought only on the other side of the world. As we load our handcarts with the smalt blue of Delft china or the yellow ochre stripes on the inside of an Iris petal, the thought of Joost somewhere nearby always has me by the throat. Even when he's not in my sights, I can picture him—the muscles in his arms tense beneath the weight of porcelain, the concave hollow of his back bowing beneath their weight. All the anatomy lessons of my apprenticeship put to questionable use. Once, when he passed us by with a crew of the burly dock men, he winked at me, and I was so flustered I dropped a crate full of dried puffer fish from the West Indies I was holding. When we cracked the lid back at the studio, we found half of them had crumbled into dust, and I took a lashing over the knuckles for it from van der Loos.

But Joost winked at me. All things have a balance.

So my apprenticeship gives me charcoal stains in the creases of my palms, knuckles scratched from catching loose nails when we spread canvas over frames, my fingers dyed the color of Admiral Liefken tulips from priming red ochre pigment, while Joost broadens out his shoulders, sculpting him a silhouette like one of those Renaissance Christ paintings in church I used to stare at so long my mother thought I might become a clergyman.

But so long as it is a woman draped across the sofa in the center of our sketching circle, I'll be, as van der Loos proclaims, the best apprentice in the Guild of St. Luke.

Though, it is mortifying to be declared thusly in front of a room full of the other boys, half of them rising to attention when our model stands at the end of the session and reaches down to touch her toes, presenting us with a near telescopic view of her nethers. Johannes's charcoal falls out of his hand and breaks in two against the floor, and Augustus already has that glazed look in his eyes of being halfway through a fantasy about taking this girl out behind the Wolf's Head and getting his head under her skirt. Though knowing Augustus he'd be so sweaty with nerves if he ever got this girl alone he'd probably slide right off her. When we boil the linseed oil for binding, he can hardly look *me* in the eyes—I can't imagine a girl would be any easier on him.

From the back of the room, van der Loos knocks a hand against the wall, so hard and sudden that all the boys startle, eyes ripped from the model. "Good lord, it's like you've none seen a woman before."

None of us want to be the one to admit that we haven't—Braam, the oldest of us, is fifteen, so up until now it's been mostly mothers and sisters and the occasional tavern whore for all of us.

Van der Loos shoos the model into the back room, then stalks forward to the center of our circle. A curtain sheltering the high windows catches on his lace collar as he passes and he swats it free.

"What's this?" He flicks at Braam's parchment, which is mostly devoted to breasts. "Is this what a woman looks like, or what you want her to look like in your fantasies, Englen? And this, Hermanszoon?" he snaps at Johannes, who reaches up like he's going to cover his work and keep the rest of us from seeing it. Van der Loos passes Augustus's easel without comment, but pauses on mine. I brace for a criticism, but instead he says, "This is well done, Constantijn," and I start—I hadn't realized he was so near to me.

He takes up my sketch and holds it for the other boys to see. "And you know why this is well done? Because it does not reek of childish fantasies. Constantijn here has sketches that are anatomical. No breasts that defy gravity or exaggerated curves. You would all do well to adopt his attitude—this is not the last naked figure we'll be drawing, and I expect a certain level of work from you." He drops my board back on the easel, then claps me hard on the shoulder. "Well done. You did very well today."

I try to look pleased, but the compliment sends my heart hiccuping. A singling out is enough reason to be taunted on our walk home, perhaps get a handful of snow stuffed down the back of my breeches. I've done the stuffing before—we all have. But to be called out for being the only boy entirely disinterested in the female body could have a different end. They drowned a guild master in Delft last year, and shaded taunts don't take long to darken into rumors. Though the danger of a jest holds little water with these rich boys whose parents pay fifty guilders a year for them to become painters, who will never have to grit their teeth when they lie with a woman or worry their minister will confront them about their unclean desires that could end tied to a millstone and tossed into the sea. Whose desires their masters condemn, but at least they're boyish.

I leave the studio that night sweating in spite of the winter cold. Most evenings, the five of us apprentices walk from van der Loos's studio along the Uilenburgergracht to Dam Square, where we break apart, following the veins of the canals to our homes, but I try to clean up as quick as I can and escape alone. I'm the first one to leave the studio—I realize halfway down the stairs I've left one of my gloves behind, but I can't muster the courage to go back to fetch it.

I'm half a flight from the gate when I hear the lumbering thud above me of the other boys' klompen on the stairs. They swarm around me on the street, like I'm a boulder in their stream. I speed up, trying to stay a few steps ahead with my scarf pulled tight around my face, but I can still hear them behind me.

"Eyes ahead, Constantijn," Braam calls. "Don't want you getting *distracted*." He strikes the last syllable like a cymbal, just as a clump of slushy snow slaps the back of my head. I don't turn around.

"Look at Constantijn, so focused."

"Doesn't even notice the girls all around him."

"Have you ever seen a girl before, Constantijn? Come out tonight and we'll give you some tutoring."

Another lump of slush hits near my feet. No wonder Braam's vanishing points are always a few inches off.

I pull up the collar of my cassock and walk faster, but my klompen slide on the stones, still slick with last night's new snowfall. I have to grip the bridge rail as I cross the canal like it's a lifeline just to stay upright.

"What do you like more, Constantijn—girls or dogs?" Braam calls, and Johannes laughs.

"Girls or chickens?" Johannes adds.

"Girls or sailors?"

"Go to hell, Braam," I say, quiet enough I think they won't hear me but I'll still get the satisfaction of having told them off under my breath.

But Johannes hears—he's deaf to instructions about canvas priming but he's dog ears for everything that isn't meant for him. "What's that, Constantijn? You're going to hell?"

Dam Square looms at last—the milky green dome of the weigh house wears a hat of new snow, militias of sharp icicles lined along the gutters. The low clouds swallow the spire of the Westerkerk over the tops of the canal houses. A breeze spools off the water, bitter and ripe—I can smell the stench of the harbor, oysters spitting seawater and herring left to fester in shining piles upon the rotting slats of the docks. My stomach heaves.

I would be smart to joke back jovially, pretend like the taunts didn't sting like rust on a razor, then say yes to a drink when Johannes suggests it. Probably would have been good to muscle down a kiss with a carmine-cheeked whore just to prove that I don't find the female form almost entirely repellent. Maybe if I look long enough it won't be; all these weeks of nude studies adding up have built up my tolerance. Maybe sinful desires can be cleansed through prolonged exposure, like colors faded from a canvas by hanging too long in a sunny corner of the house.

But instead I keep walking as the boys peel off toward the Wolf's Head, letting their taunts roll off me like the snowballs melting down my back. I duck down Raadhuisstraat and across the Singel Canal, toward my parents' house. They'll have the stove lit, peat smoking in its belly, and my sister will take my cassock and my klompen and they'll want to know about what I'm painting and my mother will have herring and none of this will matter. In a few moments, I can be home and pretend everything is fine.

"Constantijn, wait!"

Against my better judgment, in the middle of the bridge, I turn. Augustus jogs up beside me, his feet sliding on the icy planks. I grab his arm before he falls. "Thank you." He ruffles his hair, a powdered snow like the sugar dusting on oliebollen scattering over the front of my cassock. "Sorry, I..." He starts to brush it off for me, then stops, his face going red.

"What is it, Augustus?" I ask, and my voice sounds like van der Loos's, pinched and tired.

"What? Right. Yes." He fumbles around in his satchel, then comes up with my missing glove. "You left this. Back at the studio."

"Oh. Thank you." I try to take it, but he doesn't let go as fast as I think he will, and it clenches up between us like a taut sailing rope. Neither of us let go for a moment, but Augustus shies first, and the glove slumps into my knuckles.

He scuffs a toe along the ground, his klompen making a horrible scraping noise against the ice. "They're just jealous, you know. Because you draw so well."

"Is that what it is?"

"Truly. You're the best of us." He kicks a lump of muddy

snow and it bursts against the rail like a Catherine wheel. "Have you thought of your specialization yet?"

"Landscapes. Maybe. I don't know. Not nude women."

"Why not?"

"They're..." I scratch the back of my neck. "Not really my subject."

"Nor mine. I liked when we were painting the fruit."

"The fruit?"

"Fewer breasts on the fruit. I mean..." He presses his hands to his cheeks. "I'm not good at breasts."

"Most fruit is rather breast shaped, though."

"But they're not so squishable. They're more solid. So the shadows are easier on the fruits. And I like the colors." He's got his hands up in front of him, flexing them, gripping these imaginary not-breast squishable fruit, but then he shakes them out, like he's only just realized what he's doing. "God, what a conversation. If someone were to overhear us."

I laugh. "The scandal of naked fruit."

"The church would have a whole business around making dresses for apples and pears by the week's end."

"That'll be the new commodity now that the tulips have failed."

"And it would be a very specialized profession, since only those with the tiniest hands could sew these tiny dresses for the fruit."

I laugh again, almost more from surprise than at what he's said. Augustus is so quiet and nervous in class, I've never heard him speak so freely. Or realized how funny he was. When he looks up at me, the reflection of the dying light off the canal catches his eyes, the warm umber of cane sugar.

Augustus smiles, the tips of his ears poking out from under his knit cap pink where the cold nips at them.

"Well," he says, after a moment of staring at each other,

our breath fogging the air between us. "I'm back that way." He points back over his shoulder, toward the square. "Don't worry about what Braam said."

"I'm not."

"I know. But if you were. Or if you need to hear it. You're all right."

He reaches out and touches my shoulder, so quick it's almost imaginary, then walks away, leaving the cold clawing at me, each breath burning as I swallow it and coming up misty and white, warmed by my lungs.

By the end of February, the girls have become more ordinary—we can all draw hips and breasts in a creative array of positions now, most of us without exciting ourselves. We still draw the plasters, now interspersed with models once or twice during the week. When we're not sketching, van der Loos has Augustus and me glazing his undercoats for a new series of domestic scenes while the rest of the boys mix his pigments and prepare the pallets, so we spend most mornings shoulder to shoulder, our hands sticky with glaze. Augustus sometimes hums under his breath while we work, his usual twitchy hands still and steady on the brushes.

A snowstorm buries Amsterdam and we're out of the studio for three days, all of us trapped in our homes, and when we return, we're all buzzy and talkative, so the shout of someone entering doesn't register with me straight away as out of the ordinary. I'm stretching parchment on my board, trying not to smudge my charcoaled fingers over the edges, but then I hear Braam say, "What are you doing here?" And I look up just as Joost Hendrickszoon steps out from the studio doorway, his wool cap crushed between his hands.

I drop into a nonsensical crouch beside my easel, an action born purely from the panic of seeing him out of context and so unexpectedly, then fumble around for something to do so my sudden drop to the ground looks even remotely motivated. I thrust my hand into my satchel, just to look like I'm doing something, and I nick my thumb on the knife I use to sharpen pencils.

"Constantijn!"

I stand up, thumb in my mouth, so fast I knock my head on the edge of my easel. The whole thing teeters, parchment board tilting at a dangerous angle, but Joost catches it before it falls in earnest and tips it back into place for me. The charcoal falls off the edge and breaks against the floor. When Joost casts his gaze down to it, I can see the red-gold freckles sprinkled over his eyelids and, when he bends, the spot behind his ear where his hair doesn't lie flat. He's sheared it off since he started his dock work, and the short curls feather against the back of his neck.

He tries to scoop up a few salvageable pieces, and when he hands them to me, it takes a full minute to remember how to make my fingers work to take it from him. Another to recall language and form the shape of it with my tongue.

"Joost. Good evening. Morning. It's morning."

He wipes the charcoal off his palms, leaving black smears on his cassock. "How are you faring? I saw you at the docks last week."

"Did you?"

"You looked occupied or I would have come over."

"Oh. I was fetching the plasters."

"The what?"

"We were doing a study..." Halfway through this sentence I realize I had been at the docks retrieving the plaster casts van der Loos had made of naked male torsos and I go so lightheaded with embarrassment I think I might faint.

Joost raises an eyebrow. "A study?"

"For painting."

"Ah."

His eyes drift over my shoulder, like he's tiring of this conversation and looking for someone else to speak to, and my mind becomes so overwhelmed by desperation to keep him here that it latches on to the word I have been so careful to skirt for this entire conversation and spits it out. "Penises."

Which gets his attention back on me, but at what cost!? "What?"

"We were painting... We've been talking about the musculature of..." I do a mime of something oblong shaped with the unfortunate placement of right in front of my crotch. "It was just for the painting. We didn't do anything with them. Not the penises. The casts. The plasters."

"Oh. Well. I suppose you have to start somewhere."

A wild little giggle escapes me. Joost raises his eyebrows, and I look around for some sort of pallet knife on which I could fall on and impale myself. "Are you making a delivery?"

"No, not many ships of late—the snow's kept them from docking. Hard to make a living."

"Yes, hard."

"What?"

Don't say it again, I think, but of course I do. "Hard," I repeat, louder, and, Jesus, take me now. Scoop me from this earth; I shall never recover. I tug at the front of my smock, which I have somehow sweat through, and force myself to keep my eyes on Joost's face and not the pale dip of skin visible between his kerchief and collar, sprinkled in freckles the same color as his hair. "So are you, um... What are you doing here?"

"Take your seats, please," van der Loos calls. "Hendrickszoon, if you'll come with me." Joost ducks out from between the easels to follow van der Loos, and I collapse into a swoon upon my stool, so light-headed I almost tip backward. I plant my feet on the floor and try to breathe and not look around for Joost, though just knowing he's near makes me feel set aflame. I hear the scrape as van der Loos drags the sofa into the center of our circle. All I catch of his words is "return to life drawing today." I peer out from behind my easel just as he slaps the sofa cushion once, raising a mushroom of dust. "Hendrickszoon," he calls. "If you're ready."

And then Joost steps out from behind the partition, wearing the thin dressing gown, same as every woman we've drawn. My heart starts to pound its fists against my rib cage like it's trying to burst out and lay itself dramatically at Joost's feet.

Van der Loos presents the couch with an extended hand. "If you please."

It seems to take a thousand years for the robe to come off. It slides like slick oil off his shoulders, and if I thought they were a thing of beauty beneath a shirt, they're miraculous unsheathed, whorls of thick muscle coiled beneath his skin. His whole body is taut as he unfastens the sash, the studied concentration of a beautiful man who knows he's being watched but chooses to pretend he's unaware because it makes for better planes of his face. As the robe falls open, I wonder if it will be possible for me to complete this entire study without once looking any lower than the dip of his hip bones, so sharp and precise they look as though someone chiseled them.

This, I think, as I keep my eyes determinedly focused on his face while the robes thumps softly to the floor, is entirely not my fault, and entirely his, for being so pretty.

Joost nudges the robe beneath the sofa, then gives van der Loos a smile. His hands twitch at his sides, like he's trying not to cover himself. "Shall I…?"

"Prone, please, to begin. And your boots."

"Oh." Joost laughs as he looks down at his feet. "I forgot."

He kicks off his boots, and they bounce across the floor, landing in a rumpled heap before Augustus.

I duck behind my easel, close my eyes, try to take a breath, fail, try to take another, nearly pass out, give my cheeks a stern talking to about being a little less red or they're going to give us both away. Another breath, another failure. Peer out from behind the easel.

Joost stretches out on the sofa slowly, like a thing unthawing. Braam whistles, and there are a few laughs, though of an entirely different variety of those that accompanied the bare-breasted women who have previously draped themselves over this sofa.

"Quiet please," van der Loos says, then, to Joost, "You might begin with your arms above your head please." Joost obliges, stretching himself out to his full length. He's so tall that his feet hang off the edge of the sofa, and the muscles in his chest coil, his skin gilded by the sunlight curling in through the windows, brighter than usual as it reflects off the new snow piled along the sills.

Van der Loos adjusts the drapes, letting in more light, then turns to us. "Gentlemen, observe particularly the musculature here, in the torso, how it connects differently than on the female form."

Look somewhere else, I think, as van der Loos strokes a hand through the air over the ladder of Joost's abdominal muscles. *Look at his boots.*

I stare at the material in a muddy heap on the floor, the way the folds drape, the leather sole, the hole along the heel where the stitching has come loose and he hasn't yet taken it to the cobbler.

"Constantijn, are you paying attention?"

I raise my eyes from their determined study of the boots. Van der Loos is staring at me with a frown. So is Joost, less frowny. So are all the other apprentices. Braam's mouth is quivering with trying not to laugh.

"Yes, sir."

"What are we discussing?"

"His…torso, sir."

"We've moved lower." He points straight between Joost's legs. "Follow along, please."

And, because everyone is watching me, I look.

As Joost lounges upon the sofa like some god ripped from mythology, the entirety of his front side on display, I have a stern talking to with my own bits about calming down and they staunchly refuse to listen.

I try threats. *If you don't go soft, you'll have no supper*, though my body seems far more interested in sex than food.

BUT LOOK AT HIS CHEST, it seems to scream in response.

I try bargaining. *If you go soft, I'll give you a good workout tonight.*

BUT LOOK AT HIS BARE THIGHS.

I try pleading. *If you do not settle, all of these boys are going to see me go stiff over Joost and I will get more than a handful of snow to the back of the head.*

BUT LOOK AT HIS—

Think of the least arousing things possible. Gutted herring in the market. Spilled sewage in the greasy snow outside the Wolf's Head. The old woman who begs outside the church with a mouth full of rotted teeth she sometimes spits at my sister and me like melon seeds.

"If you would change, please, Hendrickszoon," van der Loos calls, and I start, nearly crushing my charcoal between my fingers—I hadn't realized we had started to sketch. Joost sits up, letting one leg dangle off the sofa and giving me another eyeful of his crotch that sends all the blood fleeing my head.

Maybe if I faint, van der Loos will let me go home. Maybe if I throw up, he'll let me leave early. Maybe if I keel over dead they'll bury me in the churchyard with "Here lies Constantijn, slain by the first penis he saw that wasn't his own."

I look at my parchment. I completed nothing from his first pose. I start to scribble frantically, tracing out the arch of his back just to get something on the page. My heartbeat is sitting in my hands—the few strokes I manage are palsied. I look around at the other apprentices, hoping at least one of them will look as uncomfortable as I am and my own fumbling can be passed off as something other than unholy lust. They all seem focused, and the room is quiet but for the soft shush of charcoal on parchment. Beside me, Augustus bends so close to his sketch that his nose seems likely to smudge the charcoal.

"Constantijn, what are you doing?"

I start so spectacularly my charcoal skates across the page, leaving a long black smudge. Van der Loos is standing over me, frowning at my board.

"Sketching, sir."

"You have yet to finish a figure."

"It's difficult."

"How so?"

"Different. Than the women. The anatomy," I tack on hastily.

Van der Loos's frown deepens. "Constantijn, are you well?"

"Yes, sir."

"You look feverish."

"It's very hot in here, sir."

"Perhaps you'd prefer to sit by the window."

"Oh, God, no," I say, too quickly, and van der Loos frowns at me. "It would disrupt my angles," I say, instead of explaining that sitting by the window would give me a view that is far more full frontal than my current.

Van der Loos scowls at me again, then at my parchment.

"Your progress has been exceptional lately," he says. "Be certain you don't stagnate."

I bow my head and van der Loos moves on. I have to do something. And that something is not trying to swallow down staring at Joost naked and not nursing the sinful desires that I have heard over and over from my ministers are a sign of being damned. I look down at my board. A few half-hearted shapes. The tip of a chin, the curled hunch of a shoulder. Maybe I am damned.

Instead of his frame, I draw his face. The shape of his cheekbones beneath his skin, the freckles on his eyelids, the shadow his lashes cast against his cheeks. The thin bow of his lips, the wide spot on the bridge of his nose from when it was once broken when Merik Engel accidentally knocked him with an oar when they were punting. Thick brows, the way his hair curls behind his ears. I draw him more from memory, even though he's in front of me, until van der Loos calls time and the class ends.

I pack up my charcoal and stow the easel, careful to look away as Joost redresses himself. I hear him laughing over something with Braam and Johannes, so it's a shock when I turn back from washing my hands in the basin and he's standing at my easel, waiting for me. The collar of his shirt has gotten tucked under the seam, and I almost reach up to fix it. I curl my hands into fists around the edges of my smock to stop myself.

"How did I do?" he asks.

"Well." My voice cracks, and I clear my throat. "You did very well. Very still."

"Was I good to draw?"

Oh, God, if ever there was a question more weighted than that—it's like I can hear grapeshot clicking within the words. "Yes."

"May I see it?"

"See what?"

"Your sketches."

"Of you?" The word *mortifying* was certainly invented to describe showing the boy whose broad shoulders you have been admiring from afar since you were young the nude sketches you have just attempted to do of him while trying desperately, desperately not to think about the nights you have kept yourself company with fantasizing about him. My first instinct is to rip the paper to shreds just for an excuse to say no.

But Joost is standing, expectant, one hand extended, so I pass over the parchment. He studies it, a small crease appearing between his eyes when he looks from the few half-hearted studies of his frame to the rendering of his face. "I thought you were only meant to be drawing my body."

"I, ah, thought I'd try something else."

"Look, you got my hair there, where it flips up." He laughed, running a finger along his bottom lip. "And my eyes are exactly right."

"They're not. The shape is off."

"The lashes, then—you've drawn the shadow of them." He scrubs one hand under his eye. "They're longer than most."

"They're not. I mean, they are. But they're so nice." I nearly jam a paintbrush through my own eye in hopes that a quick death might end this now.

Joost smiles, one cheek dimpled deep and the other smooth as porcelain. I expect thanks for the accidental compliment but it must make him too uncomfortable to acknowledge for all he says is "You'll be a great artist someday."

"So will you."

"What?"

"Sorry, I thought… I thought you were going to say… Nothing."

When I look up, he's still examining my sketch. "May I keep this?"

"No, I need it."

"Oh."

"For my portfolio."

"Of course." He stares at it for a moment longer, rubbing his hand along his chin, admiring his own beauty, which is what I was doing a few moments ago, but somehow it's less endearing when it's him staring at himself with an approving eye. He hands it back, and I shove it into my satchel.

Joost gives me his easy smile again, pushing a strand of hair off his forehead and back under his knit cap. There's a clatter behind us, and we both turn. Augustus has leaned too close to the washbasin mirror in an attempt to wash the charcoal off his nose and rattled it. Joost snorts. "I didn't know Augustus Rikszoon was apprenticed here."

"Oh. Yes. Is that…surprising?"

"I'm surprised he found anyone to take him on as an apprentice—he's such an odd creature, I thought he'd be slopping hogs somewhere." He laughs. "Do you remember, when we were young, he was so frightened of having to walk up to the altar at church he pissed himself?" He laughs again.

"Augustus is a good artist," I say before I can stop myself. In truth, I've never really noticed Augustus's drawings more than anyone else's, and similarly have no idea where this compulsion to defend him is coming from. I'd certainly be more endearing to Joost if I simply nodded and agreed, and what does Augustus mean to me? He *is* an odd thing—I've thought it myself before. Maybe because we've walked together almost every night since Braam and Johannes mocked me on the way home, and because I like the way he blushes when he laughs, no matter the joke, and the cant of his head when he listens, sometimes so far it seems he's resting his cheek upon his own shoulder. The way he remembers the things I tell him.

And who didn't piss themselves at least once when they were young?

Joost pulls his cap lower over his ears with a shrug. "He should at least be a clergyman or something that gives him an excuse to be awkward and stay away from women."

"I have to go," I blurt.

"Oh. Of course." Joost takes a step back from me, his coat sleeve drifting over an open jar of saffron pigment and leaving a smudge the color of fresh pollen along the patched elbow. "Would you like to walk with me? I'm going to Westerpark for a drink with some of the East India men. You could come, if you like."

"I need to be home. My mother holds dinner for me."

"Oh. All right, then." His face creases, like being turned down is a new experience for him. "I'll see you soon, I think. For more sessions. You can draw my face again." He wiggles his eyebrows at me, and I have to work hard to muster a smile that reaches my eyes. "Have a good night, Constantijn."

I watch him go, then take the sketch out of my satchel and examine it again, his long eyelashes, the careful strokes—I've never drawn anything so lovingly, like a constellation map of the points of his face I admired. But now the cheekbones look too prominent. The eyes too warm, the bones too shapely. I drew him finer than he is.

"Constantijn." I look up. Augustus is standing in front of me, his cassock already pulled on over his tunic, satchel looped around his neck. Beneath his cap, his hair is twisted back and stuck through with a paintbrush. A few feathery pieces have slipped free and flutter around his face. When I meet his eyes, he looks down, twisting the hem of his coat like he's ringing out wet washing. "Are you walking home?"

I crush the paper in my fist.

He looks up at the noise. "Is that your sketch from today?"

"They're terrible."

"Mine too. It was…not my best day."

"Mine neither."

"We deserve a drink."

"Yes. Many drinks. Every drink."

He laughs, then stops suddenly and it turns into more of an awkward throat-clearing cough. "I mean… Do you want to? Really?"

My eyes stray over his shoulder to his board, the parchment still stretched in place. There are a few half-hearted attempts at shoulders, a jawline, the silhouette of Joost's back curled on the couch. But the most complete drawing is not of Joost at all—it's his boots, bunched in a pile on the ground.

"Yes," I say. "I do."

Augustus and I walk side by side, mostly in silence. Slate clouds, their undersides pearled like the inside of a seashell, have fallen into place since the morning, and the last dregs of another snowstorm are tipping down from the sky, so soft I hardly feel it until a single flake lands upon the back of my neck, melts and drips between my shoulder blades. I shiver. Augustus looks over at me, and when his eyes catch the gray light, I think of burnt umber pigments made from rust-stained clay mined, ground and washed before the fire is lit beneath to stain it, a heat that could melt snow turning mud brown to the syrupy, warm gold. The color of lantern light through the darkness, bubbles of sap risen from tree bark, the veins of gold in the papery bulbs that tulips burst from. I wonder what his eyes would look like with our noses pressed together.

Augustus glances away from me as fast as our eyes met, a faint smile toying with his lips.

Just as the snow stops falling, I take his hand.

★★★★★

THE DRESSER & THE CHAMBERMAID

BY
ROBIN TALLEY

Kensington Palace, September 1726
6:30 a.m.

Susanna was accustomed to creeping about the palace in the dark.

All the chambermaids were experts at slinking along the back corridors in complete silence this early in the morning. Each was well aware of the price she'd pay if she disturbed one of the sleeping courtiers while going about her morning duties.

But on this particular morning, it was all Susanna could do not to gasp aloud when she cracked open the door to the princess's chamber, her water ewer and parcel of wood balanced carefully on her hip.

A girl she'd never seen before was seated by the hearth.

Susanna bit her lip.

The girl had to be the new dresser. The one who'd arrived the day before from the country. But she oughtn't to have been in the princess's chamber yet.

The chambermaids had been up since five, fetching the water, heating it over the fires and hauling the full ewers up the stairs, their feet already aching in their boots before it was properly light out. Dressers, though, rose late. Nearly as late as the ladies themselves. Susanna had glided soundlessly into Her Royal Highness's chamber every morning since she had entered the court's service, and never in those many years had she encountered anyone but the princess herself, snoring softly behind her canopy.

But there the new girl was, seated just as you please on the princess's very own dressing stool, her eyes cast down and her fingers flying over a bit of needlework. She hadn't noticed Susanna yet.

The girl wore a fine gown, one that had probably been passed down to her from some previous mistress, as it was no longer quite in fashion. The ornamentation had been carefully removed, of course, and an apron affixed about the waist, so there could be no mistaking the dresser for a lady.

When Susanna silently pushed the door wide, the new girl clutched at her sewing and leaped to her feet. As well she should do. Servants didn't sit in the presence of their mistresses, regardless of whether those mistresses slept. Yet Susanna had often suspected that dressers didn't consider themselves to be servants at all.

The girl—she was some acquaintance of Lady Portland, Susanna had heard—had a crop of thick dark curls poking out from under her cap, and she was awfully tall. She'd had to let out her hem. It had been mended by a skilled hand, but even so, Susanna could see where the last few inches of fabric were less faded than the rest.

Perhaps girls grew taller in the country. The air was meant to be sweeter there. Susanna had never been outside London, so she couldn't imagine what sweet air might entail.

But when Susanna lifted her eyes, she nearly dropped her ewer full of hot water right onto the princess's thick brown carpet.

The girl—the dresser—was *looking* at her.

Princess Amelia's last dresser, the one who'd run off to marry some yeoman the week before, had never so much as glanced at Susanna. If they happened into the same room, the dresser's eyes would skip right past her. As if she thought herself as grand as Her Royal Highness herself.

The other dressers were no different, whether in service to one of the princesses or to any lady of the court. Dressers thought chambermaids no more worthy of notice than the fires they lit or the floors they swept. Less, in truth. Everyone at court, dressers included, cared a great deal that their fires went on burning bright, even if they didn't give a whit how they came to do so.

Susanna went to the fire now, setting her ewer carefully at the edge of the hearth. She wouldn't allow any country girl to see her flustered, not even a girl who rose before it was properly dawn and looked lesser servants in the eye. Susanna took her parcel of wood from under her arm and reached out to lay it in the hearth.

Her arm froze when she saw it.

Neat planks of fresh, clean wood had already been laid out, waiting to be lit.

Susanna turned, sharply, back to the dresser. The girl was still watching her, needlework quite forgotten. The dresser shrugged and gestured to the bag of coal Susanna carried, as if to say she hadn't been able to find any coal herself.

Had this country dresser truly ventured into the dark winding back stairs, found the pile of extra logs the footmen kept there and carried wood into the princess's bedchamber before dawn, all in her finest passed-down dress?

Well, the court ladies always did giggle behind their fans at the odd ways of country folk.

The new girl had laid the wood out in just the right way,

too. There was nothing more for Susanna to do but lay the coal atop it and draw out her tinder pistol. Soon the fire rose in the hearth, ready to warm the princess when she began to stir.

Susanna must be gone by then, lest she risk a striking later from Mistress Keen, so she rose quickly to fetch Her Royal Highness's chamber pot and be on her way.

The girl, though. The strange new girl. She was still standing. Still watching Susanna, and blocking her path, too.

Well, there was nothing to be done for it. The pot had to be emptied, rinsed and returned to the bedchamber before the princess awoke, no matter what some dresser from the country thought about it.

Susanna strode forward with quick, silent steps, readying herself to knock the girl out of her way if she must. The pot was in its usual spot beside the princess's bed. Susanna could just glimpse it beyond the new girl's wide skirt.

At the moment Susanna reached for it, though, the dresser spun on her high heels and turned to face the bed. Susanna covered her gasp. The dresser now stood only a foot from the sleeping princess.

Tendrils of Her Royal Highness's pale hair peeked out from behind the canopy. If the new girl kept whirling about, she would wake her, and the dresser and Susanna would suffer for it just the same.

Susanna laid a finger to her lips, praying the girl would grasp the need for absolute silence. The dresser stared at her for a moment, then nodded solemnly. Thinking it safe to advance, Susanna moved again toward the pot.

The new girl reached for it at the same time.

No! It was all Susanna could do, once again, not to cry out loud. How dare this strange girl try to touch Princess Amelia's chamber pot! It was Susanna's place, her *duty*. True, she had longed to be named dresser to the princess herself when the last girl had run off, and true, her skill at fixing ladies' hair should have been enough to place her in the post, had not that awful Lady Portland swooped in—but all the same, Susanna was still the princess's own chambermaid, and that meant it was for no one but *her* to handle Her Royal Highness's night water.

But Susanna was faster than the new girl, and she was the first to lay a hand on the rim of the pot. She pulled it out of the dresser's reach as swiftly as she could without risking a spill. The girl's brow wrinkled, but Susanna turned away, thrusting the pot out to her side where the smell would be less of a bother.

Strange country girls and their strange country ways. Susanna would think no more on it.

She rushed in silent steps through the door to the servants' corridor, dumped the pot into the bucket for her to haul back down the stairs later, splashed it with fresh water for a rinse and returned with it to the princess's chamber. To Susanna's great relief, Her Royal Highness slept on, her snores as even and undisturbed as they had been all morning.

The dresser had retreated to stand before the fire, thrusting a staff into the wood and disturbing the fire Susanna had built, instead of laying out the princess's morning costume as any dresser ought rightly to do just before her mistress woke. Susanna spared a last, despairing glance at the new girl before she swept back out of the room, shutting the door behind her without a sound.

She hurried down the stairs with her bucket to prepare for the chamber's proper cleaning. She had lost precious time already that morning, and Susanna had not a moment to spare for thoughts of the new dresser and her odd, troublesome ways.

Even if the girl was as lovely as the king's very best tapestry in his privy room below.

8:30 a.m.

Mary was lost. Again.

These dark, wretched back corridors went on for miles, twisting and turning and ending in inexplicable staircases that were always filled with servants running to and fro. All of them carried candles and seemed to know precisely where they were going, and none of them spared an eye for Mary as her panic grew and her empty stomach groaned.

She had thought she knew the proper way to dress a distinguished lady. She had never dressed any so high as a princess, of course—but then, who had? She had gotten the stockings mended in time, despite the interruptions from that pretty little glaring chambermaid. Yet the princess had still found fault with Mary even before she had entirely awoken.

Mary oughtn't to have been waiting in the chamber, didn't she know, but in the dressing room, until after Her Royal Highness had risen from her bed and knelt to pray. Only *then* should Mary have entered, to draw the canopy and help the princess out of her nightgown and into her fine linen shift. How Mary was to have known this, the princess did not indicate, but she did voice, often and shrilly, that Mary was *not* to stoke the fire, even when its flames seemed to wane.

"Honestly," the princess had intoned as she thrust her arms overhead for Mary to lay the shift upon her skin, "Mistress Susanna has the charge of it. She knows how I like my fire. I don't know how they do things at Portly's house out in the country, but here you're to not to interfere with the work of the *capable* servants."

Susanna, then. The pretty chambermaid's name was Susanna.

But Mary had no time to dwell on anyone but the princess as she set about arranging Her Royal Highness's hair for her morning lessons. For days back home, ever since the note had arrived with Lady Portland's summons to come to court, Mary had done nothing but practice hair. Yet it seemed to have been of no use. Mary was skilled with a needle but had only scant experience with a young lady's toilette, and when Princess Amelia saw her reflection in the glass that morning, Her Royal Highness seemed struck speechless.

Only for the briefest of moments, of course. Princess Amelia was not known for silence.

"Tell me your name once more," the princess demanded.

Mary curtsyed. "It is Arnold, Your Royal Highness, Mary Arnold."

"Mistress Arnold." The princess turned from her. "I will now go for my morning walk. I shall pray, as should you, that the sentinels in the gardens do not mistake me for the palace laundress, despite this mess upon my head. As for you, before you attend to any other duties, you will find Mistress Susanna and have her show you how a princess wears her hair. I dare say she can teach you before this evening's ball. She must, in fact, unless you wish to be back in the country by sundown."

Mary dipped deep into a new curtsy, hoping her face fell far enough to hide her shame. "Of course, Ma'am."

The princess did not look on her again as she strode toward the door. Mary hurried forward to open it for her, but Her Royal Highness took the knob in her own hand and vanished in a whirl of silk and lace.

Mary allowed herself a silent sob, but just the one, before she hurried to gather up and put away the princess's nightgown and hair powder. She started to remove the bed linens, but then remembered how angry Susanna had grown when she'd merely tried to pass her the princess's chamber pot. Perhaps she had best leave it. Besides, Her Royal Highness had made it very clear that Mary's first task must be to find Susanna for instruction on hairdressing.

Some girls, Mary imagined, would consider it an insult for a dresser to take direction from a chambermaid. But Mary had no doubt, as she searched blindly among the dark corridors, that there was not a person in all of Kensington Palace, down to the lowest scullery girl, who knew less than she about the proper way to serve a princess.

Besides, she wouldn't much mind taking in the sight of Susanna's face once more. Even with her lips' permanent downward turn.

"Are you lost, mistress?" a male voice called. Mary turned toward the sight of a candle flame bobbing toward her in the darkness. It could be anyone, of course. All the men here, and the women, too, were strangers to her. But Mary could not afford to be cautious.

"I am, sir," she called. "I seek the princess's chambermaid."

"Which princess?" The flame grew closer. Mary could make out the shape of the royal livery. A footman, then.

"Her Royal Highness, Princess Amelia."

"Ah, you'll want Susanna." The footman was now close enough that Mary could see his face. His smile was warm and his eyes friendly, though he was a good deal taller than she, and wider, too. The long tassels on his shoulders spread from one side of the corridor nearly to the other. "She'll be at the servants' breakfast, just down the stairs. I'm headed that way myself, if you'd allow me to escort you."

"I'd be quite grateful, sir."

"It's no trouble." The footman made no effort to conceal his curiosity as he regarded Mary's cap, her dress, her empty hands. "They've not allotted you your candles yet, I see? Mistress Arnold, is it?"

"It is." Mary tried to hide her surprise. Was there nothing the servants in this strange place didn't know? "Are you in the princess's service, as well?"

"The king's, I'd wager. Not that His Majesty knows any one of his footmen from any other. My name is Halford, by the by, Barnaby Halford."

Mary curtsyed as well as she could while they hurried down the stairs. "Mr. Halford. Has the princess her own footman?"

"No, though I'm sure she'd happily take one. Their Royal Highnesses each have their own gentleman usher, though, and a page of honor and a page of the back stairs. And a dresser and chambermaid, of course."

"Of course," Mary echoed, marveling that her former mistress had thought it proper to go through life with naught but a single maid to handle her dressing, her fires and her chamber pots alike.

"Ah, here we are, then." Barnaby held a door open for her, the delicious scent of porridge wafting out. "The servants' breakfast. Though not for dressers such as yourself, of course—the upper servants' breakfast would be one floor above—but you did say you sought Susanna."

"Thank you, Mr. Halford." Mary curtsyed again and cursed her stomach as it rumbled.

She entered a room filled with chattering girls in aprons and men in livery. Three dozen servants, at least, were all sitting around a long wooden table covered in clanking bowls and spoons. The chatter faded, then halted altogether before Mary had taken three steps inside. She swallowed and tried not to show her fear as every set of eyes in the room locked on her.

Susanna was sitting between two girls whose laughter had just died off. Her face was drawn, her eyes locked on Mary's.

"Mistress Susanna, is it?" Mary stepped toward the table, doing her very best to ignore the eyes on her, even as her cheeks turned crimson. "Her Royal Highness asked that I find you."

At once, Susanna was on her feet and halfway to the door,

knocking the crumbs off her apron and tugging her cap forward. "What is it? Has her fire died already?"

"No, no, there's nothing amiss with the princess's chamber." Mary caught Susanna by the wrist before she could leave the room. It was a thoughtless gesture, no less so than her attempt to pass the chamber pot, but this touch of Mary's skin to Susanna's seemed more significant somehow. As Susanna raised her eyes to meet her own, Mary released her hand, though she was surprised at how deeply she felt the loss of their shared touch.

"The princess has asked—" The other servants had ceased to watch them, but Mary lowered her voice all the same. There was shame in the admission. "She has requested that you instruct me in the proper way to dress her hair for the ball this evening."

"Requested?" Susanna narrowed her eyes, as though this might be a trick Mary was pulling. But something in Mary's face must have convinced the maid of her sincerity, for after a moment, Susanna nodded. "Did Barnaby show you the way here?"

"He did." Mary was surprised to notice that Barnaby still leaned against the door.

"Lingering in the corridor by Lord Hervey's chamber again, were you?" Susanna's tone was scolding, but from the tilt to her head Mary could see that Susanna and Barnaby got on well.

"Aye, mistress." Barnaby inclined his head in return. "I thought he might require assistance dressing this morning."

"No need for that," one of the maids, a pretty girl with dark hair, called out. "His Lordship already gets all the help he might need with his garments from Lord Fox."

"And more besides," one of the other footmen replied. "Though if our Barnaby had his way, I'm sure he'd provide his *particular* assistance to the both of them when there were no garments anywhere in sight."

The room erupted into laughter as Barnaby good-naturedly swatted the other footman across the ear.

"Oh, don't listen to any of them." Susanna and Barnaby shared a smile before the maid turned back to Mary. "Right, then. We shall do as Her Royal Highness bids. Have you found your way to your own breakfast yet?"

Mary shook her head, chastened at how little she understood the workings of this odd place, where there were multitudes of servant dining rooms, and lords helped other lords with their underclothes.

"Fetch the new girl some porridge, would you, Lydia?" Susanna called to the dark-haired maid. "She'll need to eat quickly if we're to see to the princess's request before she returns to dress for dinner."

Frowning, the other girl spooned a small quantity of porridge into an empty bowl and thrust it across the table. Mary curtsyed in thanks and took it from her hand.

"Have you not had the care of a lady's hair before, then?" Susanna asked as she led Mary up the dark stairs. Susanna carried no candle, and seemed not to need one. Mary focused on shoveling porridge into her mouth and following Susanna without tripping over her skirts, a daunting task indeed.

"No, no, I have. I cared for my last mistress's hair, as well as her clothing, and her chamber, too. But I'm afraid I'm not yet versed in the ways of young ladies' hair for court."

"Her Royal Highness is very particular about her toilette. All the ladies are, but the princesses most of all."

They reached Princess Amelia's chamber in only moments with Susanna leading the way. Mary finished her porridge and set aside the bowl just as Susanna cracked open the door, and then, on seeing the room empty, pushed it open.

"We haven't time much for lessons." Susanna laid the curling irons carefully in the fire, thrust open the windows to air out the chamber and gathered up bellows, brushes and glasses into her arms. "I need to change the linen and you need to arrange the princess's dinner dress before she's returned from her lessons. Quick, into the dressing room."

Mary reached out to help Susanna carry the hair things, but the chambermaid cast a scalding glance her way and she withdrew her hand. She followed Susanna into the smaller room just off the princess's chamber, where Her Royal Highness's wardrobe was stored, from her finest mantuas and hoods to her simplest shifts and patches. That morning, when Mary had first seen the dressing room by the light of day, she had feared to do her mending surrounded by such splendor.

"A shame we don't have a girl to practice on," Susanna mused as she carefully set out the combs and pins on a dressing room shelf. "But no one would be able to spare the hour. Right, then. To start, I shall do up your hair the way the princess likes it, so that you may see it in the glass, and then I suppose you'll have to do up mine. Sit."

Susanna stood behind Mary and reached up to grasp her by the shoulders. Mary collapsed underneath her, startled at the other girl's strength, and knelt on the floor, careful to spread her skirts about her. She had brought only one other dress with her to court, and it was not nearly so fine as this one.

Susanna jerked off her cap and thrust it down into Mary's trembling fingers.

"Your hair is much thicker than the princess's." The chambermaid wound her fingers into Mary's curls and began to comb it through. "I do not think yours would require as much powder. Though, of course, we cannot waste Her Royal Highness's powder on your hair, or mine, so you must listen closely as I describe its use."

"Of course." Mary grimaced as Susanna tugged at her scalp, holding up one of the princess's miniature looking glasses so she could follow the maid's movements. "Do you usually pull her hair so fiercely as this?"

"Fiercely?" Susanna snickered, though Mary noticed she tugged with less force after that. "Well, I wouldn't know. I've never touched the princess's hair."

"Haven't you?" Mary watched closely, trying to memorize her movements as Susanna's fingers moved quickly from curl to curl. Susanna fetched the hot curling iron, a rag wrapped around the end to protect her hand. "But Her Royal Highness said you knew how she liked it."

"I suppose that's true." Mary caught a glimpse of Susanna's face in the glass as she spoke. Her eyes were downcast, her lips set and straight. "I've oft been in her chamber, assisting with the fire and things, while she prepared for a ball. And I've practiced dressing hair in all sorts of ways, though only on the other maids, of course. I've been trying out a special French sort of style, with flowers woven in between the strands of hair. It's long been a dream of mine to try it on the princess herself for one of the grand palace balls."

"Perhaps you should have become Her Royal Highness's dresser, then." Mary sighed. "I fear I am not fit for it. The princess was most unkind to me this morning."

Susanna tugged Mary's hair into a high, wide bun. "Her Royal Highness is most unkind to everyone. Not just servants, either. Why, yesterday Lydia heard her tell Lord Hervey himself that he looked quite the fop in his new waistcoat."

Mary couldn't help but smile.

"She's the prettiest of the king's granddaughters, though," Susanna went on, "and they say she's the cleverest, too, but she's also the most forthright. A terrible quality in a princess. The king fears he'll never find a monarch in all of Christendom who will stand to be her husband. Though we shouldn't say such things about Her Royal Highness, of course."

"Of course," Mary agreed, her head spinning. She had never imagined the palace chambermaids would know how His Majesty viewed his family affairs.

"There, now." Susanna rested her hands on Mary's shoulders where her skin met the neck of her gown. The sensation made Mary flush. "Take a look and see how I did it."

Mary did her best to view her hair in the little looking glass. Her long, dark curls sat atop her head, each strand tucked into place carefully over the wool pads Susanna had inserted to make the hair stand tall, in the fashion of the court. She looked ready to be powdered and presented to a ballroom full of admirers, if only from her neck upward. Mary couldn't imagine how Susanna had accomplished the feat in such a short time.

"Now you." Susanna settled herself onto the floor next to Mary, her legs tucked neatly underneath her, a smile on her lips. She was proud, Mary saw, to demonstrate her skill.

For a moment Mary did not wish to rise. She preferred to linger there beside Susanna. If she was not mistaken, the chambermaid's voice had taken on a slight hint of kindness as her fingers had slipped through Mary's hair.

But there was no time for frivolities. Mary climbed to her feet as Susanna slid the cap off her head, revealing soft light brown waves pinned up neatly.

Mary released the pins, letting Susanna's hair flow free. Touching the maid's hair felt intimate in a way that taming the princess's thin blond tendrils had not. Mary tried to imitate what she'd seen Susanna doing in the looking glass, but her fingers fumbled, more with nerves than inability.

"How long have you served the princess?" Mary asked, wishing, she realized suddenly, to know everything about Susanna.

"Many years." Susanna drew her cap over her hands. Her fingers, Mary noticed before they disappeared beneath the white fabric, were red from handling the curling iron. The tips were blistered, too, and the nails short. Mary knew well the effects of tending to fires and scalding ewers and rough soap day after day.

"You must have been quite young, then, when you came to the palace."

"I was born in the palace." Susanna tightened her grip on the cap. "It would have been near to the time the princess herself was born, in Hanover, you know."

Mary and Susanna—and, she supposed, the princess—were of an age, then. Her Royal Highness's fifteenth birthday had been celebrated earlier that summer with a grand ball. Mary had heard tell of it even in Hertfordshire.

"Your parents served Queen Anne?" Mary asked.

"My mother did. She worked in the kitchens. Careful, there, you missed that strand on the side."

"My apologies, mistress."

"You needn't call me 'mistress.'" But there was mirth in Susanna's voice. "You're the dresser, not me."

"My apologies." Mary bit her tongue so as not to say *mistress* again. "Is your mother here in the kitchens still?"

"No." The mirth in Susanna's voice had vanished. "She died two days after my birth. The Lord Steward had always liked her, so he did me a kindness and asked the laundresses to bring me up until I was old enough to work."

Mary knew more of that sort of story than she wished to. "Your father, he died, too, then?"

"My father spoke not of me." Susanna's words now came fast and short, as though they meant no more to her than Princess Amelia's chamber pot. "Nor of my mother. He was far too grand to be saddled with a kitchen maid or her offspring."

Mary's hands faltered in Susanna's hair. "My father wouldn't own to me, either."

Susanna turned ever so slightly, as though to meet Mary's eyes. "And your mother?"

"She died. A year or so past." A year, two months and three days. Mary slipped a pin into Susanna's soft waves. "I was to be sent to the workhouse, but a woman from my village took me for her maid instead, as an act of charity. Then, just a few days ago, Lady Portland sent for me, saying that Her Royal Highness's dresser had run off and I was to take her place. My mother had been governess to Lady Portland, you see."

"Two bastard girls in the princess's service." Susanna's voice was gentler than her words. "Would that Her Royal Highness were aware."

Mary slid the last pin into place. Her fingers no longer trembled. "How did I do?"

Susanna climbed to her feet and peered into the glass. "I wouldn't say admirably, but it represents a great improvement from your first attempt."

Mary's face sagged. "My first attempt?"

"I spotted the princess on her morning walk about the gardens. I must say, even for a princess who defies convention, I'd never seen her hair look quite so...*unconventional*."

Susanna met Mary's eyes. Her lip trembled. Soon she began to laugh. And, after a moment, Mary could no longer prevent herself from laughing, as well.

The feeling was tremendous as the tension rolled out of her limbs. Mary couldn't remember the last time she'd laughed.

Susanna began to explain how Mary should apply the powder, but her laughter did not cease, even as she puffed out the bellows. Soon she was bent at the waist with the bellows pointed high in the air puffing out tiny white clouds. She clutched at Mary's arm, much as Mary had clutched her wrist in the servants' hall that morning.

Her touch felt warmer now.

But they had work to do, the pair of them, and less time to do it than they should. Still giggling, Susanna showed Mary how to use the strange white powder—a mixture of wheat flour, lead and finely milled starch that would hold the princess's hair in place and give it a bright sheen—and then they set about their other morning tasks. Susanna stripped the bed of its linen and hung it up to air while Mary brought out the petticoat and dress the princess was to wear for dinner.

When Susanna reached for the chamber pot, Mary did not interfere, but when Mary held out her hand to catch one end of the bed linen to help lay it back in place, Susanna allowed her help. She even nodded in a gesture that might have been taken as gratitude.

The girls talked as they worked, keeping their voices low in case any servants or ladies passed in the corridors on either side. Susanna told Mary of court life, and of the other palace servants, and of the French way of styling ladies' hair that she'd attempted to learn.

During a quiet moment, Mary picked up one of Her Royal Highness's fans from a table. "What does the princess do with this, do you think?"

"Oh, she carries it about. All the ladies do." Susanna grinned and stole the fan from Mary's grasp, spreading it wide. A pastoral landscape was painted across the front, a young man beseeching a beautiful girl while cherubs danced about them. "If a lady touches the tip of her fan while looking at a gentleman, it means she wishes to speak with him."

"Does it really?" Mary couldn't quite believe fine ladies would use such trickery. "What does it mean if a lady opens her fan?"

"If she opens it and then closes it again, she's accusing the gentleman of cruelty." Susanna's smile grew wider. "And if she touches the fan to her lips, it means she wishes to be kissed."

"Certainly not!" Mary blushed bright. "No lady of the court would wish such a thing! Except perhaps of her husband."

Susanna laughed harder than ever. "You haven't yet witnessed a royal ball, I see."

The princess was due back from her lessons shortly, so Susanna finished her sweeping and slid out of the chamber, leaving Mary to attend Her Royal Highness. Fortunately, when the princess arrived a few moments later she was in much grander spirits than she had been that morning. A music lesson was scheduled for the afternoon with the princess's favorite teacher, Mr. Handel.

While Mary dressed her for dinner, Her Royal Highness chattered on to Mary about the operas she'd seen and complained about having to share the music lesson with her sisters. It seemed she was not particularly keen on her elder sister, Princess Anne, the one who would have been pretty had she not been so badly marked by the pox, or young Princess Caroline, who was meek and conscientious where Amelia was stubborn and loud. Her Royal Highness was so caught up in her complaints that she failed to comment at all on her appearance in the looking glass as she swept out the door to join her sisters in their private dining room.

Much of the day passed swiftly after that. Mary joined Susanna for the lower servants' dinner, ignoring the haughty looks from the other maids, and the two girls worked together that afternoon, cleaning the bedchamber once more and mending a petticoat Susanna assured Mary the princess would want to wear to the ball that evening.

Before Mary even had time to grow nervous, the ball itself

was imminent, and Princess Amelia was once more standing before her dressing table waiting to be laced into her stays.

Her Royal Highness, still happy from her music lesson, lay her finger beside her chin and nodded absently at one of the three mantuas Mary had laid out for her selection, to the dresser's delight. When the princess was attired—not an easy feat, given that the whalebone hoops extending beneath her skirts on either side made Her Royal Highness wider than she was tall—and a short muslin cape draped over her shoulders to protect the elaborate dress, Mary set about her hair.

The princess's threat from that morning was still clear in Mary's mind. She expected her hands to tremble as she began her work. But to her surprise, her fingers moved easily in the princess's soft blond curls. It wasn't so different from handling Susanna's hair, really. And after the morning they'd spent together in the dressing room, Mary felt startlingly at ease.

She took up the curling iron and set about imitating the techniques Susanna had shown her that morning. When she was done, she laced Her Royal Highness's hair with generous puffs of white powder from the bellows while the princess held a paper cone over her face to avoid its awful scent. Mary had no such protection, but she managed not to cough too audibly. After she had carefully applied the princess's delicate collection of patches to her cheeks, Mary decided to try out the trick Susanna had described, the new French style. She plucked a few flowers from the vase on the princess's dressing table and laced them between the strands of hair.

When she was done, Mary braced herself for Her Royal Highness's anger. But when the princess peered into the looking glass, she merely shrugged.

"It's an unusual sort of style." Her Royal Highness lifted her chin to scrutinize it. "One I've not seen at court before.

Perhaps you learned it in the country? Or was it Mistress Susanna who showed you?"

"I—" Mary hesitated. She did not want to claim the style was her own invention, but she did not want Susanna to incur the princess's wrath if she disliked it, either. The latter seemed the likelier possibility. "It was of my own invention."

"No matter." Princess Amelia stood and selected a fine lace fan from her dressing table. "We shall see what the other ladies have to say about it. For my part, though, I will say that I do prefer *this* sort of strangeness to this morning's."

Mary curtsyed. Her face colored, in relief this time.

When the princess was gone, Mary sagged against the wall. Her Royal Highness's toilette had taken more than two hours. Aside from the brief interval at dinner, Mary had not sat down since that morning. All she now wished for was her pallet, and perhaps a glass of small beer.

But the servant's door cracked open before Mary could retreat, and in spite of herself, she smiled when she saw Susanna's face peeking around the edge.

"Quick," Susanna whispered. "If we hurry, we'll get to see them arrive."

7:00 p.m.

Susanna ignored the new girl's protests and tugged her down the back stairs. Mary had never been to court before, and she did not seem to understand that the arrivals were the most crucial part of any evening. The dresser allowed herself to be led readily enough, though, smiling at the chambermaid from underneath her eyelashes. It was all Susanna could do to keep the two of them on their course.

Most nights, the arriving courtiers proceeded to the Great Drawing Room to seek an audience with His Majesty. For balls, though, the gardens outside the palace were favored instead. Susanna led Mary to a concealed spot behind a door just past the courtyard where the nobles arrived, their sedan chairs carried high in the air by footmen, to present themselves for entry.

Susanna heard Mary gasp behind her at their first sight of a grand lady sitting with her head tipped all the way backward so as not to allow her freshly powdered and piled hair to scrape the top of the litter.

"Watch how they take her out of it," she whispered to the awestruck Mary.

The fine lady was helped from her chair by her husband and two footmen. One of the footmen grasped her hand while the other unfolded the wide hoops of her mantua where it had been crushed into the chair for travel. Only when her skirt was unwound to its full six-foot width did the lady attempt to step down, her high heel digging into the second footman's hand as she rocked unsteadily to the ground.

"That's absurd," Mary whispered, horror in her voice.

Susanna grinned. "Welcome to life at court."

A few of Susanna's friends joined to watch as more chairs arrived. The girls were full of compliments for Mary and Susanna on their hair. Both of them were still done up as though they were fine ladies themselves, thanks to their practice session. Susanna smiled and tilted her head to give them a better view, but Mary barely even noticed their attentions, so transfixed was she by all the courtiers descending from their grand chairs and adjusting their ridiculous clothing.

Just as the arrivals were beginning to slow, a palace footman passed on his way to the garden, his wig tight around his ears, his arms loaded with bottles of wine. Susanna slipped one bottle from his hand with a smile. The footman winked at her in reply.

"Come," Susanna whispered to Mary. "You won't be

needed for hours yet, not until the princess tires. We have time for some amusements of our own."

Mary's eyes widened, and for a moment Susanna feared her country sensibilities would compel her to refuse. But then the dresser smiled, and soon she was following Susanna through the winding passageways to the back stairs.

The two of them found a dark, empty spot and talked and giggled their way through the bottle of wine. Susanna showed Mary the fan she'd borrowed from Her Royal Highness's dressing room, with a delicate painting of a biblical scene—Ruth and Naomi in the wilderness.

She demonstrated for Mary how ladies used their fans to ask gentlemen to follow them, and to communicate messages of love and malice, and told her stories of the absurd behavior she'd witnessed from the grandest ladies and gentlemen in all of England.

Mary told stories, too. Her former mistress, it seemed, had loved brewing potions designed to ward off illnesses, and had tested her smallpox potion on Mary, causing her to belch for days on end. As Mary laughed now, at the memory, Susanna stared into her brilliant blue eyes. She'd never seen anything so beautiful.

Mary finished her story and they fell into a contented silence. A moment passed. Then another. And then Susanna lifted the princess's fan and tapped it to her lips.

Perhaps it was the wine, or her country naivety, but at first Mary seemed not to take Susanna's meaning. Susanna tapped the fan again, and once more, then passed the fan into Mary's hand.

She saw on her face the precise moment when Mary understood. The girl's eyes grew so wide it made Susanna giggle.

It was an easy thing, then, to kiss her. As easy as laughter. Easy as a warm sun on a September afternoon. Susanna leaned in halfway, and Mary closed the remaining distance, until their lips met as equals in the empty, shadowed hall.

Mary tasted sweet, as a country girl should. Susanna smiled against her lips, and felt Mary smile in return. She slipped an arm around the other girl's waist, and the feel of her stays pressing against Susanna's palm was like another kiss. Her body grew warm.

"Ho, there, mistress. And, ah—you, too. Mistress."

The girls sprang apart at the sound of the man's voice. In the dark, they couldn't see who was speaking.

Susanna tried to think of some innocent explanation for why she and Mary were lingering in the corridors instead of going about their duties. If Mistress Keen, the housekeeper, were to find out, Susanna and Mary could both be lashed.

Then the man approached them. His shoulders were broad under his livery, and his step was quick and jaunty.

It was only Barnaby.

"Sir!" Susanna's relief echoed in the corridor. "You frightened us."

"My greatest apologies." Barnaby's lips quirked in the candlelight as he glanced back and forth between the two girls. "If I'd known what you were getting up to I'd have left you to your privacy. I merely sought to inform you, Mistress Arnold, that I've been circulating among the ladies, and Her Royal Highness has been receiving a great many compliments on her hair this evening. Our very own Princess Amelia is quite the talk of the ball."

"Truly?" A flicker of a smile passed over Mary's face. Susanna smiled, too. Even though she'd wanted the position for herself, now that she knew Mary, Susanna wanted her to stay at court for as long as she possibly could.

"It's a fact, mistress. Why, I overheard my fair Lady Mordaunt—she's one of the maids of honor, you know." Barnaby added this as an aside to Mary, holding his hands at his chest to indicate her ladyship's bosom, which Susanna had long ago noted was impressive indeed. "Her ladyship said that in *her* opinion, Princess Amelia's hair has never looked finer than it does this evening. And Her Royal Highness *herself* said—" At this Barnaby lay a finger beside his chin, in a clear imitation of the princess. Mary gasped at his impropriety. "The princess said she has received more compliments on her hair this evening than she's had all summer. She then said that as much as she absolutely *despises* everything to do with Lady Portland, the best thing that woman ever did was to acquire her this strange little country girl to be her new dresser. Princess Anne was simply *seething* with jealousy by her side. None of them could believe you'd already mastered such an interesting new style, with the flowers woven in."

"Flowers?" At first Susanna thought she'd misheard. "What about flowers?"

"I—" Mary looked away. "Susanna, I—I put flowers in Her Royal Highness's hair. You see, I was trying the French style. The one you told me about."

"Oh." Susanna didn't understand why Mary wouldn't meet her eyes. "Did you tell her it was my idea, then?"

"No, I— Susanna, you must understand, I—"

"You didn't?"

Just one day earlier, Susanna would have thought a betrayal like this would anger her. Instead, she felt herself about to cry. She'd been so rash to trust this strange girl after knowing her such a short time.

And a dresser, too. Dressers never saw chambermaids as equals. Perhaps Mary thought Susanna good enough for a bit of fun in a dark hallway, but that didn't mean she thought of her as anything more.

Susanna was such a fool. She'd let herself begin to care.

She blinked back her tears. Next to her, Barnaby looked confused, and Mary looked as though she might cry herself.

"I see the way of it." Susanna kept her voice measured and cold. "I understand everything. Now never speak to me again, and I'll grant you the same favor."

"Susanna, please, listen to me, I—"

But Susanna was running down the corridor before Mary could finish whatever lie she was about to attempt.

10:00 p.m.

"She's gone." The despair welling in Mary's soul was deeper than she'd have ever imagined. "Oh, do you suppose she could forgive me, Mr. Halford?"

"Well, I'm not sure I quite grasped all that just transpired, Mistress Arnold, but that's one question I *can* answer." Barnaby shook his head. "Susanna does not easily forgive."

There had to be something Mary could do. She couldn't lose Susanna already. She was the one good thing about Mary's new life here at the palace.

An idea began to form in Mary's mind. It might be her only chance. But she'd have to move quickly.

"Barnaby," she said, forgetting in her haste to use the proper form of address. "My apologies—Mr. Halford. Could you get me into the ball?"

"What do you mean, *into* the ball?" Barnaby's eyebrows went shockingly high. It was indeed a strange request. Only male servants attended on the courtiers in the evenings. The ladies enjoyed the sight of a handsome man in livery holding out a shining tray.

"Just for a moment. I need to— I must speak to Her Royal Highness."

"To the *princess*?" Barnaby's shocked look would have been

comical had Mary not felt so desperate. "You wish to speak to Princess Amelia *during* a ball in the palace gardens."

"It's my only choice." Mary could not help the desperation that leaked into her voice. She could not allow the ladies to continue gossiping about her marvelous knowledge of hair-styling. It was a lie, and more important, it was a lie that hurt Susanna. "Please, sir. I must convince Susanna of my sincerity."

"You really do care for her, then." Barnaby softened. "All right. It's a good thing your hair is done, at least. I suppose there's nothing we can do about your lack of proper dress, but stay close behind me and maybe I can block their view."

Mary followed Barnaby through a gap in the shrubbery and into the garden itself. Suddenly they were steering carefully through a crowd of women in six-foot-wide mantuas and men in flowing gray wigs. The courtiers stood in chattering groups, sweat dripping down their necks and anxiety glossy in their eyes.

"There she is," Barnaby whispered. Mary spotted the princess right away from the petals in her towering hair. "I must leave you here. I've been away from my post far too long."

"Thank you, Mr. Halford." Mary straightened her shoulders and tried to think of a witty way to thank him. Something Susanna would say. "I'll alert you if I hear tell of Lord Hervey growing tired of Lord Fox."

Barnaby grinned and disappeared back into the garden.

How was Mary meant to address the princess? She oughtn't be here at all. Already several ladies were casting her unhappy looks now that Barnaby was no longer shielding her.

Mary fidgeted with her dress. It had been fine once, but here among these ladies in jewel-crusted mantuas, she might as well have been wearing rags.

"Mistress Arnold?"

The sound of the voice made Mary's chin shoot up. The princess was calling her.

Mary ran to her side as fast as she could in her high heels. The princess was standing at the center of a group of ladies, including her sisters, the Princesses Anne and Caroline.

"Your Royal Highness?" Mary whispered.

"Ah, I thought I saw you skulking back there." Princess Amelia did not whisper. In fact, she seemed to raise her voice even higher as she commanded, "Fetch me a bourdaloue."

"Yes, Ma'am."

Mary scurried backward, trying to think of where the nearest bourdaloue might be. The day before she would've been astonished to hear a princess of England call out so loudly for a device in which to relieve herself, but no act of Princess Amelia could shock her now.

On a hunch, Mary glanced down beneath the shrubbery at her feet. Sure enough, she caught a glimpse of white porcelain, and another a few yards farther on. She should have guessed that the gardens were well-equipped during balls. Mary knelt, holding her breath, as she strongly suggested the gentlemen at the ball had already been employing the shrubbery for a similar purpose, but without the use of pots.

The nearest bourdaloue was the most beautiful one she'd ever seen, white with gold trimming and an array of painted flowers along its oval surface. It was amazing how such a purely functional object could look so delicate. Mary wondered what it must have been like for the painter to use his artistic gifts on such a thing.

She grasped the handle and lifted the lid to make sure the pot was empty. It was, God be praised. She slid the cover back in place and tried not to think of how many ladies had already used this bourdaloue that evening as she carried it swiftly back to the group surrounding the princess.

"There you are." Princess Amelia spotted Mary and beckoned for her to follow. A moment later, Mary and Her Royal Highness had slipped into a dark corner of the garden. They could still see the other ballgoers, but no one seemed to pay the princess much mind as she hiked up her mantua and petticoats. Mary passed her the bourdaloue in silence and managed not to flinch when she heard the princess begin to use it.

Well, Mary had come here to speak, had she not? This may be the only chance she had.

"Your Royal Highness," she began. Mary was anxious to choose her words carefully, but mindful that she only had moments until the princess composed herself again. "I must make a confession to you. The style I used on your hair today—it was Mistress Susanna's idea. That is, it was she who told me of the French technique, with the flowers. She, not I, should be the one to receive praise for it. I apologize for my misrepresentation, and if a punishment is due to me, I will accept it without complaint."

When Mary was done speaking, the princess laughed long and hard. She handed Mary the full bourdaloue and began to right her skirts. "I suspected as much. A meek little country girl like you knowing hairstyles never before seen in an English court? Well, here's what we can do. My sister Anne despises her dresser, so you can go and work for her instead. Then Mistress Susanna can become *my* new dresser. It should've been her in any case. Portly thinks she has the charge of our households, but she's not the granddaughter of a king, now, is she?"

Mary was astonished. This was even better than she had hoped for. She struggled not to spill the bourdaloue in her excitement. "No, Ma'am."

"Run and tell Mistress Susanna, would you? Have her inform Mistress Keen."

"I will, Ma'am. Thank you."

"Right then. Now, that's enough servant talk for me. I've a ball to enjoy."

The princess, her skirts back in place, strolled to rejoin her group of ladies. Mary, nearly laughing to herself in her glee, emptied the bourdaloue into a remote shrub, then returned it to its place and left the garden as quickly as her footsteps could carry her.

When she reached the palace, its back corridors were dark and empty. Mary ran up the steps, trying to look in every direction, and quickly lost her way.

"Susanna?" she whispered into the blackness after countless minutes of wandering. It was hopeless. She would never find her in this darkened maze.

"Mary?" a voice whispered back through the emptiness. "Is that you?"

"Susanna!" Mary couldn't believe her luck, but she knew that voice perfectly. She ran up to her and took the other girl's hand, even as Susanna tried to pull away. "Oh, Susanna, I'm so sorry about what I did. But please, you must listen. I must tell you what's happened tonight."

Speaking so fast she wasn't even sure the other girl would understand, Mary told her about her conversation with the princess. At first, she worried Susanna wouldn't believe her. Soon, though, as her eyes adjusted to the dim light, Mary could see the smile on Susanna's face.

"Truly?" Susanna finally said.

"Truly! You're to be her dresser. No more emptying chamber pots. Well, except the occasional bourdaloue, I suppose. We must find Mistress Keen and tell her!"

Susanna shook her head. "Not yet. She'll be busy with the ball arrangements for hours yet. We'll tell her after that. For now, I think you should simply come with me."

Mary nodded. She couldn't stop smiling.

Neither could Susanna. Perhaps she truly was forgiven.

The stairs were dark and winding. Mary didn't know where Susanna was leading her, but neither did she care. They turned down one dark corridor into another, until Mary couldn't stand to wait any longer. She caught Susanna by the wrist.

"Enough climbing," Mary said. "Do you believe me?"

"Yes, of course."

Mary could hardly believe it. "You forgive me?"

Susanna laughed. "I wanted to forgive you even before I knew you spoke to the princess. It was a struggle to think of you as capable of deceit. You're not an easy one to be angry with, Mistress Arnold."

Mary smiled and shook her head. "Then enough dashing through corridors. We're already in exactly the right place."

"Well," Susanna said with a smile, glancing above her, "in truth, we—"

Mary silenced her with a kiss.

It was darker now than it had been when they kissed before, and warmer, too. Susanna kissed her back with an eagerness that drew little sighs out of Mary as their lips moved together. She pressed Susanna back against the wall, dreaming of being alone with her again tomorrow, dreaming of the time ahead, together. Here, where the corridors were a dark, hazy maze. The perfect place for secrets to be kept.

"Hem." The voice behind them was gruff, male and speaking words Mary didn't recognize.

Susanna did, though. She broke apart from Mary at once and dropped into a deep curtsy. "Your Majesty."

The king! Mary dropped to a curtsy, too, but not before she caught a glimpse of King George, the curls of his wig cascading down over his embroidered waistcoat, his jeweled shoe buckles gleaming in the dim light.

He said something else Mary did not understand, but which drew a light giggle from Susanna. Then he turned and began to climb the stairs behind them, his heavy footfalls clumping on each step.

The girls turned when he did, ensuring they faced him until he was out of their presence. They did not rise until they heard a door slam on the floor above them. Nor did they speak for some moments after that, until they could be quite certain he was gone.

Then their laughter spilled out, despite their attempts to contain it.

"Shh. His mistress's rooms are just above," Susanna gasped out in a whisper. "I tried to warn you. He's often been known to take the back stairs to visit her."

"What did he say to us?" Mary whispered when she finally regained the breath to speak. "German, was it?"

Susanna nodded, gulping through her laughter. Of course the servants here spoke German, like the royal family themselves. Mary would need to learn it, too, now that she was to stay among them.

"He said—" Susanna choked "—he said, 'Right then, girls. Carry on.'"

Mary lost her composure all over again, collapsing against Susanna in a heap. They laughed and laughed as quietly as they could, holding each other through their tears.

"Well, then," Mary said. "We ought to follow the royal command, should we not?"

And that was precisely what they did.

★ ★ ★ ★ ★

NEW YEAR

BY
MALINDA LO

San Francisco—January 21, 1955

Lily Ma notices his hair first: parted on the left, slicked back on the sides, with a swell of dark waves on top. He has a smooth face with high cheekbones and a plump lower lip. Lily is almost positive she's seen him somewhere before, but she can't remember where. It's strangely unsettling.

The red paper lanterns hanging from the ceiling of the Eastern Pearl Restaurant shed a warm glow over the table in the alcove where he sits with three women. One of them is wearing trousers. Another is a redhead with bangs cut straight across her forehead. The third woman is seated to the man's left, and she's wearing a royal blue dress and a neat pearl choker. She smiles at him with a glint in her eye that Lily doesn't quite understand.

It's late for dinner—nearly nine thirty—but the restaurant is almost full. On a Friday night, the Eastern Pearl mainly attracts tourists seeking out a taste of the exotic Orient, as advertised by tour companies who bring them in by the busload to gawk at the neighborhood Lily grew up in. They're always given the American menu, decorated with gold dragons on the cover and filled with a dozen kinds of chop suey, food that Lily herself would never order.

Lily's friend Shirley Lum nudges her with her elbow. "You're making a mess of those," Shirley says, eyeing the loose, haphazard stack of napkins in front of Lily. They'll never pass muster with Shirley's mother, who is only letting them linger in the family restaurant because it's Friday night and they need the help.

"Sorry," Lily says. She notes the precisely pleated napkins stacked in front of Shirley. "I'm no good at this."

"Here, I'll redo yours." Shirley pulls Lily's napkins toward her. "And stop mooning over that man. He'll catch you staring."

Lily shoots an indignant glance at her friend. "I'm not mooning. I think I've seen him somewhere."

Shirley's eyes flicker toward the table that Lily has been watching. "He's handsome," Shirley says.

Lily pushes her chair back and jumps up, running behind the counter, where the cash register is located. She returns with several old issues of the *San Francisco Chronicle* in hand. "I know where I've seen him," Lily says.

Shirley's mother uses the *Chronicle* to wrap up leftovers, and sometimes Lily reads them while she's at the restaurant, lingering over the film reviews and society columns, imagining a life outside the boundaries of Chinatown. Lily shuffles through the papers, searching for something that she hopes she'll recognize on sight.

"What are you looking for?" Shirley asks.

"It might have been an ad," Lily answers. The rustling newspaper is a whisper, barely audible over the sound of conversation and laughter in the warm restaurant. It smells of fried dumplings and hot and sour soup. Outside on the street, firecrackers are going off again, even though it's too early.

Chinese New Year's Eve is tomorrow, and it'll be launched with a fusillade of firecrackers right after midnight, but the Chinatown boys can never resist exploding a few in advance.

Lily keeps an eye on the foursome as the man gestures to their waiter, holding his hand up to ask for the check. The woman in the royal blue dress has a black patent leather purse with a white scallop on the top. From within it she takes out a gold compact; it glitters like a Hollywood star.

That's when Lily remembers the section she saw him in. She flips through the newspaper with rising excitement, finally pausing on the After Night Falls column, which reviews nightclub entertainment. She scans the page, looking for the ad she vaguely recalls—but it wasn't an ad after all. Four photos are prominently featured with the column itself: three women, including Mae West, and one man. Lily surreptitiously compares the man in the restaurant to the person in the photo. The same shiny, short hair, the same nose and cheeks. The caption reads "Tommy Andrews: Club Chi-Chi Performer."

"Is that him?" Shirley asks, leaning over Lily's shoulder.

Lily scans the column until she finds the brief mention. "Tommy Andrews, the male impersonator, brings something different in nightclub entertainment to Club Chi-Chi."

Something goes still inside Lily, as if her heart took a breath before it continued beating. Shirley has gone silent. Her eyes dart back and forth from the photograph to the man at the table with the three women.

"Tommy Andrews," Lily whispers.

Shirley is a little pale.

Lily looks back at the newspaper, scanning the ads beneath the column, and there's Tommy Andrews's name again. Tommy Andrews Male Impersonator. Club Chi-Chi. 462 Broadway. That's only a few blocks from the Eastern Pearl.

The bars and clubs are packed in close beside each other on

Broadway. Lily's parents always tell her to avoid those blocks; they're for adults, they say, and tourists. Not for good Chinese girls. Not for girls at all.

But Lily has walked along Broadway before. It's scarcely five minutes from her home, yet it always feels a world away. She likes the gaily painted awnings and tall neon signs; the music leaking out from behind closed doors; the ladies in smart hats and high heels, with their stocking seams neat up the back of their silk-sheathed legs. There's something vivid about those blocks that lights a secret flame inside her.

"It's not natural, you know," Shirley says softly. "Ladies shouldn't look like men."

Lily looks up from the newspaper. "It's for show, Shirley. Entertainment."

Shirley shakes her head reproachfully. "This is the Eastern Pearl, not a nightclub."

Lily rolls her eyes. "Oh, please. There are always dancers from the Forbidden City here. Doesn't your father say all money is equal at the Eastern Pearl?"

Across the restaurant, Tommy Andrews is paying for the meal, but the other women at the table also drop dollars onto the tray—even the woman with the scallop purse.

Shirley sighs. "Let's not argue, Lily. It's almost the New Year. We should be friendly and peaceful." She is as prim as one of the St. Mary's nuns, but her jaw clenches.

Lily bites her tongue with some effort, but can't resist snapping the newspaper closed with a showy gesture. On the back page there's an article about the upcoming New Year parade, along with a photo of Miss Chinatown smiling delightedly at the camera.

"You should've entered the Miss Chinatown pageant," Shirley says abruptly.

Lily is surprised. "Why?"

The foursome Lily has been watching are standing now, putting on their coats. Tommy Andrews helps the woman in the blue dress with her coat, holding it open for her like a gentleman.

"Your father is a doctor, and he's on the parade committee. You could have won," Shirley says.

Miss Chinatown was ostensibly a beauty pageant, but the winner was determined by the number of raffle tickets she sold. Everyone knew it was about connections, not beauty.

"I don't want to be in a beauty pageant," Lily says.

"Why not? I would."

"I don't want people staring at me."

"You should be in the pageant next year," Shirley says. "And I'll help you sell raffle tickets."

"If you're so jazzed about it, why don't you enter?" Lily asks a bit sharply.

Shirley shakes her head. "I'm the daughter of a restaurant owner. I'm not going to win."

"Why not? Isn't this America? You're much prettier than me. I'll help *you*, how about that?"

Shirley seems mollified. "Maybe."

The bell hanging over the Eastern Pearl's front door jingles as the foursome leaves. Lily catches one last glimpse of Tommy Andrews pulling the door shut.

Behind Lily and Shirley, the swinging door to the kitchen opens. Shirley's mother pokes her head out. "Shirley, come help me for a minute," she says.

"Yes, Ma," Shirley answers. "Leave the napkins," she says to Lily. "I'll finish them when I get back."

Once Lily is alone at the table, she carefully opens the newspaper again and tears out the After Night Falls column. She folds it into a small neat square and tucks it deep into the pocket of her skirt.

★ ★ ★

Sunday morning, Lily wakes up to the voices of Aunt Judy and Uncle Francis in the living room. Luggage thumps onto the floor, and her brothers' footsteps pound down the long hallway from their room at the back of the flat to the front door.

Lily climbs out of bed and pushes open the pocket doors that close off her tiny bedroom from the living room, and Aunt Judy and Uncle Francis are laughing, hugging Eddie and ruffling Dickie's hair. When Judy notices her standing in the doorway, she comes across the room and folds her into a hug. She smells like fog mixed with firecrackers, the scent of New Year's Eve in Chinatown.

"You're so tall!" Judy says, her eyes crinkling at the corners as she smiles. "And half-asleep I think."

"Did you have a good trip?" Lily asks.

"We took the overnight train from Los Angeles," her aunt says. "I slept the whole way."

Lily's mother herds everyone into the small dining room off the kitchen, where she sets out a pot of jasmine tea, fried dough and steamed buns from the bakery on the corner. Judy pulls out a bag of Southern California oranges from her suitcase, and Lily's mother slices them into wedges. Her brothers shove whole wedges into their mouths and deliver wide orange smiles that inspire Uncle Francis to copy them.

The whole day is full of cooking in preparation for the Chinese New Year's Eve dinner. While Francis takes the boys out to buy a Cantonese roast duck, Lily helps her mother and Judy prepare the rest of the food. They make stir-fried rice cakes with napa cabbage and minced pork, and fish braised in a sweet soy sauce. They roll rice balls around sesame paste, cooking them in a clear broth. And for dessert, there is babaofan, or steamed eight-treasure sticky rice, which is filled with red bean paste and candied fruits. When it is unmolded from the bowl after Mama pulls it from the steamer, the sticky rice glistens, the candied fruits shining like jewels. Dad has to hold Eddie back from digging in to it immediately.

After dinner, Mama scoops out servings of babaofan and passes the small plates around the table. "We only need one more to make a lucky eight," she says.

"Seven is a lucky number here," Francis says.

Mama ignores him and gives Judy a pointed look. "Any chance we'll be welcoming a little one this year? He would be lucky number eight."

Judy laughs. "I just started my new job. I think I'd better put some time into that first."

"How is that going?" Lily's father asks. She can easily see the family resemblance between her father and Aunt Judy, even though Judy is nearly fourteen years younger than him. They have the same eyes and chin. They have the same stubborn streak that pushed Dad through medical school and kept Judy up late studying math, despite being thousands of miles away from their family in China.

"It's going well," Judy responds, getting up to refill everyone's tea.

"Aunt Judy," Lily says, "is it true that you're helping to send spaceships to the moon?"

Judy looks surprised. "Who told you that?"

"Eddie," Lily says, gesturing to her fourteen-year-old brother, who is busy shoveling babaofan into his mouth. "I think he was exaggerating. We can't go to the moon!"

"Not yet, but maybe someday," Judy says.

Lily's eyes widen. "Really?"

"Yes, really," Judy says, smiling.

"We'll need rockets to go to the moon," Eddie says. "I've read about them before—"

"Those are science fiction books," Lily says.

"They're based on real science!" Eddie responds indignantly.

"Are you building rockets, Aunt Judy?" Dickie asks, bouncing in his seat.

"I'm helping to build them," Judy says. "That's one of the things we do at the Jet Propulsion Lab. Your uncle Francis helps, too."

"But what do you do?" Lily asks her aunt.

"I do the math," Judy says. "I calculate a lot of different things—it's a little complicated to explain, but in order to figure out where a rocket will go, I have to do a lot of mathematical equations. Well, I and many other computers. Your uncle Francis works with the engineers who use the calculations we do to build the rockets."

Dickie has picked up one of his chopsticks and is using it to challenge Eddie to a duel. Eddie obliges, but before they get very far into their sword fight, Mama notices. "Stop that, boys. If you're finished with your dinner, go play in the living room." She picks up their empty plates and holds them out to Lily. "Lily, will you take these into the kitchen and wash up, please?"

Lily knows it's her mother's way of getting her and her brothers out of hearing range—the adults always wait till they're gone before they say anything really interesting—but Lily stands up and begins stacking the empty dishes. As she clears the table, Dad steers the conversation toward Uncle Francis and Aunt Judy's new house in Pasadena, which they bought only a few months ago. Lily carries the bowls and plates into the kitchen, piling them into the sink and turning on the water, adding dish soap. It's her job to clean up after dinner, although sometimes her brothers help dry.

When she turns off the water she hears her mother saying "I wish we could move, but he doesn't want to."

Lily wipes her hands on the dish towel and tiptoes to the kitchen door to listen.

"It's not that," Dad says. "You know we can't move. My practice is here in Chinatown. This is our home."

"Our home," Mama says derisively. "Last week the immigration service stopped him on the street."

"It wasn't so bad," Dad says mildly.

"What happened?" Judy asks.

Lily can't follow everything her father says, though the English words *alien registration card* are sandwiched between his longer answer in Chinese. Government immigration agents often stopped Chinese to ask for their identification, but Lily didn't know it had happened to her father.

"They didn't believe he was a doctor!" Mama says.

"They believed me in the end," Dad says, sounding tired. "They were doing their jobs."

"They were bothering you for no reason," Mama says. "Everyone in Chinatown knows who you are. If those agents don't believe you from the start, they won't believe anyone. We should move."

"Moving isn't that simple," Dad says. "There are people who don't like Chinese everywhere. Think of how difficult it would be to live in a place where there are no other people like us. And how many non-Chinese will go to a Chinese doctor?"

"Judy and Francis had no problem buying their house," Mama says defensively.

"No," Francis says. "But we read in the paper that some others have had problems. The Americans in a neighborhood voting that the Chinese should leave, things like that."

"We're Americans now, too," Judy says quietly.

"You know what I mean," Francis says.

There's a moment of silence, and then Dad says in a low

voice, "I haven't heard from Didi or Jiejie in over a year." Didi is Lily's youngest uncle, and Jiejie is her eldest aunt; both are still in Shanghai.

"I haven't either, but what can we do?" Judy says. "We can't try to contact them now. We'll be seen as Communist sympathizers."

A chair scrapes across the floor, and Lily's mother says, "I'll get more tea."

"I'll get it," Judy says. "You sit."

Lily scampers back from the door, returning to the sink. She is busily washing up the bowls when Judy enters the kitchen, empty teapot in hand.

"Time for more tea," Judy says, setting the teapot on the kitchen table. She picks up the empty kettle from the stove and comes over to the sink. Lily moves to the side, and Judy fills the kettle from the faucet.

"Can I ask you something?" Lily says.

Judy puts the kettle on the stove, lighting the burner beneath it. She leans against the counter as Lily continues washing. "Of course."

"Are you the only Chinese girl at your job?"

"So far," Judy says. "But not the only Chinese. There's Francis, too, although I don't see him much during the day."

"Do you like your job?"

"Yes. I do. All the women I work with are wonderful. You know why?" Judy puts her hands on Lily's shoulders and steers her toward the small kitchen window. "Look out there. Look up."

Lily's soapy hands drip onto the counter. "I can't see anything. It's dark."

Judy chuckles. "Yes. But in that darkness, behind those clouds are stars. It's not really dark, Lily. That's space. There is so much light there—all those stars. You just have to know how to see it. That's where we're going, and I'm going to help us get there. All the women I work with—did you know all the computers are women? We're working together to get there."

Lily peers out the window, but above the city lights there is only the smudge of black night sky. "How? Are you going to send people to space? Like in those books that Eddie reads?"

"Maybe someday. Can you imagine?" Judy's voice swells with emotion, but as hard as Lily tries, she can't imagine what it could be like to leave planet Earth. She can't even imagine what it would be like to leave San Francisco. Her whole life has been bound by this city, except for a few weekend trips with her parents to Carmel or Half Moon Bay, where they watched the Pacific crash against the shore and ate a picnic of cold Chinese buns on the beach. On those trips, she did her best to imagine China on the other side of that vast stretch of blue, but even with Chinese words tumbling in her head, it was hard to envision the land her parents once called home.

"What do you want to do when you graduate high school?" Judy asks unexpectedly.

"I don't know." Lily adds impulsively, "But I don't want to stay here in Chinatown forever."

The kettle is beginning to hum as the water heats up. From the living room, Lily hears her brothers' voices chattering as more firecrackers pop on the street.

"You don't have to stay in Chinatown. There are so many things you could do," Judy says.

"Like what?" Lily says skeptically. "I heard what Dad said. It's hard for Chinese here. What if they deport him? Or all of us, and we have to go back to China?"

"That won't happen," Judy says decisively, shaking her head. "You are an American citizen. You were born here, and they can't force you to leave. You have all the rights and opportunities of every American." Judy takes a breath. "As a girl in China I never imagined I could have the job I do now. I'm helping to build rockets to space. Anything is possible here, especially for you."

Lily meets her aunt's eyes. "Anything?"

Judy looks determined. "Yes."

The kettle begins to whistle, and Judy squeezes Lily's shoulder before she goes to pour the boiling water into the teapot. Lily continues to wash the dishes, but after her aunt leaves the kitchen, Lily pauses. She dries her hands and turns off the overhead light before going back to the small window. The kitchen is in the top rear corner of the flat, the only room with a view down the streets away from Chinatown, toward Market Street.

Lily thinks about the newspaper article she took from the Eastern Pearl. Tommy Andrews's face is as exotic to her as the idea of rockets launching into space, but Tommy Andrews is real. Tommy walks the streets of San Francisco, just like her.

Lily doesn't look up at the dark night sky. She gazes at the city lights, glowing through the fog like stars on earth.

There's a cramped little bookstore on Columbus between Chinatown and North Beach. The first time Lily went into it, she was with her brother Eddie, who was looking for more science fiction novels. While he pored over *Mission to Mars* and *Sentinels from Space*, she picked her way through the packed bookshelves to the back of the shop, where she found a spinning rack full of dime novels. The covers were lurid, with half-clad women and swarthy, looming men, and titles like *The Devil on the Mountain* or *The Castle of Blood*.

There were also books with two women on the cover. On one, a girl in a negligee knelt demurely on the ground, eyes cast up over her shoulder at the slightly menacing woman behind her. *The Sappho Sisters* the title read. "This sorority is like no other." On the cover of *Strange Lovers*, the tagline declared, "She couldn't escape the unnatural desires of her heart." The cover showed one woman, the strap of her dress slipping off one bare shoulder, swooning in the arms of another woman.

Lily flipped through the pages with her heart in her mouth, keeping an ear out for Eddie. She skimmed the story, her face creeping with heat, until she came across a scene that riveted her in place, half-hidden behind the rack of paperbacks. She went back to that bookstore three times to keep reading *Strange Lovers*, but on her third visit the book was gone, and the bookseller gave her a queer look and she realized she couldn't go back.

She remembered that one scene from the novel as if it were a movie she'd watched in the theater. In the dark corner of a studio apartment in New York, a girl named Patrice tried to resist her feelings for an older woman named Maxine, but Maxine had seen through her subterfuge and told her, "You're like me, Patrice. Stop fighting the possibility." Then Maxine had kissed her, and the words on the page were imprinted in Lily's mind like a sailor's tattoo. *The sensation of Maxine's mouth against hers was a delight far beyond shame.*

Rain slicks the streets the morning of the Chinese New Year parade, but as crowds gather in the early evening to watch the procession up Grant Avenue, the drizzle dries up, leaving a cloudy sky and damp pavements that cause the firecrackers to fizzle on contact. Lily's family has prime seats in the grandstand, and Eddie is one of fifty boys who will carry the fire-breathing dragon up the streets. As the St. Mary's Chinese Girls' Drum Corps stops in front of the grandstand to perform "Chinatown, My Chinatown," Lily says to her mother, "I'm going to meet Shirley by the bakery."

"Bring her back here," Mama responds. "Don't go anywhere else."

"I won't," Lily says. She picks her way down the grandstand seats to the street. Mama forced her to wear a qipao—all the Chinese girls are wearing them today—and the dress's tight skirt makes climbing down the steps difficult. She passes a little boy about Dickie's age, clutching his burning sparkler a moment too long. He yelps as it singes his fingertips, dropping it onto the wet street, where it hisses out.

Although the audience in the grandstand is mostly Chinese, the crowds along the sidewalks are not. There seem to be thousands of people lining Grant Avenue, and Lily finds the raucous throng exhilarating as she swims through the crowd. The chattering conversation, the cheers as the marching bands go by and the cacophonous beating of drums break against her in waves, as if she is being tumbled about in the Pacific itself.

Lily finds Shirley in front of the bakery just as the float bearing Miss Chinatown comes up the street. Shirley drags Lily to the front of the sidewalk to watch Carolyn Lim, seated on her throne and surrounded by the runners-up, tossing confetti into the masses. She is dressed in a gold-embroidered red qipao almost exactly like Lily's.

"You should be up there!" Shirley cries.

"No, you should be," Lily responds, and Shirley giggles happily.

The climax of the parade is the twenty-five-foot-long dragon that slinks its way up Grant Street, its gold silken back undulating and its electric eyes flashing through the twilight. The children nearby shriek in mingled terror and excitement at the sight of the creature. Lily cheers, clapping for her brother Eddie even though she can't see him. The dragon is trailed by a truck bearing a generator to keep the eyes lit, the noise of the engine a dull growl beneath the cheering.

After the dragon passes, Lily and Shirley head back to the grandstand to meet Lily's family. Lily's mother has an extra ticket to the Miss Chinatown coronation ball for Shirley, who is beside herself with excitement. They are almost at the grandstand when Lily sees Tommy Andrews turning away from the spectacle on Grant, one hand on the elbow of his companion. Lily recognizes the handbag the woman is carrying—that distinctive white scallop on the glossy black patent leather. She's wearing a belted black raincoat and a cocked hat with a little net, and as she and Tommy leave the parade, something white flutters from her pocket onto the sidewalk.

Shirley is far ahead now. Lily darts toward the spot where the couple turned off Grant and finds the item that fell to the ground. It's a handkerchief, and its tumble to the street has left the white cloth stained with a few dark wet patches. In one corner, the handkerchief is embroidered with a cursive letter *L*.

Lily runs after them, following them up Pacific Avenue. "Miss!" Lily calls. "Miss, you dropped your handkerchief!" The woman with the handbag doesn't seem to hear her, so Lily puts on a burst of speed and reaches out to tap the woman's arm. "Miss? Your handkerchief?"

The woman halts and glances over her shoulder. Her face is lit by the edge of the streetlight; she looks surprised. "Oh! Thank you."

Tommy Andrews turns back, too. Lily wants to look, but she tries to keep her gaze on the woman with the handbag. She holds out the handkerchief. "My name starts with *L*, too," Lily says breathlessly, and immediately feels like a fool.

"What's your name? Ling? Isn't that a Chinese name?"

Lily flushes. "My name is Lillian."

"Lillian," the woman says. "What a lovely name. I'm Lana. What do your people say, gong hay fat something?"

"Gong xi fa cai," Lily says, her heart sinking with embarrassment. "Happy New Year."

"Happy New Year," Lana responds. "That's a beautiful dress you have on."

"Thank you," Lily says. She should turn away and go back to her family, but she says, "Can I— May I ask, were you at the—the Eastern Pearl last week?"

Lana's eyebrows lift. "The Eastern Pearl? That restaurant over on Kearney?"

"Yes." Lily hears the last bits of the parade, the crowd laughing and clapping, but this stretch of Pacific feels like a quiet little cocoon. Behind Tommy, the street goes uphill, and the damp pavement sparkles in the streetlight.

"Is that where you took us?" Lana asks Tommy.

"I think so. Is that your family's restaurant?"

Lily has to look at Tommy to answer. Tommy's face is shadowed by the building looming over them, and Lily wishes she could see more clearly. "No," Lily answers. "I was there with my friend. I—I've seen your picture in the paper."

"Have you?" The tone of Tommy's voice is sly as a secret.

Lily trembles. "Yes."

"You ever been to the Chi-Chi Club?" Lana asks.

Lily shakes her head. "No, miss." She adds boldly, "But I'd like to go."

Lana gives Lily a slow, deliberate smile. "If you ever stop by, you tell them I sent you, all right? Tell them Lana Jackson sent you."

"I—I will. Thank you, Miss—Miss Jackson."

Tommy says, "We'd better get going. The others are waiting."

"Thank you for bringing me my handkerchief," Lana says.

"You're welcome."

"Maybe we'll see you again some time," Lana says. She

resumes her trek uphill, tucking her handkerchief into her coat pocket.

Lily turns away, but at the corner she glances back. Tommy and Lana are walking side by side. They're not touching, but the careful distance between them makes Lily almost certain that they're together. *Strange Lovers*. The thought sends a quick thrill through her, like a firecracker sparking in her veins.

She forces herself to go back to the grandstand, back to the lights and the crowd and her family. She sees Mama scanning the crowd for her, relief breaking over her face when she finally spots Lily. "Where have you been?" Mama demands. "Shirley came back without you."

Shirley looks at Lily curiously, and Lily says, "I saw a lady drop her handkerchief so I went to give it back to her." Mama's forehead furrows critically, but before she can say anything, Lily continues, "Aren't we supposed to be helpful and be good American citizens? Isn't that what this parade is about? Showing everyone that we're trustworthy and honest?"

Mama looks dubious, while Aunt Judy, who is standing nearby, swallows a smile.

"Already practicing your speech for next year's Miss Chinatown pageant?" Shirley teases her.

Lily says tartly, "Anything is possible."

★ ★ ★ ★ ★

AUTHOR'S NOTE

Although all the characters in "New Year" are fictional, two of them are inspired by real people. Lily's aunt Judy is inspired by Helen Ling, who was one of the first (if not the first) Chinese American women to work at the Jet Propulsion Laboratory as a computer. Helen became a supervisor and hired many more women, including other Asian Americans. You can read about Helen and the other women computers of JPL in Nathalia Holt's book *Rise of the Rocket Girls: The Women Who Propelled Us, From Missiles to the Moon to Mars.*

The character of Tommy Andrews is inspired by the male impersonators who performed in San Francisco's nightclubs—including many that catered specifically to lesbians—in the 1940s and 1950s. The Chi-Chi Club was real, and performers like Tommy were featured in the *San Francisco Chronicle* as male impersonators. For more about San Francisco's lesbian and gay communities, read Nan Alamilla Boyd's *Wide Open Town: A History of Queer San Francisco to 1965.*

Finally, San Francisco's Chinese New Year parade was modernized in the 1950s by Chinatown leaders partly as a way to destigmatize Chinese Americans during the Cold War. The Chinese in San Francisco deliberately used Western stereotypes about Asia to render Chinese Americans as peaceful and nonthreatening, which was imperative during an era when Chinese were routinely harassed due to American fears of Communist China. I am grateful to Chiou-Ling Yeh's paper, "'In the Traditions of China and in the Freedom of America': The Making of San Francisco's Chinese New Year Festivals," in the June 2004 issue of *American Quarterly*, for many of these insights.

MOLLY'S LIPS

BY
DAHLIA ADLER

Seattle—April 10, 1994

My parents love to talk about where they were when Kennedy was shot. They love it in particular because the answer is that they were making out in a closet at school when they were *supposed* to be watching the parade on TV with their classmates, but I've heard their friends get swept up in it, too. It's a marker for their generation, I guess—even bigger than John Lennon, though they'll also happily tell you where they were for that (reading me my favorite bedtime story—*Frog and Toad Together*). I always thought this was a particularly morbid way to remember things.

Now I get it. I know I'll always remember where I was when I heard Kurt Cobain killed himself. It's been only two days, but I just know I'll recall every microscopic detail with brutal precision.

Because it's the moment I realized I was in love with my best friend, Annabelle.

She's the one who told me, because of course she was. I was lying on my bedroom floor and blasting music—Pearl Jam's "Black," specifically, which feels like an extrashitty betrayal in retrospect. If I'd known she was coming, I would've had on Nirvana or the Vaselines or the Melvins or even Mother Love Bone.

I knew it was bad when she didn't even comment.

"He's gone, Molly" was all A.B. said, and her voice was vapor and then so was she. I don't even know how she found her way into my arms, how long it took my T-shirt to get drenched with her tears. I didn't need to ask who "he" was; I'd been preparing myself for this inevitability since news broke of his overdose in Rome last month. My brother, Ben, had said, "Watch this, Mol. Next member of the 27 Club. I'll put money on it."

I hated him for saying it and told him to fuck off, but the truth was, I knew not to take that bet—and not just because Annabelle would've abandoned me for life if I had.

She, unfortunately, did not share the vision of Kurt's imminent doomsday. "He has a daughter now," she'd said so many times, tracing glossy magazine photos of Frances Bean with her finger and a wistful sigh that told me she would've given anything to trade places with the blond infant. "He'll fix himself for her. Watch."

I watched. It broke my fucking heart.

I love Nirvana, too, in case that isn't clear, but not the way Annabelle does. I don't have plans to tattoo their logo over my heart when I turn eighteen, or their lyrics around my arm and on my foot. But I can list you every drummer they've ever had, in order, and sing you anything by heart, including the songs I never heard until Annabelle and I parked ourselves in front of the TV to watch their *Unplugged* performance on MTV last fall. I can tell you which of their songs is a Shocking Blue cover and what inspired "Polly," and probably reenact the entire video for "Smells Like Teen Spirit."

Would I be at Seattle Center right now if Annabelle hadn't begged me, though? Would I be standing here in my flannel shirt and knit cap, surrounded by a crush of grieving bodies and the scent of wax, my heart thudding in my chest every time Annabelle squeezes my hand or lets out a sniffle or smiles despite herself at the sight of all the different Nirvana T-shirts and signs?

Probably not.

But here we are, surrounded by hundreds or thousands of other fans in Nirvana tees and flannel, some bawling their eyes out, some howling to no one and some too stunned to react at all. There are mini vigils everywhere, little crowds sitting around candles and signs and flowers.

"We should've brought stuff," Annabelle sniffles in my ear when we pass each one, on the pavement, on the grass. "Of course we should've brought stuff."

I wish I'd thought of it—anything to make her smile. The need to help her through this is a fiercely fluttering thing in my chest, if only just to feel her clammy palm in mine again. She grasped it only once, quickly, when we first entered, and the tingles that shot up my arm were decidedly un-best-friend-like.

Now that she's let go, my hands are cold.

I have no idea how this happened, or why I suddenly can't look at my best friend without my eyes straying to the Dr Pepper–scented sheen on her lips. But when she collapsed in my arms two days ago and I kissed the top of her head, all I could think was that I wanted her to look up. I wanted to kiss her again, somewhere it counted. I wanted to kiss away every tear—but really, I didn't want her to have any to begin with. I wanted the fact that she had me to be enough.

But of course I'm not enough. We're here because I'm not enough. She'll never love me like she loves a man she'll never meet.

The sound of overhead-speaker static stops us in our tracks, and chills ripple down my body as I recognize Courtney Love's voice—or at least a teary, stuffy-nosed distortion of it—filling the air. This time, I grab A.B.'s hand, and I'm relieved when she squeezes it and lets me hold it close to my heart.

"I don't really think it takes away his dignity to read this, considering that it's addressed to most of you." Courtney's words are only decipherable because the crowd is stone silent. "He's such an asshole. I want you all to say *asshole* really loud."

I glance sideways at Annabelle, wondering if she'll do it, if she'll desecrate her hero like that. But I don't wait for her before I do it myself.

"Asshole!" I chime in with I don't know how many other voices. Feeling A.B.'s nails digging into my palm, remembering the way her entire body shuddered as she cried on my shoulder the other day, how can I think he's anything but?

Courtney continues on, and it feels like a kick in the gut as I realize what she's reading is his suicide note, his very last words. Next to me, Annabelle weeps quietly, tears streaming down her smooth cheeks, her eyes like polished copper.

We're quiet as Courtney reads on, interjecting her own anger every few lines, and then, suddenly, Kurt's widow breaks down, and now I'm crying, too, wondering with her what she could've done, what would've saved him. And next to me, Annabelle cries louder, harder, red splotches blossoming on her cheeks.

Without thinking, I gather her up in my arms and whisper, "I'm sorry," over and over again while she soaks my shirt for the second time in three days. I don't know what to do to make this better. I don't know what else I can do. I don't know what Annabelle needs. I don't know why this is destroying her from the inside out like she just lost her father, her mother, her sister.

Her best friend.

I don't know how to save Annabelle from this pain I don't quite understand.

"A.B.," I murmur into her ear. "It's okay. I know it hurts, but it's okay. You'll be okay."

"I won't." She's shivering in my arms now. "I won't."

"Annabelle." I stop while I choose my next words carefully. I don't want to say his death doesn't matter. It does, to her, and to me, and everyone gathered here and everyone who couldn't be.

But the crack forming in my heart at the knowledge I don't matter *more* is stealing all my thoughts.

"Talk to me" is all I manage.

"You won't get it." Annabelle wipes her nose on her sleeve. "No one does."

"Try me."

She hesitates, then reaches into her pocket and pulls out a piece of paper. No, not paper—liner notes. Well-worn ones I immediately recognize as being from Nirvana's *Incesticide*. She doesn't say a word as she hands them over, then hugs herself into her flannel shirt.

There's nothing scrawled on them, no words but the text itself. I scan it in case there's something I've forgotten, but there's nothing new. I know these words; probably every Nirvana fan does.

Whatever Annabelle's trying to get me to see, I'm failing. I hate, hate, hate that I'm failing her, today of all days.

I look up into her teary blue eyes, trying to convey all the sadness and guilt I feel. "I'm sorry, A.B. Whatever it is, I don't..." I can't bring myself to say "I don't get it," so I just don't finish.

"The end," she says in a rasp.

My entire body ices over. "The part about the girl who was raped to 'Polly'? Ann—"

"No," she says quickly. "No, not that. The part before."

The part before…where Kurt (well, "Kurdt") basically tells homophobes, racists and misogynists to fuck off. It's a good part. It actually makes me feel a little bad for calling him an asshole a little bit ago. But I still don't get it.

"I've never had anyone stick up for me like that."

Her voice is so soft that I almost have to ask her to repeat it, but then I process her words. Really process them.

Oh my God.

"You're not talking about the 'women' thing, are you?"

She shakes her head. Or maybe her head is still and it's the rest of her shaking.

"Annabelle." My voice comes out in a whisper, and I reach out to stroke her hair before I can stop myself. I don't even know what else to say.

"Do you hate me?"

"Do I— *Annabelle.*" I step closer, bringing my other hand to her face so that my palms lightly cup her cheeks, which are flushed and tear-sticky and so, so soft.

She jerks back, out of my grasp. "You don't even know the worst part. How much I actually hate that album."

Of course she'd think that was the worst part. "Annabelle. It's pretty inarguably their worst. I mean, other than 'Sliver,' 'Aneurysm,' and 'Molly's Lips'—"

The words die in my throat as she wrenches her gaze away from mine and another tear slips down her cheek.

After what feels like endless silence, she finally speaks, broken and brittle, her eyes on some far-off point in the sky. "It's like it was mocking me, you know? That song."

That song.

My heart hammers in my chest as I think about all the different ways I could interpret her meaning, and the only way I want to, which rises above them all. "You mean 'Molly's

Lips'?" I feel like I need to shout over the rushing in my ears, but my words come out a whisper anyway.

She gives a jerky nod. "I'm sorry. I'm *sorry*, Molly. I have tried so hard not to, and I'll keep trying, just please don't..."

The rest of her words are drowned out by that rushing, joined by the pounding in my rib cage. Is she saying what I think she's saying? I'm trying to process her words but my brain is nothing but static.

"Mol?" Her voice is timid, tentative, nervous.

And suddenly I feel anything but.

I grab the flaps of her flannel shirt and mash my mouth to hers in what's probably the least romantic kiss of all time, both our faces damp and the crowds around us both cursing and celebrating a dead man. But it's perfect, still, the way her arms wrap around my neck and squeeze me like I am a lifeline and I squeeze her right back the same way and then we finally remember that we know how to kiss like normal people and we do but it's so much better than normal and in fact it's actually everything.

She pulls away, just a few inches, just far enough for me to see a glazed look in her eyes that I don't think has anything to do with her tears. "Mol? Really?"

"'I'd take you anywhere, I'd take you anywhere, as long as you stay with me,'" I say with a grin, brushing her damp hair out of her face so I can kiss her again.

"Did you just use a Nirvana quote to flirt with me, Molly Oliver?"

"Of course not. I paraphrased a Vaselines quote to flirt with you, Annabelle Mason. Nirvana just covered 'Molly's Lips.' They can't be blamed for your years of anguish."

A smug, know-it-all smile curves her mouth. There have been times I've dreaded that smile, but now it's beautiful to see on my Annabelle, and I am ready for whatever factual shredding she's about to toss my way. "*Actually*, Kurt changed those lyrics slightly from the original Vaselines version, so those *were* uniquely Nirvana lyrics, smartass."

I sigh. "Dear Annabelle, I am so sorry I tried to out-Nirvana you. Now will you please kiss, kiss Molly's lips?"

She does.

It's all too short, but then again, we *are* at a vigil. We came to pay our respects and to say goodbye, and hand in hand, we walk through the crowds to do just that. When we pass a particularly full and colorful cluster of candles and mementos, including a guitar, A.B. squeezes my hand and says, "Hold up a second."

I stop and watch as Annabelle pulls a bright-red lipstick from her pocket. She applies it messily to her lips, not caring how boldly she goes outside the lines. Then she pulls the liner notes back out and plants a kiss right over her favorite paragraph, leaving a flaming lip print. She sets it down right next to the neck of the guitar, then grabs my hand again.

"Okay," she says, then takes a deep breath. "Okay."

The crowd is getting wilder, the huge fountain teeming with kids hollering chaos, the candlewax-and-incense scent in the air mingling with scorched fabric as people burn their flannel shirts. The "asshole" chant continues, only partly drowned out by the Nirvana songs flowing from the loudspeakers, and Annabelle and I walk slowly and take it all in. And then the whispers begin, everyone spreading the word that Courtney Love is handing out Kurt's clothing, and without exchanging a single word, we double back in the direction of the rumors, hoping to catch a glimpse of bleached hair and runny eyeliner.

I dodge a girl wrapped in yellow police tape, dancing in the middle of the grass with her eyes closed and her hands waving, as if "Scentless Apprentice" were a rave jam. We don't see any sign of Courtney, but we're caught in streams of people slowly filing past us, talking about heading to Viretta Park.

"Do you wanna go?" I ask Annabelle, bracing myself for her enthusiastic "Yes!" I don't know that I want to spend the rest of the day creeping near the Cobain house, especially since it'll probably be crawling with cops. The fact that I'll be returning home reeking of weed and incense is bad enough. But I also know there's no way I'll say no to Annabelle, especially not today.

"Nah," she says, and she couldn't have shocked me more if she'd stripped down to nothing but her choker and Doc Martens on the spot. "I've got a boom box, an *Unplugged* tape and a quiet garage. I can think of better ways to celebrate Kurt today. Let's go."

We turn back to the crowd, to the speakers, to wherever the essence of Kurt Cobain drifts over this space, and blow kisses into the wind. "Peace, love and empathy," Annabelle murmurs, and then we fade away.

THE COVEN

BY
KATE SCELSA

Paris, 1924

It was Gertrude Stein who first introduced us to the coven.

I had been hearing about it for years at this point of course. There had always been talk of witches in the eleventh arrondissement. The excited whispers would start every year in early October, children daring each other to walk down certain streets where it was rumored that the witches held their secret séances. After Halloween the children always lost interest. For most people witches were a seasonal topic.

I never thought much of them. Witches or people.

Until Vivie brought me to Gertrude Stein.

Vivie had made it her mission to gain access to the salon of the legendary writer. She finally succeeded by claiming to be a long lost niece. Alice B. Toklas, Gertrude's de facto gatekeeper, didn't believe the story for a second. But she let her in to see Gertrude anyway. And that is how things usually worked for Vivie.

I often met Vivie after school in her favorite café. She was always sipping an espresso and scribbling furiously in her notebook. She had a few affectations that I put up with, some more reluctantly than others—the uninterrupted writing in this corner of the Café Select, drinking coffee late into the night. The hat that she stole from her brother that she liked to tip just so, down over one eye. The way she had started walking with her hands in her pockets, as if life was just a stroll for her.

Actually, I liked that part. I liked the hat, too.

I had been planning on trying to kiss Vivie for a month at this point. The idea occurred to me one day and then I just decided that I would do it. I was simply taking my time. I watched the other women in the café with jealousy—the girls who held hands and wore pants and didn't seem to care what anyone thought. I wanted to say to Vivie "We are like them," but what we had felt like a magic spell that I was afraid to break.

And Vivie might have kissed me already if she wasn't so busy teaching herself to be a "great writer."

"Like Gertrude Stein," she said.

On this day when I met Vivie in the Café Select she had just come from another afternoon at Gertrude's salon. She always looked brighter when she left there, as if a little flame had been lit behind her eyes. I tried not to feel jealous that someone else could make her that happy.

She saw me come in to the café and waved. I was foggy today. That was what we had come to call it. Days when a cloud seemed to descend over everything around me. My thoughts went slowly, tripping awkwardly over each other to get where they needed to be. Moving through space became an exercise in walking through water. Vivie could always tell when I was having a foggy day. She noticed things like that.

"Going slow today," I said before she could.

It was hard to say exactly when the problem started. The fog had crept up on me over the past year, like a nagging obligation. Days that felt a little "off" had led to strange visions, auras of color circling around objects and people. Then the feeling of dread that accompanied this underwater life, as if somehow I really was walking around on the bottom of the ocean, and it was only a matter of time before I realized that I didn't know how to breathe down here.

"I talked to Gertrude about you," Vivie said when I finally sat down at her table.

"Oh, really?" I said. I picked up a café menu and looked at it, not surprised to see the familiar words swimming in front of me. Things didn't like to stay in place on my foggy days.

"She wants to meet you," Vivie said.

I had not yet been admitted to Mme Stein's famous salon myself. I was not a writer or an artist, so why would the woman known in these cafés simply as "the Presence" want anything to do with me?

"I'm supposed to bring you to her," Vivie said, "so she can decide for sure if you're ready."

"What do I need to be ready for?" I asked.

"I guess—" and with this Vivie took my hand "—you just have to have an open mind."

She smiled at me from under the brim of her brother's hat. That smile that was my only true heart and confidant and home all wrapped up into one person.

I looked down at the open page of her notebook. It was filled with words but also strange symbols. Circles in circles. Five-pointed stars.

"My mind's open," I said.

The next day I found myself on Gertrude Stein and Alice B. Toklas's famous doorstep at 27 rue de Fleurus in the sixth arrondissement. Vivie held my hand on the walk there, and I couldn't tell if she was doing it to help me keep up with her through my fog, or if she was feeling what I was: actual electricity firing between our fingers. It took everything I had to pay attention to where I was stepping.

The fog was a little better today. The electricity helped. It always helped. Back when the fog started, my mother took me to all of the doctors that she and my father could afford. But no one could find anything concretely wrong with me. I took pills that made me tired. Drank tonics that tasted like dirt. Nothing made a difference.

"You've just got to be tougher, Dean," my father would say.

So I stopped telling them about it. It didn't seem significant in the face of what we had just experienced anyway. The knock at the door that had confirmed all of our worst fears. That our family would never feel whole again. My brother, who had been so excited to go and see the world, would not be coming home. Not ever.

Vivie was the only person that I told about the fog anymore. And now, at her insistence, I would tell Gertrude and Alice.

"You know they're married," Vivie said to me as we stood on the doorstep, still holding hands. She hadn't rung the bell yet. I wasn't sure what she was waiting for.

"Who?" I asked.

"Gertrude and Alice. Not actually married by law. But in practice."

"Oh," I said. I wanted to say "I know, Vivie, like us. Like we will be one day." But I didn't.

She rang the bell and a small birdlike woman with severe hair and even more severe eyes opened the door.

"Madame Toklas," Vivie said. "So nice to see you again."

Alice B. Toklas nodded at us and opened the door all the way.

"She is expecting you," she said.

Still holding my hand, Vivie led me down a hallway and into a drawing room, where the Presence herself was perched in a chair that was slightly higher than the others. Her throne. The walls were covered in modern art, outrageous cubist faces made of shapes and women's bodies with many breasts and even more eyes. Gertrude Stein was dressed all in black, as if she were in mourning, the buttons on her shirt done all the way up her neck. It was old-fashioned, in contrast to her shorn-short hair and the outrageousness of the art.

A young man was pacing in front of her, talking and gesturing.

"I just don't understand how long I have to wait for the world to catch up," he was saying.

Alice came in and motioned for the two of us to take a seat. Vivie led me over to two chairs in the corner.

"These things take time, Hem," Gertrude was saying. She smiled at us. She didn't look like a woman who smiled much, but when she did it was like a glorious secret. As if maybe you were the only person she had ever smiled for.

"Anderson says I'm a genius." The young man was sweating. He hadn't noticed us enter. "Scott says it, you say it, so why can't I sell any books?"

"Yes, Hem, I told you that you were a genius and you've never let me forget it," Gertrude said. "Now, if you don't mind, I have some other guests to entertain."

The man stopped pacing and looked around the room as if he didn't believe her.

"Oh," he said when he saw us.

"Come back tomorrow and you can tell me more about your genius," Gertrude said, waving him away with her hand.

"I can't stay?"

Gertrude shook her head.

"Definitely not, genius. Ladies only."

He stood there for a moment, not quite believing that he

was being told to leave, then turned around and walked out of the room.

"Sorry about that," Gertrude said, turning to us. "Ernest is a sweet kid, but he doesn't know when to just shut up and listen."

Vivie nodded, as if she understood.

"So," Gertrude said. "This is Amandine?"

"Dean," I said.

"Vivie has told us a lot about you," Gertrude said.

Alice settled down in a chair across the room and began knitting. These women were different from the girls holding hands that I saw in the cafés. Gertrude and Alice seemed to exude a sense of living history with their black clothes and severe expressions. In her corner, Alice was weaving something into her knitting that looked like feathers.

"I've heard about you, too," I said to Gertrude. "I mean, everyone knows about you." This seemed like the wrong thing to say and I found myself blushing.

"Have you read my work?" Gertrude asked me.

I looked to Vivie, not sure if I should tell the truth.

"A little," I said.

"Well, it's not really meant for the layman," Gertrude said. "So I wouldn't blame you if you hadn't read it. It'll become much clearer…after." She smiled again, and even in this somber room, with Alice knitting her mysterious feathers, I found myself wanting to trust Gertrude Stein completely. I saw why Vivie spent so much time here. Gertrude's attention felt like an honor that was not given lightly.

"Vivie tells us that you've developed some unusual symptoms," Gertrude said, all business now.

"I get foggy," I said. "That's what we call it. It's better some days."

"With the moon," Alice piped up from the corner.

Gertrude waved away the suggestion.

"They will determine," Gertrude said to her. "Do you know when it started?" she asked, turning back to me.

"About a year ago," I said.

"Around the time that your brother did not come back from the front lines," Gertrude said.

I looked at Vivie. Evidently she had told them everything.

"Yes," I said.

Gertrude got up and went over to a desk. She took out a piece of paper and wrote something down on it.

"Vivie, are you able to get her to the eleventh arrondissement this Friday at midnight?"

Vivie looked at me.

"Yes," she said. "We'll have to sneak out, but we can do it."

She looked so sure of herself, so excited for us to be the ones receiving instructions from this formidable woman.

"What will we be doing there?" I asked.

Gertrude walked over to us and handed Vivie a piece of paper with an address on it.

"Meeting the coven, of course," she said.

Vivie met me in the alley next to my apartment building at eleven thirty that Friday. My mother and father had been asleep for hours. I tiptoed past the cat and simply locked the door behind me. I ran down the stairs, feeling free of the fog for now, my mind actually clear for the first time in days. The stairs below me were just stairs, contained in their own shape. The street outside looked only like itself.

Vivie was leaning up against a wall, her hat tipped down over her eyes. I was breathless when I got to her, but seeing her silhouetted in the dark against this midnight street, I wasn't sure if it was from exertion or excitement.

She looked up when she heard me. She looked worried for a moment, then she smiled.

"I thought you might not come," she said.

"How could I miss the coven?"

And then for a second I thought that maybe this was it, this was the moment when Vivie would kiss me. Or when I would be bold enough to kiss her. Now, in this darkness, and with the promise of more magic to come.

But she just took my hand again.

"You ready?" she asked.

I nodded.

Vivie had brought money for a taxi, knowing that the metro wasn't safe for two girls traveling alone at night, and that any fogginess might slow us down. I didn't ask her where she got the money. Probably the same place she got her hat. Her older brother, who indulged this mini version of himself with whatever she asked for. Her brother, whose bad eyesight would always protect him from having to fight. Even if he had wanted to go to war, he had to stay home, safe, with his family.

Vivie hailed a taxi and when we got in I could already feel the fog returning. I had been naive to think that the excitement of this night might banish it. The glow of the streetlamps outside the taxi window took on colors and expanded, refusing to stay in place.

"You okay?" Vivie asked as the taxi started moving along the Boulevard Saint-Michael.

"I'm okay," I said. I looked up at the sky. The moon was full.

The taxi stopped at a gate on a particularly deserted block and we got out. Ornate stonework crowned buildings that resisted the small amount of light that emanated from the wrought iron streetlamps. The shadows of cats stalking their prey moved among the cobblestones.

I had never been to this part of Paris before, and definitely not to this street, which seemed to stretch back in time hundreds of years.

We stood together in front of the large iron gate and looked at the oversize door knocker.

"Do you think they're really witches?" I asked.

"Only one way to find out," Vivie said.

She raised the knocker, then dropped it, letting it ring out across the small courtyard. The taxi had driven down the street and turned off at the corner. We were alone. No other cars. Only quiet and the watching cats. And then the gate opened.

A young woman in black mourning clothes like the ones that Gertrude had worn locked the gate behind us and led us through the courtyard. A stone arch brought us to another interior courtyard, surrounded by the large fortresslike building, a spot that couldn't be seen from the outside.

I held tight to Vivie's hand.

In the center of the interior courtyard there was a circle of women, also in black. They stood as another young woman walked in a formation around them, holding a burning bundle of twigs.

The girl who had led us this far turned to us.

"Wait here," she said.

She went to the center of the circle, where a group of candles were set up on an altar, and began to light them.

I looked at Vivie. She stared wide-eyed at the circle of women. The light from the candles was illuminating something perfect and unrepeatable in each of their faces. A few wore cloaks with hoods pulled up around their heads, their faces hidden in shadow.

The one girl finished swirling smoke around the circle, the other finished lighting the candles and one woman began to speak.

"We thank the local spirits for allowing us to gather here tonight, to honor our moon and to purge ourselves of that which no longer serves us."

Vivie and I watched from outside the circle as the witches conducted their ceremony. A wind kicked up as the hour moved past midnight, and I noticed, as if it were a faraway fact about someone else, that my fog from earlier had lifted. The candles flickered without auras. The breeze was made of air and not water.

Finally the woman who had spoken first turned to us.

"We have visitors tonight, sisters," she said to the group. "Come forward."

Vivie and I stepped toward the circle, and it opened to make space for us.

"You are in need of our help?" the woman asked.

"Dean needs you," Vivie said. She seemed to want to say more, but something stopped her, perhaps the severe look on the woman's face as she turned to me questioningly.

"Is that true?" she asked.

"I guess so," I said.

The woman closed her eyes then, tilted her head up toward the full moon, which seemed to be getting closer somehow, as if it would like to join this unusual gathering.

"A rose is a rose is a rose," the witch woman intoned. The wind was picking up around her. She opened her eyes. "On the full moon we give up that which no longer serves us," she said, "so that we may clear a path for the energy of existence to move through us freely. This is not a cure, but a reclaiming of self."

She took a step toward me.

"What do you need to rid yourself of?" she asked me.

I let go of Vivie's hand and stood on my own then. The air stilled, and from somewhere nearby I could smell jasmine. Vivie had brought me here, and I may not have believed in magic before this night, but I wanted to now.

"Doubt," I said. My voice was strong when I said it and it surprised me. I hadn't known what I was going to say before it came out.

The witch smiled.

"Very good," she said. She came over to me and handed me a piece of straw. "Here is your doubt," she said. "Burn it."

I took the straw and stepped forward toward the largest of the center candles, a white pillar of wax. I let it touch the flame. It started to burn and I dropped it into the light.

Your brother's pain is not your own.

The words wrapped themselves around my ear, becoming my entire existence for just a moment. No one had spoken, but I heard the words as clearly as if I had said them myself.

Let go of that which cannot be held.

In that moment, something seemed to take off from me, as if a large bird had been perched on my shoulders and had now been released back into the heavens where it belonged. My body became so light I thought it might merge with the air and blow away.

I was light. Everything was light.

Then one of the witches was laughing, and then they were all laughing, and then they were running, one by one, away from the candlelight, back out of the courtyard.

I looked to Vivie, whose eyes were so bright with the reflection of the flame. I wondered if she had seen it, too. The thing that flew away from me. I wondered if she had heard those words.

"Where are they going?" I asked the one black-cloaked figure who remained.

"We purge through fire, then purify through water," she said. She took down the hood of her cloak and revealed the unmistakable face of the Presence. Madame Stein herself.

"Follow me," she said. "A swim under the moon binds the magic." She looked at Vivie. "Although there are *other* ways to bind a magic spell."

She smiled and walked toward the place where the others had gone, back out and under an archway. In the distance, I could hear splashing and laughing.

"Should we follow?" I asked and turned to Vivie, but I barely got the last word out before she was kissing me, a desperate, perfect kiss that caught me off balance and pushed me backward. She caught me and held me tightly to her, my body filling with moonlight, a cleansing fire that spread out from my heart and into every part of me.

Vivie pulled away and looked at me, her eyes searching for something.

"Okay?" she asked.

I smiled.

How could she not know how sure I was of her?

I took her hand and pulled her in the direction of the witches.

★★★★★

EVERY SHADE OF RED

BY
ELLIOT WAKE

England, Late Fourteenth Century

The first time we kissed, our bodies bronzed in the emberlight, our skin a mosaic of shadow and fire, Robin cupped my face and said against my lips, "I'm not like other boys, Will."

It was the first kiss of many. I would remember his words, years later, before the last.

But I never actually heard his voice.

Speech was touch and sight was without sound after the illness: a pulse of air stirring my hackles, a glimmer of light playing over his mouth. My ears heard nothing, but the rest of my body learned new languages. For me Robin spoke concisely, carefully, so that I could read his lips. I treasured every word more than gold.

"Look at this, Will."

He stood in the torch-thrown shadows of our forest hideout, surrounded by his stolen hoard. Coins spilled over the edge of a coffer when he lifted it. Robin laughed, his eyes fiery with a hundred mirrored suns. I felt his laughter like I did the doubloons clinking and rolling across the moss oak floor: golden sounds, bright and round, rumbling off into the shadows.

"We're rich," a boy said, and another, "We're kings."

"And *queens*," Alix quipped.

They slung their arms around her, hoisted her to the rafters, crowing, "Long live the queens."

Other words I couldn't decipher swirled around me, a cloak of hot breath. My heart filled my whole chest.

We had done this: Robin's lost boys and lost girls, the children society had thrown away. We'd woven together a family of orphans and outcasts and exiles. Not one of us shared blood. Not one of us would balk at spilling our own blood for a brother or sister.

"Fools," Little John roared, slamming his staff against the planks. Coins leaped like molten droplets. A foot taller than the tallest of us, with his head swathed in brilliant white scarves and a pearl earring gleaming against rich brown skin, John seemed like African royalty. "Kings are weak men who think gold and gems give them power. Shiny bits of broken earth." He picked up a coin, flashing its bright eye back and forth. "This is not power. We took it from them and it may be taken in turn from us. It is nothing, friends. Nothing compared to what we possess. With all the gold in the world they could not buy what we have. It makes us mightier than kings."

"And how, pray tell, are we mightier than kings?" asked Alix.

Little John tossed the coin into the hearth fire. "We are free."

A pensive silence spread through the room.

Robin's eyes swept over us without seeing. In the honeyed light of the hearth his smooth face shone, hairless and fair. He'd laugh when I would nuzzle him, graze my coarse jaw against his soft throat. When I would hold his face and kiss him, hard, telling him everything with my mouth, yet without words. When I would press him down into the sweet straw that made our bed.

My beautiful boy, full of laughter and light. But not now.

His gaze pierced through me. He was whispering—no one else would hear, but I read his lips.

Again and again he repeated, *We are free.*

Smoky green haze drifted through Sherwood Forest, as if fire quickened in the leaves, licked from bough to bough and burned coolly, giving off a pale light. Here under the canopy, the sun dissolved into fog. Wraith shadows glided through the gloom, prowling.

Us. The forest gods.

Distantly, a horse nickered. I did not hear it; Alix signed to me from a tree across the path. I crouched on a branch high above the others. My eyes were sharpest.

There.

A furlong away, the white murk opened like a ghost's mouth, and from it emerged dark shapes: carriage, beasts, riders.

I signaled the numbers and arms of the men. Alix slithered down the trunk.

My role was over.

I rubbed my thumb over the virgin yew of my bow, twanged the cord with my fingertip. Robin never forbade me from fighting but he may as well have. "I need those keen eyes of yours where they will do the most good," he'd said, but what I heard was "where there is the least threat of harm." Robin's pet, the others mocked, good-naturedly. Pup. Pony. Broodmare.

"Say that word again," he'd told the girl who voiced that

last, "and I'll cast you out. You can fend for yourself come winter."

So she didn't say it.

Not that he could hear.

But sometimes she would look at me—Rashida, her skin tawny from the desert sun of her people, her eyes rimmed with kohl—and her lips would make a silent oval: *Whore.*

You can hurt a boy like me without speaking a single word aloud. All you have to do is hold it in your mouth.

Road dust rose from the horses' hooves, the riders' black whips licking the air like snake tongues. They rode fast, knowing the stories about the forest. It wouldn't matter.

First we took their horses.

Nets flew out of the brush, burlap sacks weighted with stones. Each one found a beast's head. Blinded, the animals slowed and swayed, leaving their riders easy game. We disarmed the men with staff strikes and lassos on catchpoles as Little John rushed in to throw hoods over their helms. It was done in seconds. The carriage driver called his team to a halt, staring wide-eyed.

On a branch overhanging the path, a mass of leaves and vines uncurled lithely and became a boy who dropped light-footed to the dirt, sauntered left a few paces, then right, then bowed, his deep hood shadowing his face.

I could not see his lips move, but my heart knew his words.

"Gentlemen," he'd be saying, "welcome to Sherwood Forest. I am Robin, lord of the woods, prince of thieves. I noticed that your horses travel under a heavy burden. Permit my friends to lighten the load. Keep your calm and you will not be harmed."

As he spoke, we moved. Alan, once a cutpurse whose fingers had been removed by the Sheriff one by one till all he had left were thumbs, approached the carriage with a smile.

Alix's swordswomen put silver blades to the throats of any rider who looked apt to resist robbery. Rashida, formerly a courtier whose weapon was words, slung herself onto the driver's seat and wheedled him for information.

We knew our roles well. We performed them with aplomb.

All but Will Scarlet, whose only task was to simper after Robin.

I ground my teeth. That wasn't me anymore. Not the cringing, lily-hearted son who so disgusted my father. Not the boy who'd tangled his limbs with those of another boy, and rolled through the crackling summer grass, and let my head fill with blue sky and bliss—then cried when a farmhand told my father, and again when my father made me watch every lash the other boy took. Forty lashes, but forty-five marks on that boy's back—five of which were mine. As I watched him writhe I could still feel his taut muscles moving against my skin, smell the salt and sea musk of his sweat.

My father had said, "If it happens again, I will kill him."

Then you may as well kill me, too, I'd screamed with my hands, stabbing my finger at my own heart.

My father's face did not change. Calmly, he answered, "A widower does not slay his only heir. But if I must, I will remove your manhood and marry you to a nobleman, as befits a woman."

That night I crept into the stable. In the last stall was my father's prize stud, painted silver blue with moonlight. I left no letter. Months later, while scrubbing piss and ale from filthy floorboards, I spied a scrap of parchment tacked to a tavern wall:

A Handsome Reward is offered
for the return of a White Stallion
belonging to the Lord of Scarlock.

Perhaps I hadn't given him due credit. He knew which of us held the higher value in breeding.

My name was Scarlet now. No longer a lord, but a mere boy.

One who loved another boy.

Alan ducked out of the carriage and said something I couldn't parse. Robin glanced up into the trees, seeking me. I dipped a hand into my tunic lacing and fished out the medallion: a bronze fox, tarnished with fingerprints. The symbol of Locksley. Robin's house. One eye was missing but the other was a ruby, and this caught a stray shaft of sun, bursting into a rose of light. I whisked the medal back and forth, signaling in code: *The way is clear.*

Nervously, a lordling climbed out of the carriage. A hand reached after him, slim and white—his sister, perhaps. Alan bent over that hand and kissed it, grinning. Below me, boys scattered the horses into the wood—we could not keep them; horses left tracks—while swordsgirls tied up the men-at-arms with leather scraps. Tuck, who'd abandoned his noble titles because a friar need not wed nor bed and he longed for neither, swung a heavy velvet sack, and I imagined the music it made: fine chimes of silver, dulcet bells of gold.

The children faded into the forest, our clothes the color of leaf and bark, blending, becoming one. In moments all that remained was Robin in his hood, his face unseen.

I had waited too long. I was supposed to retreat when the others did.

But I never missed this part.

Robin snatched the whip from the carriage driver. As he climbed atop the coach his cape flickered, a patchwork of leaves and flowers and fur. He looked like the forest made flesh. An avatar of the living wood. The whip cracked, coiled around a tree branch. He looped it over his forearm and leaped into the green air and, like magic, vanished. Though I'd seen this trick a hundred times, I could barely track him as he swung up into the canopy. If not for one flaxen lock of hair slipping from his hood, I'd have lost him.

My golden boy.

The riders stirred, loosening their bonds.

Time long past for leaving.

I shimmied down a chain of grass ropes, my rabbit-skin boots supple and swift. The men would mask my noise in their attempts to free themselves. I knew how loud I was by nature's response: a startled bird winging away in a rainbow streak, a scuttle of paws kicking up dirt. Sometimes sight is a more powerful way of hearing than sound.

Before I disappeared into the undergrowth with the others, I saw it.

A torn parchment.

I knelt slowly, my heart thrashing. At Scarlock Manor I had learned to read and write, the privileges of a lord. Most of the others couldn't. Robin himself struggled. He'd ask me to read for him and then curse and ball his fists in frustration. It puzzled me.

"Your father is a lord," I'd signed, miming a crown, fingers to forehead like antlers. "Did he not teach you?"

"Why would he teach me?" Robin had snapped.

Patiently, I'd signed, "Because you are his heir. His only son."

Robin had stared at me, expressionless. Then, quick as a fox, he embraced me. I could not see his lips to translate, but he said something over and over against my chest, three short words. Three knives rattling between my ribs.

My heart still trembled to think of it.

Now in my hands was something else that shook my heart. Mud blotted the ink, obscuring words. What I could read was enough.

"A Handsome Reward is offered," it began, and at the bottom it ended, "Report any Sightings to the Sheriff of Nottingham."

The lordling's name was Nicholas.

His tale had come through our usual channels: gossip in pubs, coins pressed into sweaty palms. One afternoon, rumor said, Lord Hamish had returned early from the hunt, his horse maimed, to find his son, Nick, in bed with a serving girl and a stable boy, the three tangled together like some unholy chimera.

Lord Hamish did not possess the mercy my father did. Nick unlaced his shirt to show us the scars: crimson weals, angry and boiling in the firelight. So Robin rescued him. Contrived an invitation for Nick to court a noble daughter across the forest. On their passage through our wood, we ambushed.

Later we would bolster the ruse: cut the finger from a cadaver, slip on Nick's signet, courier it to his father.

Hamish lost a son; we gained a brother.

It set off a friendly contest, the others removing bits of armor and clothing to tell the stories of their own scars: parents who'd disowned them, whoremongers who'd betrayed them. Robin watched with a solemn face and when it came his turn, said simply, "My scars are on the inside," and stalked out of the house.

I followed him into the spiced dusk air. Summer waned, days shortening, sunlight deepening into poignant shades of amber and marigold. A final decaying richness before death. I tried not to read portents into it but my thoughts were cagey, feral.

In the pocket of my breeches the fragment of parchment lay folded. It burned against my thigh like a coal.

When Robin caught sight of me he smiled, that sly, rakish smile that had made my belly tighten the night we first met, years past, both filching eggs from an innkeeper's hens. I'd sold the white stallion for mead and meat. Robin had stolen the horse to return to me. We raced it out of town as the watchmen chased, my chest molding to his slender back, my arms around his waist, both of us laughing.

On a hilltop we watched the distant torches swarm madly like fireflies against the night sky. I set the horse free in the woods, and Robin's eyes twinkled. "Come meet my brothers and sisters," he said, and I thought, *Anything that keeps me near you.*

Years passed, but my blood still fired at his smile same as the first time.

Robin tilted his head toward the wood. We walked into the trees, hands linked. I felt the air buzz with insect song and my body hummed in harmony. At the creek, Robin guided me to a tree stump, opened my shirt. His hands were small and elegantly formed. Water ran through them, liquid threads of mirror, like mercury.

"You don't have to," I said, but he silenced me with a kiss.

Sometimes, in a thunderstorm, a lance of white fire would spear down from heaven and split the stone heart of an ancient tree, a crack so deep it seemed to come from the core of the earth. You could feel the skin of the world tense against it.

Robin's kiss felt like that.

Gently he tore his lips away and washed my neck, my chest. I shrugged the tunic off. His fingers traced the terrain of my body, each ridge and slope of muscle. They raked through the trail of hair at my belly as he kissed me again.

"Robin," I said aloud, and from his smirk I knew I'd moaned his name. "I found something."

That somber look returned. As if he already knew.

I drew the parchment from my breeches, unfolded it. "It's a bounty. The Sheriff is offering a reward."

"For who?"

"Who do you think?"

Lord Scarlock was wealthiest of all our fathers. The only one who could interest the Sheriff in his personal plight. It must be his bounty, and the quarry must be me.

"It's been years," Robin said. "He's let you go."

His eyes focused on the water beading on my chest. I could not read his tone.

Perhaps something's happened, I signed. *Perhaps Father's fallen ill. Realized his holdings will be picked over by his cousins, like vultures cleaning a carcass. Maybe he wants his heir back. By force.*

Robin rolled his shoulders languidly. He pulled at my belt.

"Are you bloody listening?" I gripped both of his wrists in one hand, speaking with my mouth. "This is serious."

In the green-blue gloaming his face appeared delicate and fey, almost nymphish. There was a beauty to him that bordered on the unreal, a fineness that made girls heady, drunk on longing. It did the same to me, of course.

"You're not the one they're looking for, Will."

"How do you know?"

"I know."

I opened my mouth and again he kissed me, but this time I could not resist.

My lips crushed against his, tasting the piney rosemary sprigs he chewed. Every muscle in me flexed to draw him closer. I pulled him down into the doe-soft grass, our legs entwined, our hands clawing at each other. Atop me he felt lean and strong, dominant. My body was wet clay to him, responding fluidly to every touch, and every touch circled toward the center, the root of the ache. When he finally grasped between my legs I thought my teeth might shatter.

Robin pressed his cheek to mine. Blond hair spilled around us, a veil of sun.

He whispered something.

All I sensed was heat, lips skimming my ear. He knew I could not understand. But still he crooned to me as he unlaced my breeches, put his hands where I needed them. Made my hackles dance and my skin sing. Language is not only words. We speak with our whole bodies, with gesture and glance, with touch. We had told each other a thousand times with steady hands and the searing insides of our mouths: "You are the boy I love."

Now he told me again as I stared up into the night, the stars switching on, disintegrating the sky into glitter, a dark body slowly consumed with light.

Misgiving woke me from half sleep. I lay alone on the pallet, Robin's bedroll cool to the touch. He'd been gone awhile.

I tugged my pants on and padded barefoot through the camp. We never stayed in one place long—no sense making the Sheriff's job easy. Our village was oilcloth tents and crude log lean-tos. The hideout had once been a priory; now the timber rotted, and moss bearded the fieldstone. Robin loved it: the natural reclaiming the unnatural, just like us.

At the outskirts of camp a willowy silhouette stood in the moonlight, idly twirling a staff while he kept watch. As I neared, Tuck planted the staff to sign, *Evening, Will. Can't sleep?*

I'm looking for Robin.

Haven't seen him. Tuck raised a bushy brow. His eyes were bright and intelligent, but warm, too. *What's troubling you, my son?*

It was a joke: Friar Tuck, the boy who did not believe. He'd turned to the order to escape an arranged marriage, threw away his lands and legacy without a mote of faith in his heart. When I'd asked him why, he'd said, "Could you imagine wedding a woman, having children and being happy? No. For you, happiness is being with a man. For me, happiness is being among friends. Love takes many forms, Will Scarlet. If I must lie to the world to be true to my heart, then I'll lie. I'll cheat, I'll steal and I'll do it with a smile. Love is the only higher power I answer to, and my love is no less for being chaste."

Tuck knew the language of hands and had helped me teach the others. In the order, the brothers lived for days, weeks, months in strict silence, communicating only through signs. Quiet smoothed the ripples from the pond, he said. His mind grew calm and clear. The words he spoke with his hands took on deeper significance. An entire day would pass and the only word he'd have shared with another soul was *please.* Imagine the world like that, he said. Imagine if all we could share was kindness.

I touched the paper in my pocket. *I'm in trouble, Tuck. The Sheriff's after me.*

Are you certain?

I showed him the bounty.

My eyes aren't as sharp as yours, he signed, *but I don't see a name.*

His gaze flicked over my shoulder. I felt a presence, turned.

Rashida strode into the moon-washed clearing. Her hair hung loose, a midnight cowl sweeping around her long, leonine face. Flowing white robes trailed her like silk spun from sheer moonlight. Often our expressions settled into the grooves of our strongest traits. In Robin it was mischief; in me, stubbornness. In Rashida it was pride.

It took a moment for me to notice the torn parchment in her hand. The other half.

"The name is right here," she said.

May I see it?

Rashida smiled. A breeze snapped her robe and I pictured a cat lashing its tail. "What is it worth to you?"

I have nothing that you don't also have, I signed. We kept no coin for ourselves. All of our wealth was shared.

"Don't you?"

She glanced at the medal on my chest, the bronze fox. Reflexively, I cupped it against my heart.

This was a gift, I began, feeling my throat clench.

Rashida clucked her tongue, exaggerating for my benefit. "I have no need of baubles. What I want is your post. Let me climb the tree and be Robin's monkey." She was still smiling. Beneath the glaze of moonlight in her eyes, they were bloodshot. Strange.

Tuck shifted his weight. "That's not wise, sister."

"Just once. That's all I ask."

Done, I signed and extended my palm.

"Trade me."

With utmost reluctance I unknotted the leather cord. *I want it back.*

"I give you my word," she said, and I could see the wryness curling the sounds in her mouth.

When she left Tuck twirled his staff again, anxious. *This is unlike her. Rashida has a good heart.*

I knew she did. Sometimes we found young girls in the carriages we stopped, girls with burnished nut-brown skin and sparrow bones, wearing petticoats and girdles and the face paints of highborn ladies, like dolls. Rashida would offer them refuge. Too often they refused, afraid of coarser treatment at the hands of brigands.

Once we discovered a girl of eleven years, her belly swollen with child, her eyes bewildered and dull. She would not leave the coach. On my watch that night I spied Rashida leaving camp. I followed her into the woods to a hollowed stump, lightning split, its edges blackened. She crawled inside and I listened to the silence in my head till she crawled out again, her face wet and streaked with dark paint like fingers of shadow.

I knew there was goodness in her. She despised me for what I symbolized: the light-skinned men of wealth, the lords who enslaved women as playthings.

I could not blame her. Yet those same men hated me, too.

Tuck was saying something, but I was fixed on the paper. I tilted it into a moonbeam. There it was in iron-gall ink, a black tinged with rust as if with blood. The friar leaned over my shoulder.

See? he signed, his tension slackening. *It's not you after all.*

But my nerves were not soothed.

The bounty listed a description: hair the color of summer wheat, eyes the color of sun filtering through the canopy. A height that would reach my shoulder. A name.

It was the name that made me afraid.

"Lady Marian," it read, "of Locksley."

Weeks passed before Rashida had her turn playing hawk's eye. It felt both like no time and all time.

The pace of life quickened as we stocked provisions for winter, mended boots and cloaks, chopped firewood, buried caches of dried meat and nuts and berries. Not all of us would survive the cold. I wondered who we'd lose this year—it was never who you thought. Alix once coughed blood for months while Rashida sat at her bedside, dabbing her forehead with a damp poultice. Yet Alix recovered and in the spring thaw, a boy named Joren tiptoed across a frozen lagoon until it cracked, and he fell in and drowned.

Perhaps this year it would be Nick. We bathed together in a creek and he caught me staring at his naked chest. His scars had healed fully, turned invisible. Still strong and well fed from his lordling days. He flushed as I watched him dress and it didn't occur to me until later that he must presume lust on my behalf.

Absurd. What I felt for Robin burned stronger than anything, even the fever that had taken my hearing.

"I wish I was like them," I told Tuck as we watched Alix and Rashida sharpen their swords. Their bodies moved in rhythm, one girl beginning a motion that the other completed. "Women who are lovers aren't looked at with revulsion."

"Women are seen as less than men. That's why they're permitted indulgences—they're pretty pets. Is that so much better?"

"Then I wish I was like you. Unbeholden to carnal desires."

"And you'd be seen as less than a man, too. A man who does not serve God must serve his earthly father, and give him grandchildren."

"Is there no way for men like us to be happy, then, Tuck?"

He shrugged. "I'm happy here. This is the most I've ever been myself. Aren't you?"

I thought of Robin, those three words he once voiced into my chest.

Of course, I signed, forcing a smile. *Like Little John said, we're free. We can be our true selves with each other. No gold or gems could buy anything more precious. No king's crown could tempt us.*

He gave me an odd look. Perhaps my eyes had betrayed me. Perhaps he had sensed some undertone in the movement of my hands, some quaver of fear, of dread.

That night in Robin's arms I kissed his smooth throat, unmarked by the apple of Eve's deceit. I touched the leather bindings beneath his tunic. I traced the dashing lines of his face, chapped by sun and wind but still finer than any other boy's. "I'm not like other boys, Will," he said, his lips glistening from the touch of mine.

I pinned him flat to the straw and said, "It doesn't matter. I love you."

We stared at each other, stunned. Then I said it again.

"I love you." I laughed. "I love you."

He kissed me, smiling against my mouth with disbelieving joy. The riddle had been solved. Those three words rumbled the same way in my chest as they had when he'd spoken them.

Rain needled through the trees, a vast, inescapable flaying of the earth. Leaves ripped free and fell, all harvest colors—pomegranate, beet, radish—every shade of red, like heavy succulent drops of blood. Red was the color of passion, and of treachery.

Strange to see this green place changed. Undressed.

I drew my cloak tighter. Midway up a towering spruce, Rashida, playing my part of lookout, clung desperately to slick bark. I crouched on the forest floor, indistinguishable from a dozen other sodden hoods. An ideal time for this—Robin would never know we'd switched roles.

Beside me Alix narrowed her eyes. One gloved hand stroked her sword hilt over and over, as if soothing an animal. We'd told her of the ruse and she'd merely shrugged. Something else nettled her now.

What is it? I signed.

Alix frowned. Her fingers curled around the hilt. *Bad feeling.*

I felt it, too.

The air smelled like metal. The earth underfoot flinched, braced. It was like the moment before lightning, but not the purifying, enlivening charge of Robin's kiss—this was the indrawn breath before calamity.

Inside my cloak were the two halves of the bounty, sewn together.

...for the Safe Return of a Maiden
to her Loving Lord Husband...

I swallowed thickly.

Alix flung a hand skyward and I gave a start. I read the conversation between her and her lover. *Riders, carriage. How many swords? One score. How far? Don't know. How far?*

Rashida kept shaking her head. Alix glowered at me as if it were my fault.

Twenty men was greater than expected. Nicholas had sworn this minor lord could call upon no more than a dozen. Still, in the rain and confusion we would outfox them.

I cradled my bow beneath my cloak and prayed it would be over soon.

Riders entered the road without warning. They moved at a calm canter, but something seemed off—the animals were tall, roped with muscle. Draft horses. Blankets had been tossed over their sides, but here and there I caught the gleam of enameled armor.

No lord's vassal owned a war horse.

Who were these men?

Before I could alert Alix, the riders came abreast of us. Nets and bolas whirled out of the bushes. A heartbeat later Little John and his boys waded into the welter of horses and men and neatly disarmed them. At first I cringed—four to one, poor odds—but the riders milled, confused. One man dropped his sword without being touched. He looked me dead in the eye as he did it, his gaze hard, and I thought: *His gloves were wet. He fumbled.*

It would make no sense to intentionally throw down his weapon.

When the riders' hands were empty, Robin made his grand entrance: a bough unwrapping itself, revealing a boy.

Something made me look up at Rashida, then.

She was not watching us, or the riders. She was staring up the road in the opposite direction, mouth agape.

When I turned to trace her gaze I felt a chill slip inside my cloak, so strong it almost felt like a blade going in.

Then chaos.

Horses pounded behind us, a pincer attack. The disarmed riders drew second swords. The carriage driver, huddled in a rough-spun farmer's cloak, stood and sedately unfastened it, revealing inch by inch the scaled black armor beneath, the wyvern-pommeled longsword, the silver star of office.

The Sheriff of Nottingham.

She stepped lightly into the road. Her men disarmed us in turn, cleaving our catchpoles with brutal bastard swords. In a twinkling, all of the lost boys and lost girls had cold steel at their throats. All but me and Robin.

My side gave a twinge, and I stumbled. Had I felt a chill? There was heat now under my shirt.

I moved toward Robin.

The Sheriff's head was bare, her auburn hair braided tight. Her eyes were the color of frost on dead grass. She stalked with serpentine grace, the longsword bobbing over her shoulder.

"I don't understand," Robin said to her, wonderingly. "I thought the Saracen betrayed me."

Nick Hamish stepped out from behind us, wiping a blade on his cloak. "You thought wrong, milady," he said, and flicked an arc of red into the rain. "I convinced the Saracen to swap places with your lookout. Her kind are ever eager to prove they can do more than spread their legs. Those fine powders she paints on her face—I saw how they reddened her eyes. She can't see any better than this boy can hear. You have many weak links in your chain, milady. It was quite easy to snap."

Of course. Nick's scars "healing" so miraculously. Rashida always competing with me, desperate to prove she was more than her past. Nick had struck at our weak points masterfully. How had I, of us all, been so blind?

It felt as if a wild dog had sunk its teeth into my side. I groped at my tunic.

"Will," Robin said, rushing to me.

Our hands found the wound together. Blood bloomed, welling in our palms in luscious wet petals. It was beautiful, I thought. Ominous but beautiful, like the autumn leaves. All of this red. Every shade, draining from me. Vermilion, crimson, scarlet. My namesake.

When I looked at Robin's face I saw that he was screaming, sobbing.

Eerie that such passion could rack him while my head remained silent.

The Sheriff bent over me. At some point my body had folded to the ground. With her this close, I saw lines mapping worry across her face, a wrinkling of regret.

"Look, Lady Marian," the Sheriff said to Robin, and I imagined her voice: smoky and soft, elegantly viperous. "Your lover is wounded. I can save him, if you return to your betrothed husband."

Robin's tears were like nothing I had seen. When he cried over Joren and the others who died, it was calm, almost peaceful—an acceptance of nature's inevitabilities, of all things ending. What more could we ask but to live and die free men? This was different: his face was twisted, his teeth bared and his eyes filled with a wild, mad light, an untethered terror. He looked so afraid. My Robin had never looked so afraid.

"Lady Marian," the Sheriff said again. "Your husband, Lord Scarlock, is waiting."

Robin did not look at her. He touched my chest, where the foxhead should have been.

"I don't understand," I said, or tried to, but perhaps my lips moved without sound. "Why is she talking about my father?"

"Will, listen to me. I must do what the Sheriff says."

Why? I mouthed. *That's not your name. That's not you.*

His chest heaved. He scrubbed a hand across his eyes. "Someday, please forgive me for this. I know you'll despise me. But I have no choice. I can't let you die."

I don't understand, I mouthed again.

"You do. I know you do. I'm sorry, Will."

Faintly I felt hands lifting me. Robin's face receded, strangely small and elfin, fragile. He lunged for me but the Sheriff held him back with a strong arm.

I was too weak to lift mine and sign. I just kept saying his name.

"Robin. Robin."

He held my gaze as the forest closed around us, screaming my name over and over, and I did not shut my eyes even as darkness crept in at the edges. I knew the air trembled at a higher pitch when he spoke. His throat held no apple. His face was beardless, soft. These things had been used against him, fashioned into a name and a fate that were not his. My birth name was not mine anymore, either. It didn't matter. Like Tuck said: if we must lie to the world to be true to our hearts, then we would.

A face bent near mine. Something pressed into my chest. The foxhead. Rashida gazed down at me and signed fiercely, *You better bloody stay alive, Scarlet. At least until you get our Robin back. Do you* hear *me?*

Then her mouth compressed in a pained smile, and she brushed the hair off my forehead.

I'll find him, I whispered breathlessly. *I promise, Robin. I'll find you.*

The last thing I saw was the green roof of the forest dulling into gray and falling down around me, and then darkness. But in the darkness all I saw was my beautiful boy. My golden boy, my Robin. No other name fit him, and never would. Sometimes sight is a more powerful way of hearing than sound.

★★★★★

WILLOWS

BY
SCOTT TRACEY

Southwyck Bay, Massachusetts, 1732

The shock of red hair against the black ocean froth disappeared beneath the surface as Benjamin remembered a time when his own hair had been that same shade of fire-dark. A time when he'd stood on the Highlands and let the wind ruffle the hems of his skirt and pulled his hair back and tangled it into loving knots. He had been she then. Her name was Mariot, and she knew well what it was like to sink beneath the swell.

It had been many years since Benjamin had been alone in his own head. Memories of other lives, other versions of himself, grew with every year. He was the only one in Southwyck who knew himself in that way, who knew that one life was never really the end.

"Mercy Elizabeth Dare has been committed to the waters that once stole away our children." Reverend was in a frightful mood. He was more theatrical than his father had been as guiding hand for the village of Southwyck, and even when drowning a girl of fifteen he felt like the act needed something more. Words. So many of them.

Benjamin watched the last traces of her disappear beneath

the water, and soon even the bubbles that could have carried her last words had ceased. The waters churning below them were unforgiving as ever—the ocean would take her and hold her deep where none would harm her again.

In other villages, witches were drowned, or, if they refused to plead, were pressed to death. Elements of a natural world. In Southwyck, they preferred a more immediate solution to the problem. A small cliff at the tip of the headlands overlooked the shredding rocks below, and the cursed fell as quickly as the innocent. Over the years, the rocks gorged on so much blood they now kept a crimson cast, a stain to the stone that announced their intent and hunger for the castoffs. The rocks were hungry, and soon they would feed on Benjamin.

"Blessings on the family Dare in their moment of acceptance," he continued. His rum-roughened voice was no more pleasant now than when he had been cups deep the night before with Benjamin's father and the other elders. A night of drinking always preceded a morning of Return.

That was what they called it when they dropped one of their children off the high rocks that overlooked the inlet of Southwyck. The Return. The Elders taught that because of their burdens, the people of Southwyck held vigil.

The children born in Southwyck were not like children born in other villages. Not for many years now. The children born in Southwyck were as dangerous as girls whose tears would summon storms, or boys who left fire in their wake, even when a thing should not burn.

There were other curses that were worse. Curses like a girl who could not be lied to, or a ten-year-old boy who gathered secrets that no one meant to tell.

"Long has the village of Southwyck prospered even in the face of its burden." The Reverend's eyes swept the crowd, looking for signs of emotion, of weakness. But if the Dare family did not weep, then neither did any other.

It was less than one hundred years since the curses began, and the age of plenty succumbed to the age of strife. When Roanoke fell, Southwyck thrived.

"The life of Mercy Dare is one drop of water in the bucket. We must remain watchful, for our enemies lie all around us. They hope to see us fail. They hope to see us falter." The Reverend's drinking voice came out—louder, more boisterous. "But we are in control."

The more dangerous the curse, the faster the Return. But it was only the Reverend who decided when a life should be sacrificed. Only he who saw a girl that inspired honesty in those around her, and sought to silence her one last time.

Mercy hadn't cried. She hadn't given in to her fear. The Returned always knew it was coming. It wasn't them who protested, Reverend said, but the curse inside them. It wanted to live; it wanted to thrive. All good children of Southwyck were stronger than their curses.

"Since my grandfather's day as the founder of Southwyck," Reverend continued, "obscenities have plagued us. Only in our iron will do we prosper. Only through our vigilance will we maintain."

The Dare family remained stone-faced at the center of the gathering. Southwyck did not understand mercy, and even less compassion for a child named such. Her fate had been sealed as a child of the curse.

She was not a heathen like Benjamin, one who accepted their curse as a matter of their life. She was one of the unlucky few—the ones who could not hope to suppress it. No amount of prayer, no pleas for understanding could stop what had ravaged Mercy's life. Father had thought he could deny Mariot, that if he did not think and speak of her, he would prevail against his curse, as if she was a door in his mind that he could close and bar away forever. His father didn't understand. He was Mariot and Mariot was him.

A part of Benjamin knew he could have tried harder. The other voices in his head urged him at times to keep his head down, to keep his thoughts to himself. But he had always been different, would always be *other.* He spoke of things learned in other lives, told stories that he had been told as an urchin striving to feed himself at a monastery. He flouted the secrets of the town every time he opened his mouth.

The truth. Mercy's was a curse of honesty. Just as she herself could not lie, those around her found themselves unable to deceive each other. She was a threat to a town as strict as Southwyck.

The village gathered around him, but Benjamin felt as alone as he had ever been. Despite memories of other lives and a vastness inside his head that was sometimes shelter in the storm of his life, he was not meant for Southwyck. They watched him with haunted eyes. Silence Goode and her daughter Temperance, who had sewn the gowns of every Returned this year. John Thomas and his wife, Agnes, dry-eyed though their sons had taken competing dives two summers back-to-back. Susanna and Deliverance, the widows Byram, had not stopped staring at him during the entire service.

It was hard enough to stand by and do nothing, but worse when the entire town watched and imagined that you were the one dropping off into the water, disappearing beneath the tide. He was glad that Sebastian, the outsider, had not attended. He would hold his tongue, of course, but any who saw his face would read the contempt there.

Benjamin did not care what the people of the village thought of him, but he cared very much about Sebastian. The blacksmith's son was no native of Southwyck—he'd come in on the ships and grew into his role as apprentice. Being born outside the village meant that while he had learned of the curses, and of the Return, he could not understand them the same as the others. He saw cruelty in what they insisted was vigilance and kindness. Bearing witness at the Return of Mercy Elizabeth was just a reminder of that hideous truth. Once the Returns were a rarity, only one or two a year. Mercy was the fifth since the spring thaw. Five times that the children of Southwyck—children susceptible to the curse—witnessed. The Reverend said the Return was to save them. The truth was a midnight ache: it stayed buried inside until the sun disappeared and the world grew quiescent, and then it rose, unrepenting. Unwilling to hide any longer. The Return was their future, their inevitable goodbye.

Leaves fluttered on the wind, torn from branches by a vigorous push off the ocean.

Father's hands clamped down upon Benjamin's shoulders, holding him in place. They were closest to the swell, facing the Reverend, and behind him in the distance, the town itself. Reverend's eyes kept falling to Benjamin.

"We must not let our cursed souls rule us," he said, and his eyes never left the boy's. "For though this land is cursed, we are still the caretakers. So long as the Withers surround us, so long as the New World grows beneath us, we will not let them win. We will not give in to the flames of iniquity."

Things broke apart soon after that, though Benjamin's father's hands would not release him to the day. And when the Dares came up to them, there was a rare moment of compassion across Mr. Dare's face. His parents expressed their condolences, but Mr. Dare waved them off. "Acceptance of a thing makes it easier," he said. "No amount of resisting ever kept the winter from coming."

Mr. Dare gave Benjamin a long look as he passed.

Benjamin remembered what it had felt like to drown. The water closing in over his face, the stones at his feet pulling him down into the fathoms.

Inside him, Mariot shuddered.

Benjamin was seven when he first remembered wearing a dress and letting it flap in the summer breeze on the Highlands. The people of her village would smile at Mariot as she passed, she of the quiet and thoughtful nature. Her only claim to whimsy was on the days when the wind rushed through the village. She would always take a moment to herself, close her eyes and let the wind carry her spirit away.

There was never much she felt the need to say and measured the words of her life as though they would run out.

It was another person to share his skin with. Another version of himself. They were the same, but in many ways they were different. Until that time, he had been a normal child, and did as his parents commanded, but Mariot had signaled his curse's unveiling. The others rose and fell with the tides, but Mariot was the rock upon the shore.

With each new life he remembered, Benjamin changed more and more, but Mariot was always the strongest and the closest to him in times of trouble. Each of them drew something else out of him, or perhaps they brought their own traits into him.

Some of them were hazy mornings seen through the fogs of dawn. Not Mariot. Growing up with her in a different corner of his mind, he felt like he was more Mariot than Benjamin with only one difference. Mariot had been quiet and reserved, and every act was careful. Benjamin himself jumped first and looked for the rocks later, the way rash younger brothers could sometimes be.

Any other town would have called him a heathen. In Salem, he would have died outright. But in Southwyck, the others avoided him. In a town that brimmed with curses, Benjamin was an outcast. There were more curses than blades of grass, more than all the raindrops in the summer swells. But curses made you suffer, and that was the bedrock of Southwyck. Those were the teachings of the Church, and the truths that all who prayed for salvation every Sunday knew.

There had been curses in Southwyck for at least three generations. It was the first of the Massachusetts colonies, the longest-lasting, for no matter how severe the winter squall, nor how vicious the drought, Southwyck survived. The curses survived.

The first generation knew nothing about the things that slithered through the woods. Ones you did not trifle with. The ones who leveled curses.

They heard the tales of Roanoke, and the elders of Southwyck would nod their head in understanding. There was a price for dealing with darkness.

Heresy in Southwyck was pliant like the willows that wept at the town corners, their blossoms swaying with curse-driven winds. In other places, in other times, heresy was foundation and stone, but in Southwyck it changed by the day. The tolerance of the village was weighed by the Reverend's scale, on where his judgment fell.

Most families kept their secrets locked up tight. They confided in the Reverend, and let him make his decisions. But every survivor of Southwyck knew to hide their curses and never to speak of their shame. Except for Benjamin. Everyone recognized the disgrace of the miller's son.

Father kept his hand gripped on Benjamin's shoulder all the way back into the village. The town moved in slow procession, each family closing in on itself. They all knew what the curses would do, and they all knew the sacrifice that entailed.

Mercy Dare had died, but her family's suffering was not at

an end. Curses could not be killed: they merely slipped from their chain of bones and crawled into a new victim. Another Dare would fall upon the sword.

Benjamin knew there was a warning there for him. Even in a town full of oddities he was an outcast, and it was more than just his curse. When he tried to speak of it, his mouth could not shape the words to describe the pit in his stomach. He was just a Return that hadn't drowned yet.

It bothered him often, the strange feeling. No matter how much he drew on Mariot, or Claude, or any of the others, they had never felt how he did. The feelings were foreign even among his other selves. They were them, and he was him, and even among himselves he could not find respite.

Benjamin knew better than to confide in his parents, a truth he'd learned many years before. An innocent time. "I let the plague take me," he'd whispered to Papa, the words twisting in his mouth as tears streamed down his face. "Ah begged Him to unmake me. Then ah died." Father could not place the accent, though Benjamin remembered the kingdom of Castilla and of a boy too scared for war.

Father had switched him bloody for that.

Benjamin shook his head, clearing away the dark memories. He scuffed his foot through a puddle as they passed, and Father yanked him closer, hating even this momentary step out of line.

Reverend had never liked him, Benjamin thought. There was something wild in him, something that the slick man who hid behind his learnings and his books could not break upon the rocks. Benjamin had more in common with the willows that swept across the border to the woods, the trees that swayed and never came down no matter how virulent the storm. No matter what they did to him, he bent and survived.

The Reverend didn't like those who questioned, or those

who thought deep. Benjamin was the only one in town who did not swallow the lies that put the rest to an easy slumber. Benjamin saw the Returns for what they were: not just a sacrament, but a message for the witches that created them. The curses were witchborn, the only legacy they had left. Silencing them, one last gasp of air at a time, was the only power the Reverend had.

The truth was that no matter how many bodies sank into tumultuous waters, curses did not drown. They ached to live, and traveled from one life to another. Sometimes they slept, waiting until a family had another child. Others found an already cursed child and quickened inside him, growing stronger.

At first, Benjamin believed as the village did—that the Return was the only way to control the curses that castigated them. But now he saw the look in the Reverend's eye when he chose their death for them.

The Reverend thought he was without peer, as though the whole of him was more than all the others. But Benjamin was full of many others and was not limited to a life of just one.

There had been a time when he thought everyone was made up of a dozen different lives all blended together like blood into the water. But the more he remembered, the more he realized how different he was. And with that difference, he learned the most important attribute in Southwyck: shame.

He learned to read faster than every boy in his class; the lessons were taught by Brother Malley to all the young men in town. Southwyck boys had to be smart. The expectation was superiority from the colonists in almost everything. It was the only way to protect the town and its secrets. But Benjamin didn't need to learn to read, he only needed to be reminded how, and English somehow seemed easier to learn than many other languages he knew. The people of Southwyck didn't like that he was smarter than the other boys, or knew things they had never learned. For him, it was remembrance rather than recitation.

It had always seemed to be that way, too. Things just got easier for him with every new lifetime he remembered, though none of them were as close to him as Mariot. She, at least, felt like a sister, and the lines between them that had always been blurry grew hazier the older he became.

It made the town wary, he knew. So he tried to keep his head down. Benjamin learned what happened to boys who kept speaking out of turn. He learned how to hide the beatings, how to pretend to his parents that everything was fine. If it wasn't a beating from one of the other boys, it was a beating from Father.

He spent his days staying out of his parents' way, and out of the town's sight. Most boys his age helped their fathers or worked in town. Benjamin didn't associate with others his age—or of any age. Too many lifetimes had made him too perceptive for even the most world-weary of adults.

"I thought it would be me," he said to his parents as they neared the family home. Over his head, they shared a look.

Father cleared his throat. Mother pulled herself away from them.

It hadn't been him today, but it would be him soon enough. That was clear. The Reverend had boldly said as much in front of the entire town. He was strange, and even a town grown from strange seeds had no way to deal with him.

There was one place, though, that celebrated his oddness. As a port town, Southwyck maintained itself through vigorous trade from incoming ships, and there was a hunger in the colonies for books. In books, he found memories that had gathered dust in the corners of his mind, and found riddles of history he knew to be false. It was surprising how much the world lost even in a day.

Reading gave him a sense of self. There were enough minds to share his head with, but there was little of Benjamin in there. Books allowed him to find his own curiosities and interests that separated him from the others. Without them, he would have drowned years ago.

It was also through books he met Sebastian.

"What would you wish for?" he asked drowsily. Though they were lying head to head, Sebastian had his hand tangled in Benjamin's hair, and he traced his fingers through it.

"What?"

"They say before the flames consumed them, the witches spat, and the ground turned dark. That was how the curses began. But they also say that if you brought them tithes of the harvest, they would plant your dreams in the furrows left behind, and come spring there was little they could not realize. If they were here now, what would you ask for?"

It was an unpleasant truth that the town accepted so blithely. They had spurned the witches that had given them favor, and the curses were their repentance. But wishes were a fanciful thing, even for a boy who had lived countless other lives.

It was not a question that Benjamin had ever considered before. That any of them had ever considered before. The part of him that was Mariot, the part that was Claude, all of them recoiled at the openness of the question. It was a question that grew out of hope: dry cracked ground they had never thought to water before.

If they all had one thing in common, it was that they would not know what freedom felt like if it came to call upon them.

He didn't answer. Sebastian was slow to speak himself and it did not bother him when Benjamin let a thought grow at its own pace.

Benjamin stared up at the willow trees in the distance, and

how their branches ebbed and flowed with the wind. He spent a good long time thinking it over, calmed by the feeling of Sebastian's fingers rubbing absent circles against his scalp. There was a dream he had, one that returned night after night. In the dream, he could not separate Benjamin from Mariot, and it grew so confusing that he tore himself in two and emerged as something else.

"I would be as mercurial as nature herself," he said once his thoughts grew still. "Some days I am a deafening storm inside, while others I am nothing more than the possibility of a frost weeks before harvest. I am never sure what a new dawn will bring. But this is a place where people hide from nature, tucked underneath their blankets and old-woven thoughts."

Sebastian stirred, and Benjamin looked up when the hand in his hair disappeared. "I would bring you to thaw," he whispered.

It was so honest, and so naive, that Benjamin wrapped himself in Mariot and let her soothe away his sudden rush of feeling. She was always better at masking her emotions than he was.

Sebastian was a dusty-haired boy who'd come off one of the ships when the blacksmith took him in. Even then, the smith had seen the potential for heft in his frame. The smith's wife and son had died the winter before, and the village talk was that he was lonely. Sebastian saw to that.

He was one of the strongest boys of their age, and the girls in the village would not stop competing for his attention. Being a blacksmith's wife meant a secure future and each of them devised new ways to chance upon the boy, hoping to catch his eye. How they doted on him when he came into town. It made Benjamin ill.

Benjamin had never had a friend before. The others, Claude especially, had many friends during their lives, but for them it was still different. They bonded over similar natures, or a life of similar understanding. Benjamin had no peer in child or adult. No one understood him. He didn't understand the things that interested them, and he couldn't talk so they could understand. He was as much an outsider as Sebastian.

Until Sebastian married, and his children were taken by the same curses as the others, he would always be treated like a stranger in Southwyck. Bringing in new blood was only one way that the town tried to leverage the darkness they passed on to their children—sacrifice another.

Benjamin would never marry. He knew it, even if the rest of the town thought it for a different reason. He was not built like the other boys of the village, any more than Sebastian. But the blacksmith's son was better at hiding behind a mask, at pretending he was like the rest.

But the two of them, they were something like friends. Sebastian wasn't one for talking, but he would listen as Benjamin told him all the things he'd read about that day. He couldn't read as well as Benjamin could, but books fascinated him in a way foreign to the people of Southwyck.

They drew together, a pull that swallowed them until they were all that existed in the world. Benjamin woke every day wondering what he'd have to talk to Sebastian about, wondering when they'd see each other next. But sometimes he worried, and he fretted, and he let himself listen to the gossip around town. That he was an oddity, and soon they would do something about it. But even on those dark days, when he hid himself away, it was Sebastian who found him.

Sebastian knew the truth about the town, about the curses. He knew about Benjamin, and Mariot, and all the others. He had never once questioned, never once turned away. There was always a thoughtfulness in his eyes. A wonder.

After the Return, after his parents had returned to their work, Benjamin wandered across the village and slipped underneath the willows and escaped into the woods. The two of them had many places to hide away an afternoon—since Sebastian could shape iron twice as fast as his mentor, he often freed himself early.

They were near the brook, almost as far as one could get from town without heading farther inland, both of them lying in the grass. Benjamin knew the Return would have Father driving himself into a fury. He would lie low until the fires had calmed. Sebastian had already finished his work for the day, so the pair had all their lives ahead of them.

"They want me to be something other than me," Benjamin whispered.

Sebastian said nothing. Some thought the blacksmith's boy simple, but it was just that he chose his words with a sharp-eyed precision. Each was a precious gift he was loath to give away. In some ways, it reminded Benjamin of Mariot, of the way she would wrap up her thoughts and tuck her words into her pockets, only sharing what she could bear to part with.

Not that Sebastian was dull. Sometimes Benjamin could make him laugh like no other, and he could speak whole sentences using only his expression. His eyebrows had a way of communicating complex thoughts in simple gestures, an economy of movement that kept his cherished words to himself.

"Reverend says there are more curses now because we're wicked," he added. "Sometimes I think we're all going to drown."

"We could leave," Sebastian offered, his voice a quiet reassurance.

Benjamin shook his head. "They would come after us." It went without saying that if one left, the other would follow. They had been in tandem since that first meeting, circling one another in ways too elemental to understand. Confusion and fear fluttered in his chest. Benjamin, who had lifetimes of memory to draw upon, could remember no one pulling him in the way Sebastian could. Though he had the memories of all those lives, the feelings were harder to hold on to, slick and numbing like spring thaw.

"We could go through the Withers."

At the mention of the forest that pressed in against the town, Benjamin sat up. "Be serious." It was a pointless chide—Sebastian was never not. Nothing left his lips he hadn't studied and hammered at until it passed muster.

The stories said the Southwyck of now was not the first, and that the village was first planted in a grassy meadow east of the Withers. The inlet where the Returns fell was once part of the original town, but during the time of their grandparents, the ground had swallowed many of them up and the sea rushed in to take them away. That was why Reverend wanted to drown them. It was where the curses belonged.

Benjamin wasn't sure about all that, but he knew the stories about what lurked in the Withers better than most. As a child, he'd eyed the woods in the way of forbidden things, and snuck across the threshold whenever he had the chance. Last year, after one of the worst winters in memory the woods had all but come alive with an elemental malice. Children, animals, even full-grown men and women had disappeared. It had been months since anyone hunted Withers game.

People had tried to head down into the colonies, to map the extent of the woods, but it was hard to judge its distance. The woods seemed to ebb and flow like the tide, some years grand and others insular.

Everyone knew the Withers was the source of the curse, or at least all that remained of one. It was where the witches had lived, and where they had died when the town turned upon them. It was the witches who had cursed the town and left a mark on each of their souls. Towns like Salem boasted of wars won against the witches, but if they killed even a single witch, she was a stunted and malformed thing. The witches of Southwyck had never stopped being a threat, even after they were killed.

The witches gave the Withers its power. It was where they laid their heads, and it was said even now, generations later, the woods protected their old home. Some said the witches had been sisters, others claimed rivals. Others believed there was only one, while two or three was the more common guess.

"You don't cross through the Withers," Benjamin said, still aghast at the idea. You could enter and play in the fringes, but you never crossed the forest. The same way you were never to cross a witch.

"They'll hunt you down," Sebastian said, a quiet protest; it was possible he was not referring to the town, but was agreeing about the witches.

"There's a better way." Benjamin had to believe that. He was a boy now, on his way to becoming a man; he had to find another option. "There must be."

As Benjamin approached his home, the boisterous laugh of the Reverend boomed from the windows and warned him away.

They were preparing for a funeral before his body was even cold. He knew what the Reverend's presence meant. The elders of the town would meet, the Reverend would supply his next victim and then the town would arrive at the coast.

How could his mother do this? His father? Mariot and her mother had been close, like sisters, but ever since he had first remembered her, his own parents had looked at him like an empty grave waiting to be filled. Betrayal had a jagged edge, and it scoured him deeply.

The village would not act unless his parents had given their assent, but already in the distance, he could hear the sound of men with axes. A tree taken from the Withers, offered to the sea as penance. They would tie him to it, but it would dash apart the moment he struck the rocks. Mercy had sat on the stone walls that lined the main path through the village and watched as they cleaved her coffin from the woods.

Benjamin would not be so passive.

The smithy was on the other side of town, close to the inlet in case of a wayward flame. Sebastian had it easy—sneaking away took him little time at all, while Benjamin had to cross the entire village to make his escape. A trek across field and stone, outrunning expectation and demand. He slowed his steps and lingered on the path to the waterfront.

There were no ships due until the following spring if travel held. It had been a year since the last ship from the Old World had come. There would be no escape on the sea. Ship captains and crew were always outlanders, visitors to the prosperous village who never stayed themselves. They dropped off cargo and fresh blood from time to time, but even the brief visits to Southwyck impressed its curse upon them.

And yet, they could not deny the prosperity of the town, and how a visit there always seemed to refill their coffers. It was the way the town had always been—surviving when all else would wither on the branch. It could have been another curse altogether: letting them thrive so that their suffering could be even greater. Eternal damnation was less demanding a mistress than hunger or survival.

Benjamin suspected that the curses were more like plants than people knew. When there was more sun and frequent rains, plants grew hale and strong, but when they received too much sun, or the rains were too hard, they rotted.

There were only two ways out of the village, and if he could not escape by sea, then he would have to flee by the roads. Except Sebastian was right—they would not only go after him, but they would catch him. No one had fled by road and escaped since his grandfathers' days. The Withers swallowed up all but a narrow path farther into the mainland.

A hand on his shoulder caused him to jump, but when he turned, it was only Sebastian, looking sad but determined. There was a bundle tied up in one of his giant hands. He already knew.

"Through the Withers to the west, we can make it to York in a few days." If the town followed them, it would take weeks by road to circle around the enormity of the woods. "There's always need for a smith, and there will be work enough for you."

Benjamin had many skills he could draw upon. Though the emotions of the other lives were hazy and fractured, the dexterous movements of hand and body came easy to him, and a dozen lifetimes worth of distraction were available to him.

He heard tale of cities large enough where all you had to do was cook all day and people would come and feast. He knew his numbers, and while he wasn't the strongest in penmanship, he knew enough to fake it. Plus he had met no one who knew as many tongues as he did.

But if he ran, it would not just be him punished. Sebastian would suffer.

"I don't know," he murmured. Shyness honed like instincts over lifetimes overwhelmed him, and he found himself tucked into corners and shadows not even large enough to cover the unwelcome width of his shoulders. Decisions weren't for him to make. Those were for others. He was an imposter.

"There are towns that know nothing of curses," Sebastian promised. "Where you will be exceptional and nothing more. And no one will look down on you for being yourself."

Impure, they called him sometimes. As though there was a purity in curses, and his had somehow wallowed in the sty.

"They will kill you," Sebastian said, plain of fact and dry of tone. "We're going."

And that was that.

They had always been an odd pair, too similar sometimes, and too far at odds the other. It was something that Benjamin enjoyed, because for every movement he made, he felt as though Sebastian always moved in tandem. Whether they came together or moved apart, there was always a kind of synchronicity to their steps. To their lives.

Only now they were leaving, and the town would catch fire. Once they realized that Benjamin had fled, cursed justice would be swift. They would not let him cross the Withers for fear of what would happen to his curse. Would it rebound and decimate the town where it struck, or would it fizzle like candles in rain? Would it kill him, or would it kill someone else? None could say for certain, not even the most holy among them.

"I've traveled with my father," Sebastian confided as they skirted the woods. The town would expect them to take the road, but Sebastian's plan was straight across the heart of the haunted wood, a heart that Benjamin hoped would hold its beat for their journey. "There are many towns, some even smaller than Southwyck. Others so large you could not believe. Any of them could be our shelter. There are months yet until the first frost. We will be fine."

The woods were heavy and thick at first, with roots dragging their knuckles aboveground to pull at their balance. The underbrush grew heavy and nipped at every inch of exposed skin. Within a mile, Benjamin was a worry of wounds.

The deeper they went, the quieter the woods became. It was unnatural, and they both knew it. It had been too late the moment they'd stepped into the woods: the Withers had claimed them now.

There were many stories of the Withers. Some claimed that the willow trees that permeated the forest were where it drew its name. Others said the town had tried to scrub witchcraft away from its history, and all it could manage was to bring witches to wither. A few, the Reverend being one of them, claimed Wither was the name of the witch who had first plagued the town.

Benjamin had always been practical of thought. Haunted woods to keep a town in line. The Withers was what you named a wood you wanted people to stay away from. And stay away they did. There had always been a path through the wood, and a name like the Withers kept them on that path. And if they strayed, then they saw the reason a town like Southwyck had a wood like the Withers.

They heard shouting once or twice. Soon the men of the village would bring out the dogs. Soon the pursuit would become a hunt. For his crime, Sebastian would now share Benjamin's fate. All in the village knew of the bond the two boys shared, even if not a one of them understood it. They would know that if Benjamin and Sebastian were both missing, then they were together.

These were the things they were thinking when they came upon the cottage.

These were the things they feared when they saw the figure in the glass.

These were the terrors that stole their breath when the witches beckoned them inside.

"Two by two, boys of blue," the woman who settled at the table said, a pile of weaving around her. Her eyes were spring-sky blue, and her piercing gaze made the air rush from Benjamin's chest.

"A bit more than two, and not quite boys," the other whispered. She had a rasp in her voice that scratched the words to bone before they escaped her mouth.

Sebastian took them in with a calm that did not sit well with Benjamin. He was always so tranquil, even in the most heated of conversations, while Benjamin could barely catch his temper with both hands and a head start. But this was different. This was not a battle of wits with the Reverend, or the struggle to make any of the townsfolk realize that he had so much more to offer than heartache.

"You're supposed to be dead," he said, a simple statement of truth. He was the only one struggling; everyone else in the room already seemed to accept it as fact. Sebastian, in fact, looked entranced, the same way he'd looked when one of the Southwyck girls had brought him sweets hoping for a smile. Benjamin liked this even less.

"Are we?" one of them asked. Rasp, Benjamin decided. It was the only way to tell the two apart, to define them by their differences.

"Flame," the other one said in response, and they both nodded in memory.

"More than fire," the first continued. "More than water. Quite a bit of effort, wasn't it? Swinging hands, broken hearts, sorrow, sorrow, sorrow."

"Reasons."

Benjamin stepped forward, placing himself in front of Sebastian. There were two of them, and two of the witches, but he could be enough for both. His father had always told him he tried the patience of a dozen saints. "Let him lie. He is not one of us. He has no curse to bear. He is innocent."

"Innocent," one of them scoffs. Stare, the nickname fit, what with her unblinking way of watching. "You should repent."

"Not so innocent is a boy who steals away a sacrament," the other continues with an eye waged on Sebastian. "An orphan spitting in the face of all he has." She shifted to look at them both. "Nor as innocent as growing boys in rushing waters when they think no one is around for miles."

The two of them looked to one another, and Benjamin felt his skin warm. He had always carried his shame on every inch of his body that could be seen, even as it rushed across the skin that he kept hidden. His body became a furnace that could not suppress. No one had been in the woods that day. No one had seen what they had done, or what they had been to one another.

Yet still, somehow they knew. They knew about the way that Sebastian had cupped Benjamin's face, about the way their heartbeats raced against one another. His fingers had been like a promise, but his lips tasted like forever.

"I…see," Sebastian said, even though there was no way he could. The admission only made Benjamin burn hotter.

"They will kill them," Rasp murmured, a small sound of protest. "You know how they like to do that. They think the blood will tame what they cannot." There was something unsaid between them, a cloud of conversation that neither of the boys could penetrate.

They stared at each other, against each other, witch eyes matched. The air inside the cottage grew warmer, and Benjamin dropped his gaze to the gnarls in the wood table. That was when he realized what bothered him about the two women. There was weaving on the table, the skein itself covered in a heavy dust, and though Rasp moved her hands across it, it left no mark behind. Stare walked in a pattern, but her feet did not disturb the dust on the floor.

"You *are* dead," he realized aloud.

"It is the peculiar nature of our hell." Stare looked up at him, letting her white hair shroud her face. "Suffer though we must, and punished oh-so-well, our bones are ground to dust."

"The town will come for him," Sebastian said, voice unyielding. "Can you help him?"

Stare swiveled her head toward him, mouth soured in contempt. "As though we ever cared a lick for the whining of Southwyck."

"Bleating gnats," the other agreed.

"But you cursed the town," Benjamin said. This was not what happened when witches came to claim you, or when revenants woke hungry in the night.

"Curses flew, that much is true, but humans never earned our spite. Their bleating let us sleep at night."

The other rolled her eyes, rasping voice explaining, "They came at us with fire and stone, but they did not concern us. They got in the way, casualties of their own making, but what were they in the face of our own survival?"

The boys looked at one another. *Did you understand? Did you?* Neither of them could nod their head, even though they needed no words.

"They learned their lessons well. They learned that survival of most was preferable to the end of all."

It was too close to the mantra of the town for Benjamin's comfort.

"You know what they intend to do," Sebastian said, resolute. "Can you protect him?"

There was something in the way— "Did you plan this? Did you know they would find us?" Benjamin demanded, terrified and furious all at once.

Sebastian didn't answer him, but the twin cackles of the witches was all that he needed to know. "Coming to us for mercy," Rasp whispered. "How interesting. It has been many years."

"And you once granted wishes," Sebastian continued. "I would wish for his protection."

Benjamin grabbed him by the arm, a blast of cold and icy fear washing over him. "He means it not," he protested. "You don't make deals with witches," he growled to the other boy. "Especially now."

"I like them," Rasp pronounced. "And if we shelter them, then we can still claim their deaths, can we not?"

"Shelter them this night, and in the morning they take flight."

Rasp nodded. "There is that. Then there is no help for it. Only another curse will suffice."

The two witches glided through the front door, out into the clearing that surrounded the house like a perfect circle. "You would be our hands in this world, the caress at day and the fist at night. No longer will Southwyck be your fear, but your charge."

Set apart from the house, almost at what Benjamin judged to be the center of the circular field around them, were a pair of rosebushes. They were few in the town, but Mariot remembered them, as did some of the others. But all of those memories contained roses in bloom; there were none here.

"Once this land was known for the roses that blossomed here, unlike any other that exists in the mortal shell. But now only two remain, and they will not bloom again for many years." Stare eyed them with a deadly expression. "Tend this garden and know you tend your own lives. Flee us, and flee our sanctuary, and winter frost will be your fondest memory."

"Stay here and you'll protect us?" Sebastian asked. "And the Withers?"

"The woods will shelter you under their bowers. You will stand when all else cowers," Stare replied.

"It will be many years before we can slip our chains again," Rasp continued. "But we will always know what happens in this place. You will do as we instruct, and we will house you for all of your days. The animals will feed you, the woods shall be your home, and Southwyck..." The woman turned, and Benjamin had the instinctive realization she was looking back toward the village.

"That is the secret to survival. Teach fear to those who taught you to be afraid."

★ ★ ★ ★ ★

THE GIRL WITH THE BLUE LANTERN

BY
TESS SHARPE

Northern California, 1849

Everyone in Pollard Flat knew better than to venture into the North Woods. But that Thursday afternoon in November, Ella Gant's dog—an oafish beast named Virgil—broke his leather lead and darted through the trees, disappearing into the forest, and Ella had no choice but to follow.

The first snow had come and gone, leaving the forest floor wet and slippery. Mud and pine needles stuck to the hem of her calico skirt and the soles of her boots. Dampness seeped through the leather as she called out Virgil's name, her voice echoing among the trees. She tried not to pay mind to the shadows that stretched long and dark across the forest floor as the sun began to set.

"Virgil!" She strained her ears, desperate for the sound of his paws thumping through the brush, but all she could hear was the beating of her own heart and the swish of the wind through the tops of the pines.

She couldn't leave without Virgil. He wasn't a clever dog, but he was sweet in his own way, and more important, he'd been her mother's favorite. There had been nothing she could do when the fever took Mama, but Ella certainly wasn't going to let her beloved dog get eaten by a bear—or worse.

People in town spoke of the North Woods in whispers and mutters, as if using a normal voice would summon trouble. The mountain that lay beyond the forest had no name; it was untouched, unreachable, as if an ocean separated it from Pollard Flat.

Every year or so, some reckless miner would set out to explore the mountain, lured by tall tales of nuggets the size of goose eggs and streams glittering with gold dust. When greed was greater than fear, no warning was enough. But each time a man disappeared into the North Woods, dreams of gold shining in his eyes, he was never seen again.

No one reached the mountain if the North Woods didn't want them to. Or so they said.

Ella turned in a slow circle, desperate for some sign. She cupped her hands around her mouth. "Virgil!" she called, trudging ahead through the tangle of pines. Her skirt and petticoat were already an inch covered in mud. Her father would be angry when she got home. He'd think it foolish to follow the dog here, of all places.

Ella bit the inside of her lip, pausing to catch her breath. It was a good thing she'd stopped caring what her father thought, then. When Mama had fallen ill, he'd dragged his feet in sending for the doctor, worried about the cost. Ella couldn't help but wonder, in her darkest times, if she'd managed to convince him to send for the doctor earlier, just maybe...

A loud splash followed by raucous barking filled Ella's ears.

"Virgil!" she shouted, hiking her skirts to her knees and running toward the sound. But when the barking was joined by laughter, she skidded to a halt. Goose bumps spread across her skin, and her heart sped up like a rabbit's.

She crept forward, her legs shaky as she pressed herself against a pine tree and peeked around it.

A wide creek cut through the forest, its banks steep and sloping into huge shards of slate rock that rose from the water. Virgil was perched on top of one of the stones in the middle of the creek, bathed in the light coming from a blue lantern set on the other side of the bank.

Virgil barked, crouching down, his tail wagging furiously. Ella watched as the water below him broke and a girl bobbed to the surface, her laughter filling the air, twining with Virgil's happy barks.

The girl's back was to Ella, so all Ella could see was a tangle of wet dark hair floating around her. She raised her hands out of the water, her fingers moving in a complicated dance. A strange hum filled the air, and Virgil froze, staring at the water as ribbons of light rose from the surface of the pool.

Ella's eyes widened as she realized it wasn't light but gold dust, beckoned from the water as if by magic. The fragments and flakes glinted in the lantern light, wrapping around the girl's hands like a friendly cat's tail.

How was she doing this? Was it some sort of trick—or were the old stories true? The whispers of creatures whom the forest welcomed, ones who guarded the mountain, keeping it safe.

Ella stumbled backward, her foot landing on a branch that broke, the crack echoing through the clearing. Both the girl's and Virgil's heads whipped toward the sound and Virgil barked, bounding off the rocks and toward the bank. The girl did not follow, but instead stared into the forest, as if she could see through the trees…as if she could see through Ella.

Virgil had sniffed Ella out and galloped up to her, planting his muddy paws on her stomach, his fur soaked through. Ella grabbed his collar, tying the lead tightly around it. She was just about to turn and run when a musical voice broke out through the quickening darkness.

"I like your dog."

Ella didn't know what to say—or if she should say anything at all. She licked her lips, suddenly aware of how dry her mouth was.

"It'll be dark before you know it," the girl continued. "Do you have a light?"

Ella screwed her eyes shut and shook her head, even though she was hidden from the girl's line of sight from the trees—unless she really could see through them like some sort of witch.

Virgil barked, and Ella opened her eyes. In front of her was a bobbing cloud of gold dust, imbued with a light that glimmered and glowed. Her stomach twisted, partly in fear, partly in wonder. There was something strangely beautiful about it—like a golden dust devil.

"That'll guide you to the edge of the forest," the girl said.

Ella heard splashing behind her, like someone pulling herself out of the water. She peered around the tree and for the first time, she got a good look at the girl.

She wore a strange sort of dress, no more than a shift, really, that left her arms and shoulders bare despite the chill in the air. Her dark hair fell in wet ropes down to her waist, untamed by braids or ribbons. Her eyes were large and green, her small nose pointed, and her chin stubborn. But most extraordinary, the thing that made Ella's stomach drop, was the golden sheen of her skin, specks of gold sprinkled there like freckles, sparkling in the lantern light. When the girl lifted her wet hair off her neck, Ella saw long stripes shimmering on her back, as if someone had dipped a paintbrush in molten gold and stroked it down her skin.

The girl's eyes lifted, meeting Ella's, who sucked in a breath, flattening herself against the tree.

"You should go." The cloud of gold dust shimmered, as if it agreed.

Ella shivered and silently obeyed, tugging on Virgil's lead, following the gold light as it drifted through the pines, guiding her back home. When she reached the edge of the forest, the cloud bent into a ribbon, like the ones the girl had summoned, sped back through the trees and disappeared.

Ella stared, her head spinning as she tried to make sense of what had just happened. She hadn't imagined it—she knew that much to be true.

Which meant…

She didn't know what it meant, she told herself firmly, tightening her fingers around Virgil's lead. She marched down the road, trying to ignore how the hairs on the back of her arms were still standing straight up, even when she arrived at their cabin.

A candle was lit in the window, and she could see the silhouette of her father through the curtains, a bottle raised to his lips, like always.

Ella shut Virgil in the barn with her father's horse and their milk cow, Betsy, before smoothing a hand over her hair—it must look a fright—and opening the rough-hewn cabin door.

"Where've you been?" her father slurred. "Where's my dinner?"

"I'm sorry, Papa," she said. "Virgil got away from me. I had to chase after him."

He sighed, taking a swig from a nearly empty bottle of whiskey. He'd been to town, then. Had he spent all his gold on spirits, or had he thought to leave her enough for the flour and salt pork she needed? Mr. Teller, the man who owned the general store, wouldn't give her credit anymore. Not until she'd settled her account. And there was only so much she could do when her father drank away any gold he pulled from the creeks.

Getting through this winter seemed harder every day. By next week, there wouldn't be a cup of flour to be found. There hadn't been salt in the house for weeks, and the last time she'd had a pig to butcher, her Mama was still alive.

Ella kneaded the dough for the few biscuits she'd scraped together, folding it eight times, like she'd been taught. As her father sat by the window, drinking silently, she placed the biscuits on the cast iron griddle, put it in the oven and fried up the last of the salt pork. A few minutes passed in silence, Ella still dazed by the image of the golden girl.

"It's ready, Papa," she said, setting a plate on the rough-hewn table.

He grunted, getting up and sitting down at the head of the table. He ate quickly, and then without another word, left the room, heading to bed.

Ella waited until she could hear his snores from his bedroom, and then sneaked out to the barn with the scraps of her meal gathered in her apron. Virgil pranced back and forth when he smelled the food, licking at her hands as she fed him his meager dinner.

Late into the night, she stayed in the barn despite the cold, Virgil's head in her lap. She knew she wouldn't be missed, because her father had forgotten how to miss people…or maybe he'd never learned.

The second snow brought the cold and Christmas, and Ella spent long days on the gold claim, her father silent and stony, Virgil her only friendly companion. She took in sewing from some of the ladies in town, chipping away at the debt at the general store. Mr. Teller was kind about it, slipping her small packets of food when she least expected it.

The winter was long, and it was March before the snow finally melted for good, the green of the forest peeking through the drifts. Ella was grateful for the sun, for the coming warmth and spring. Winter was all cold and hunger, stretching food as far as she could, ignoring her father's angry grumbles.

Sometimes, at night, Ella thought ahead, to the next winter, and her stomach churned. She'd gotten used to the pains in her stomach, but her bones stuck out under her skin now, and her dresses hung off her like sacks. She wouldn't survive another winter like the last, so she made a plan.

One afternoon, she waited until her father was deep in the bottle before sneaking out to the barn where he kept his mining pans. She packed two of them, along with a blanket, a flint and some dried meat. With Virgil in tow, she slipped into the North Woods, her desperation finally greater than her fear.

"Find the creek, boy," she whispered to Virgil.

Maybe it was foolish to let a dog lead, but she had no cloud of gold to follow this time, and Virgil had found the creek the first time.

His nose to the ground, ecstatic at being free in the forest, Virgil pulled her through the trees—and Ella followed.

It seemed as if they walked for hours. There were times she was sure they'd passed the same spot two, three times. But just when she was sure he was taking her in circles, the sound of water splashing down slate rock filled her ears.

Ella felt a burst of triumph. They'd found it!

She approached the creek cautiously, but then when she saw no one near, she scrambled down the bank, pack in hand. Virgil splashed ahead of her, lapping up water before climbing the rocks to sun himself.

Ella set her pack next to the water and untied the pans from her rucksack. She straightened, about to hoist her skirts and wade into the water when a voice rang out. "Don't!"

Ella jerked in surprise, her eyes searching the creek, trying to find the source.

The girl flecked with gold stepped out from the shadow of

the forest. Her hair was as wet and unruly as before, the gold in her skin luminous in the light that filtered through the trees.

Ella wanted to run away and move forward at the same time. It was a strange, torn feeling that overcame her, making her heart flutter. "Why not?" she asked, surprised at how steady her voice was.

The girl's head tilted. "It's not yours to take."

Ella frowned. "Is this your claim, then?"

"It's mine to protect," the girl said.

"I don't see you working it," Ella said, because the winter had taught her to be ruthless. The cold had settled in her bones and the hunger still gnawed at her dreams, whispering that soon, all would be lost. "You got papers?"

"Humans deal in laws and papers," the girl replied. "We have no need."

There was a chilling note in her voice, one that made Ella remember the tales of the North Woods, the lost men who never came back, the whispers of the guardians of the mountain who knew the forest better than any human soul.

"So, are you going to stop me?" Ella asked, propping her hands on her hips.

The girl's eyes widened. Even from across the creek, Ella could see how green they were, like pine needles in winter, a deep, dark color that spoke of secrets. "If I must."

Ella moved forward, toward the water, and the girl's hands flew up. "Don't!" she said again, this time with true fear. It made the hair on the back of Ella's neck rise. "If you step into the water, you can't go back."

Ella stopped, her eyebrows drawing together. "You're lying. Virgil came back."

"Animals are different," the girl said. "If you want to see for yourself, you're welcome to wade in. But if you do, you're ours."

Ella shivered, stumbling back a few steps. She sat down hard on the creek bank, dread filling her.

What was she to do if she couldn't get the gold she needed? Her father was useless. Now that the snow had melted, he spent more time at the saloon than up at the claim. Winter would be here again before she knew it. They'd starve or freeze or maybe both if she didn't do something.

Tears filled her eyes and she struggled to hold them back, not wanting to cry in front of the girl, who looked at her like she was something strange and fascinating.

"You have no greed in your heart," the girl said.

Ella sniffed, still trying—and failing—to hold back her tears. "I don't know what you mean."

The girl smiled, and for some reason, the way it lit her eyes soothed the twist of despair in Ella's stomach. "It doesn't matter."

Without another word, the girl dived smoothly into the pool of water below, disappearing beneath the surface. Ella leaped to her feet, and, as the seconds stretched, began to worry. She hovered near the water's edge, but the girl's warning was fresh in her mind, and she didn't dare venture farther.

Suddenly, the girl bobbed up, water dripping down her face as she swam to Ella's side of the bank. She walked out of the water, toward Ella, and again that curious feeling of wanting to run away and rush forward filled her. This close, she could see every gold freckle, every gilded streak. The weave of her dress was rough, but the cloth itself looked impossibly soft, even soaked with water.

The girl held out her fist, uncurling her fingers. Nestled in her hand were four nuggets, all the size of Ella's thumb.

Ella gasped. "How do you do that? What…what are you?"

The girl just smiled, reaching over and taking Ella's hands. Warmth spread through her, which was odd, because the girl's skin was cool. She pressed the nuggets into Ella's palm and they seemed to buzz against her skin, not angrily, but pleasantly.

"You just have to do one thing for me," the girl said.

"What's that?" Ella asked.

The girl smiled, her eyes filling with a sly sort of mischief. "Bring your dog back for a visit some time?"

Ella told no one. As spring melted into summer, she paid off her debt at the general store and then some. Her father couldn't be bothered to notice much, and when she told him she'd taken in some more sewing, he believed that was the reason they suddenly had proper food and even a small flock of chickens.

Once a week, Ella slipped into the North Woods. She no longer needed Virgil to guide her, the invisible paths of the forest becoming familiar, only to her. Most days, Oriana—for that was her name—was already waiting for her.

They would lay on the sun-warm rocks on the creek bank and stare up at the bits of sky visible through the canopy of leaves that towered above them. They would toss sticks for Virgil to chase and laugh when he shook water from his coat all over them.

Once, when Ella arrived, Oriana was nowhere to be found. She waited until nearly dusk, her heart pounding strangely in her chest with each minute that passed without the golden girl's arrival. It was strange to think, but she felt more at home here, with Oriana by her side, than in her real home.

When Ella returned the next week, worried that an empty creek bank would await her, a glorious sort of happiness settled inside her when she saw Oriana already there.

"You came," Ella said.

"I'm sorry about before," Oriana said. "I had a meeting."

"I didn't know you had meetings," Ella said. Oriana wasn't very forthcoming about certain things. Ella knew there were others like her, who guarded parts of the forest, and even others who guarded the mountain itself. But Oriana would get quiet if Ella asked too many questions, so she tried not to push.

"Not always," Oriana said. "Only when the elders are concerned."

Ella frowned. "Are you in trouble?"

Oriana looked down at her hands, biting her lip. "They're not happy you keep coming back."

Ella's stomach sank. The idea of never coming back, never seeing Oriana again… She'd rather spend a thousand winters half-starved and huddling next to Virgil for warmth.

"I didn't mean to get you in trouble," Ella whispered.

Oriana shook her head. "It's not your fault. They think you're all the same. I thought so, too. Until…"

She reached over and took Ella's hand in hers, stroking her fingers down the inside of her palm. Ella gasped, every feeling in her body focused on that spot, and when Oriana pulled away, Ella's skin glistened with gold.

"They can't do anything unless you cross the water," Oriana said.

"And if I do?" Ella asked, because there were nights when it was all she dreamed about. She dreamed of seeing Oriana every day, playing with Virgil together. She closed her eyes and saw lazy days in the forest, floating in the water, talking, touching, her loneliness becoming just a memory.

"Then you're ours," Oriana said. "Then you're mine."

"Is that so bad?" Ella couldn't help but wonder. She thought she might like belonging to Oriana. For Oriana to belong to her.

"It's a choice," Oriana said softly. "It's a different life."

Ella thought of Oriana spinning the gold out of the water, at the strands of gold dust that she'd twist into animal shapes, dancing them across the water to make her laugh. "Yes," she said. "It is."

As fall settled over Pollard Flat, Ella faced the coming snow with dread.

"It'll start storming soon," she told Oriana at the creek. Virgil lay between them, his tongue lolling out as Oriana rubbed his stomach. "Once it snows, I won't be able to come until it's spring again."

Oriana stilled, a stricken look falling over her face. The gold flecks spread across her nose seemed to dim for a second. "I didn't realize," she said.

"I wish it wasn't so," Ella said quickly. "But the snow gets too deep up at the claim."

"You'll come back as soon as the snow melts, though, won't you?" Oriana asked.

Ella placed her hand over Oriana's. "Promise," she said.

It was nearly Christmas when her father discovered the stash of gold hidden in her room. His yelling filled the cabin, and he accused her of horrible things: whoring, stealing, milking his claim dry. The gold dust scattered across the floor as he threw his hands in the air, and all Ella could think of was Oriana, of the beauty of her gift, of the generosity of her soul.

Her father finally drank himself to sleep, still muttering about how Ella's mama would have been ashamed of her. Ella waited until he was out cold before she made her move. She didn't pack much—a few extra dresses, a bedroll, her mama's pearl brooch—before she and Virgil headed out into the night.

The North Woods were near impossible to traverse in the dark, even with a lantern, but there was no alternative; there was only moving forward. It took longer than usual to reach the creek, but she got there eventually.

"Oriana!" she whispered in the darkness. "Are you there?"

Frogs croaked in the dark, crickets chirping in between, but there was no other sound. Ella peered into the darkness, anxious, her eyes straining. "Oriana," she called, a little louder.

A light flickered in the distance, and her heart leaped as the dot grew larger and larger, until Oriana appeared through the trees, carrying the blue lantern.

"Ella," she said, surprise in her musical voice. "What are you doing here?"

Ella hoisted her pack on her shoulder and stepped toward the creek. One more step and she'd be in the water.

The point of no return.

"Ella..." Oriana warned.

Ella looked at her. Her skin glistened in the lantern light, and her eyes, her face, every part of her was beloved to Ella. She'd shown her kindness when she'd so desperately needed it. Given her hope when she had none. Made her laugh when she'd thought she'd forgotten.

She stepped forward, the water rushing around her ankles. "I love you," she said, wading farther into the water, her skirts clinging to her legs. Ella crossed the creek, pulling herself up onto the opposite bank, standing in front of Oriana, who grasped her arms as if she couldn't quite believe she was there.

Ella closed the space between them, her lips brushing against Oriana's. Her eyes drifted shut, Oriana's arms wrapping around her tight. She never wanted her to let go.

"I am yours," Ella whispered as they pulled apart, their noses bumping together.

Oriana smiled, and all around them, gold dust spun from the water, surrounding them in a glittering halo, and Virgil leaped at the cloud, trying to catch it with his teeth.

"And I am yours," Oriana said. "Always."

★★★★★

THE SECRET LIFE OF A TEENAGE BOY

BY
ALEX SANCHEZ

Tidewater, Virginia, 1969

"En garde!" My sister, Delia, and I jab and clink butter knives. She's fourteen. I'm sixteen. Our black-and-white TV blares a rerun of *The Fugitive*, about a doctor falsely accused of murder, and we're having a sword fight to the death—anything to break the boredom of the steamy, hot summer afternoon.

Drill sergeant Mom is in the kitchen making ice-cold limeade—a ruse to keep us troops cleaning and doing house projects during our alleged vacation. Today's chore is polishing the silverware, and we've gotten giddy from the fumes. Delia plunges her knife at my chest. I sputter, stagger, hit the carpet. *Thud.* I lay lifeless when the doorbell rings.

Wanda, our mud-colored dachshund, leaps off her tattered pillow and waddles to the living room, barking to rally reinforcements. I spring up from the dead. Delia and I scramble past each other. On the front porch a young stranger has appeared, like a genie conjured from a magic lamp.

He's lean and sinewy, looks like he's college age with sideburns and an anti-war T-shirt. A roguish mop of sandy blond hair curls over his ears, and—

Delia gasps. "He's got an *earring*."

I blink along with her. No guy wears an earring in our edge-of-nowhere southern Virginia coastal town. He'd be guaranteed to get gawked at. Called names. Or worse.

Wanda is up on her hind legs, peering out the screen door, tail wagging. Delia huddles behind my shoulder, hiding the wine-colored birthmark on her neck, and whispers in my ear, "He's awfully cute."

Pretending not to hear, I sidle up to the door. For a moment his gaze holds mine. His eyes are blue with little sparks of green, and something in them makes me blush.

"Hi, sorry to bother y'all." His voice is soft and lilting, and his smile gleams as bright as one of the Monkees'—Davy or maybe Peter. "My car broke down and I wondered if you could please call a mechanic for me."

"Um, sure." I swing back toward the hallway phone, bumping past Delia. Mom comes out of the kitchen, wiping her hands on a dishcloth, and Delia explains what the stranger wants.

While I'm on the line with Bubba's Texaco, our genie bends down and coos at Wanda through the door's wire mesh. She dances from one foot to the other to the rhythm of her tail. She's in love.

I twist the phone cord, my fingers trembling a little. The guy *is* cute.

"Bubba's sending his son, Charlie," I tell Mom, hanging up the phone.

She's prepared a tall glass of iced limeade for our guest and whispers to us her contingency plan. "Julio, wait outside with him, but be careful. Take Wanda with you." Mom has learned from TV that a stranger at the doorstep could easily be a convict escaped from the nearest chain gang. "Delia, you stay here and help me finish with the silver."

"Can't the silver wait?" she protests. "I want to go talk with him, too." Her eyes signal me for help.

She and I are best friends. I know that's unusual for a teenage boy and his sister, but for us it feels natural. We're almost always together. Tromping through the marsh behind our house collecting cattails. Riding bikes to the drugstore soda fountain. And mostly, living in her room. Listening to the radio. Dancing to *American Bandstand*. Daydreaming about any place but here.

"Mom," I argue, "I doubt an ax murderer would wear a T-shirt that says Make Love not War."

"We don't know anything about him," she says in her made-my-mind-up tone.

I debate whether to stage a solidarity strike for Delia. Outside the door, our possible lunatic killer has shaken off his flip-flops and taken a seat astride the porch steps. The sunlight makes his earring sparkle. I shrug at Delia, rake my bangs back in the wall mirror and push open the door.

Wanda instantly toddles past me to sniff and lick the guy, her tail whipping a million miles an hour.

"Hey, there, pup." He laughs and takes her head in his hands and kisses her forehead in the same place I sometimes do.

"The service station is sending a mechanic," I say and hand him the limeade.

"Aw, thanks, man. It feels like a hundred degrees out here." He presses the cold glass against his forehead. "My name's Cliff, by the way. Cheers."

"I'm Julio." I lean on the porch railing and while he gulps his drink, I study his earring. It's a tiny diamond stud.

"You like it?" he asks. "You'd look good with one."

My face warms. "Not around here. You'd get jumped. Where you from?"

"Raleigh. I was going to NC State but I got sick of all the lectures and papers and sitting on my butt. It's like that ad—you only go around once in life, you've got to grab for the gusto." He lets Wanda lick the cool moisture from outside his glass. "You ever heard of *A Midsummer Night's Dream*?"

"Naw—oh, wait. Maybe on TV. Is it like Shakespeare?"

"Yeah. We did a campus production. I was Puck. You remember the elf? He's like the lead."

I nod yes, mostly remembering the TV actor's legs. He wore these tights that showed his every muscle while he leapt around sprinkling dream dust on people while they slept, so they woke up in love.

"Everybody said I was great," Cliff continues. "The school paper said I should be on Broadway. And I thought, heck, why wait? Follow my heart, you know? I packed up my car, grabbed my guitar and New York, here I come. You ever been?"

"Not yet. I want to." It's my dream. I tell him how Delia and I joke that we're going to run away there like those kids in that book who hide at the museum, sleep on an antique bed and fish coins from the wishing fountain. Our favorite TV show is *That Girl*, where she leaves her hometown for Manhattan. To escape. To become somebody.

I'm still blabbering when Cliff glances at the screen door and breaks into a goofy face—eyes crossed, tongue poking out.

Delia laughs from inside. She's changed into her yellow sleeveless turtleneck, rolled up high. The color makes her sunny face look even brighter. She's so pretty but she doesn't see it. Too many kids have picked on her for that stupid birthmark.

"Cliff's on his way to New York," I tell her, and her face grows even brighter.

"Really?" She tells him how last summer we wrote to the tourist board for brochures, and the day they arrived we practically carpeted her bedroom floor with all the glossy maps and pamphlets, plotting our escape and the adventures we'd have. She wants to be an artist. She already draws great. I want to be a writer, but there's nothing to write about here. Nothing ever happens.

While she's yakking I look at Cliff. His eyelashes are as long and curly as a young girl's, but his jawline is strong and handsome.

He catches me looking at him, and I instantly glance away, blushing again. I'm a chronic blusher.

"Delia?" Mom calls from the living room. "Let the boys talk and come help me, please."

"Yes, Mother." Delia rolls her eyes and tells Cliff, "Just call me Cinderella." It's one of her standard laugh lines.

Cliff obliges. "Nice to meet you, Cinderella."

In the quiet after her leaving, he scratches Wanda behind her ears, sitting with his legs spread wide, like Dad always reminds me a guy should sit. But I always forget.

"You've got nice eyes, you know that?" Cliff tells me.

I turn away, certain my cheeks are on fire.

He chews the last of his ice. When I look up again, I notice his peace-symbol ring.

"Um, you want more limeade?" I ask.

"Naw, thanks, but I gotta pee really bad. Can I use your bathroom?" He slides a hand across his jeans to the crotch, and I strain not to look.

"Sure, yeah, um, I better ask Mom first. She's scared you might be a kidnapper or something."

"You never know, man." Obviously, he's playing, but his twinkling gaze makes me wonder: Is he telling me something?

He pins me with his grin and it feels like he's seeing inside me. When he hands me his empty glass, his fingers brush mine, and a current rushes through me.

I nearly trip on the doorway threshold as I hurry inside. My whole body is tingling. From the kitchen comes the rattle of silverware being put away. I lean against the wall to steady myself. Does he suspect about me? Is he making fun of me?

"What's the matter?" Delia asks, coming out and seeing me. "Something wrong?"

"No, nothing. Nothing." My double "nothing" obviously means *something.* I haven't been able to tell her about me yet. I haven't said it aloud to anybody, not even myself. But I'm pretty sure she knows. She's always sharing her *Tiger Beat* magazines with me, and when I asked if I could tear out the color picture of Bobby Sherman without his shirt, she only gave me a sideways look. Some days I want to throw open the window and just shout it out for the whole world to know.

"Julio?" Mom calls from the kitchen.

I put a finger to my lips for Delia to keep quiet and yell back to Mom, "Can he come in to use the bathroom?"

"No, señor." She appears in the doorway, flashing her dark Cuban eyes at me. "Not till your father comes home."

"But he needs to go really bad."

"Then show him out back." She means the azalea thicket between our backyard and the marsh. It's where Delia and I used to play hide-and-seek, and explorers, and pirates, where I would sneak up on her and pretend to capture her, and she would squeal with glee.

"Mom, you're being ridiculous," I start to say when an idea stops me cold, and I do an about-face. "Okay." I check myself in the mirror again and dart back outside.

On the porch Wanda is lying on her back, her paws paddling the air while Cliff rubs her chest. Her black lips stretch in something like a grin, and I feel as restless as those paws.

"No offense," I tell him, trying to calm my breath, "but Mom says you can't come inside till Dad gets home. You can pee out back, though, where I go in emergencies, when the bathroom's busy. I'll show you." I don't give him a chance to hesitate. "Come on, Wanda." I skip down the front steps, and luckily they follow behind.

Halfway toward the side of the house, a guy shouts in sing-song from the street. "Hey, girly boy!"

It's Butch Becker, hot-dogging past on his bike. Ever since grade school he's made fun of how I walk and talk, leading to four shoving matches, two full-on fights, one black eye (mine) and one bloody nose (his).

Mom says to ignore him. She always tells me I'm too impulsive, that I need to learn to control my emotions. Meanwhile *she's* the one who sobs at movies, and yells at us, and who eloped with Dad when she was sixteen.

I decide she's right. I shove Becker out of my mind, refusing to let him derail me, and keep walking.

"Over there," I tell Cliff, pointing across the backyard to the azalea bushes. They're head high and thick with leaves. Without daring to look at him, I announce, "I gotta pee, too."

As I lead him into the underbrush, the branches close in after us, hiding our tracks. Twigs crackle beneath our flip-flops. The ground smells moist and rich. Soon we're out of view of the house. My heart thrums with excitement. What if he truly is a kidnapper? What if he takes hold of me and tries to do something? What if he's too strong for me? Cicadas cling to the pine trees surrounding us, whirring as loud as police sirens.

In a cave-like clearing barely big enough to fit us, I turn and face him. The sun streaks through the canopy overhead and dapples his soft golden hair. His shoulders seem heroically broad.

I swallow the knot in my throat. I want him to capture me. Throw me to the ground. Press his body against mine. Rub his face on my cheek.

It's a scene I've imagined a million times. While smoothing my hand across the bare-legged underwear model on page eighty-eight of the Sears catalog. When Mr. Kelsey, my PE teacher, got on all fours on the mat to show us wrestling moves. Watching Robert Conrad, the twinkling-eyed star of *The Wild Wild West*, wrap an arm around the waist of a prairie schoolmistress.

Cliff squints at me with a confused look. Maybe I should let him pee first. Then a grin tugs at his mouth. He knows my thoughts. He's had them, too.

My body hurtles out from under me. My arms vine around him. Touching him. Feeling him. I dig my hands into his back and burrow my face in his shoulder. Breathing in his scent. Of lime. Of sweat. Of guy. My senses are alive with him.

His body tightens at first, but then it softens. He's holding me. In his arms.

I look up. His gaze locks on to me. And I think, *There's someone else like me.* I'm not the only one. I want to kiss him; I want *him* to kiss *me*. I press against him. A huge feeling swells up inside me. Like a geyser about to burst. It's too much: his warmth, his touch. I can't do this. I shouldn't be doing this.

I pull away. Spin a one-eighty. As I run toward the yard, branches scrape my face and sides like a tangle of outstretched arms drawing me back. I stumble on a root, trip, fall, pick myself up again.

I break out onto the open lawn as if I've just run a hundred-yard dash. I bend over and rest my hands on my sweaty knees. While drawing in deep drafts of air, I attempt to stop my world from spinning.

Why did I do all that and not kiss him? He must think I'm

the planet's most confused and immature kid. And he's right. I should just keep running. Into the house, into my room. Hide in the closet till he leaves. I whirl around and, startled, leap nearly out of my skin.

"Sorry," Delia says, steadying the little wooden tray she's carrying. "Mom thinks he looks hungry." She leans across the toasted sandwich and glass of milk. "Are you going to run away with him?"

"I wish," I say and dust off my cutoffs. I'm tired of wanting to escape. I'm tired of feeling alone in the world, even with Delia. I want to be with a guy. Somebody like me.

"I think you should go with him," she whispers like a conspirator—like she doesn't merely suspect about me; she *knows*. "I can tell he likes you."

My skin tingles with fear and excitement as Cliff steps out of the azaleas. I expected him to be angry, but he's smiling his Monkees smile. I look down at the grass, feeling even more immature. And Wanda trots ahead of him, her nose twitching toward the sandwich.

"Mom made you a snack," Delia tells him.

"Wow, is she always so nice to kidnappers?"

"You're our trial run," Delia says.

"I'm going inside," I mumble, unable to look at him.

I turn away, take a step and get twirled around as Delia loops her arm through mine.

"Come." She's handed Cliff the tray and steers us toward our rusty ancient swing set.

The contraption is nearly as old as we are—a single swinging carriage shaped like a cradle, with two wood-slat benches facing each other. Even though it was made for little kids, Cliff is slim enough to squeeze into a seat while Delia helps him balance the tray.

"Man, this is good." He chomps into the sandwich as

though he hasn't eaten all day, and then holds it out to us. "Want a bite?"

Delia and I decline. We already know Mom makes a groovy-good chicken salad—sweet with mayo and pickle relish. I've learned from her how to make lots of dishes.

While Cliff is eating, Delia pumps him with questions: What do his parents think of him going to New York? Does he know anybody there? What's he going to do for money?

He says his dad thinks he's nuts but his mom gave him a little cash to tide him over; he's got a college friend who's home for the summer in Brooklyn; he can always make money as a waiter.

I listen quietly, wishing I hadn't been such a dope in the bushes. There are so many things I want to know about him. But I already know the most important thing, the thing that bonds us.

When he downs the last of his sandwich with milk, Delia sets the tray on the ground and tells me, "Get in with him. I'll push you."

"The thing'll collapse," I argue, but Cliff tugs my arm.

"Aw, come on."

The frame groans as I pack into the seat facing him, wedging our knees between each other's thighs.

Delia pushes us, the swing moans and whines and the lawn and trees drift past. He and I are so close it's hard to look anyplace other than his face. And in his eyes I see a different world. Neon lights. Broadway marquees. Soaring skyscrapers. The hustle and bustle of sidewalks. A world with a place for him and me.

"Delia?" Mom's voice calls from the kitchen window. "Come back inside, please."

"Coming," Delia calls back. Then she wags her finger at Cliff. "Take good care of my brother. He's the only one I've got." And she gives me a wry little smile. "Send me a postcard."

I narrow my eyes and grit my teeth at her: it's my "shut up" look. Wanda toddles after her toward the house.

"What did she mean by all that?" Cliff asks.

"She's kind of kooky," I say and wedge my hands beneath my arms. Beneath us, the swinging carriage whines and wobbles and stops.

The sun is making his skin golden and his lips turn rosy pink. I imagine again what it would be like to press my mouth to his.

"Which is your room?" he asks, glancing toward the house.

"The one on the corner." I point and imagine it's night. He's whispering through my window. I hurry to him, quietly remove the screen, help him climb inside. And our arms entangle like in the azaleas.

Bringing myself back to the present I ask, "Why do you want to know?"

He grins. "So I know where to find you."

I try to keep my voice from trembling. "Are you going to come back through here?"

"Maybe," he says. "If you want me to." Something suddenly occurs to him, and he tugs off his peace ring and presses it into my palm. "Here. I want you to have it."

"Really?" At school, guys and girls give each other rings all the time, but it's the first time anybody's ever given me one. And inside I feel a sensation I've never felt before. A closeness that's beyond physical.

"Which finger should I put it on?" I ask.

"That's up to you."

I slide the band onto my wedding-ring finger. I know that's cheesy, but I want to feel like I'm his, like I feel right now.

"Can I go with you?" I ask. I know it's a crazy idea, but

the words tumble out of my mouth. "I could help you with stuff like rehearsing your lines for plays."

He leans back in the carriage. "I doubt your parents would go for that."

"We don't have to tell them. I'll just go with you. They can't stop me."

"What about your school?"

"I'll go to school while you're at work, and then come home and clean and make dinner for you."

He rubs a palm across his cheek, like Dad does when he's trying to figure me out.

While I wait for Cliff's answer, my body feels like it's going to snap in two. And when his fingers stop over his mouth, I grab his hand, yank it away, lean into his sun-drenched face.

It's my first time to mouth kiss. His lips feel as soft as camellia petals, and his breath tastes sweet as milk. For an instant, nothing exists but us. The sun, the wind, the clouds, the sky. It's all here just for us. For this one moment. And when at last we pull away, I ask again, "Can I go with you?"

He shakes his head no, but his eyes twinkle yes. "I don't know who's crazier, man—you or me."

"Does that mean yes?" I ask. And in the distance, a truck horn honks.

"Julio?" Mom calls out from the house. "The mechanic is here."

I clutch Cliff's hand. *"Please?"*

He nods and whispers, "Yes."

"Yes?" I ask, to be sure.

"Yes," he says louder, more urgently.

I jump up after him. The swing chain finally snaps with a *clack*! The carriage crashes beneath us. He takes hold of my hand and keeps me from tumbling to the lawn. A *guy* is holding *my* hand. Strong. Firm. Tender. I never knew a hand could feel this good.

Together we run to the side of the house, past Dad's tomato plants, bumping into each other in a giddy rush. Escaping.

I'm escaping as we fly down the driveway and a bird dives down, fluttering in front of us. I'm escaping as I hear Mom call to me. Everything around me becomes a blur. I've spent so many hours imagining running away that to finally be doing it feels like I'm in a dream.

In the street ahead, Becker races by on his bike again. Whips his head up the driveway toward us. Sees Cliff and me holding hands. His eyes spring wide.

I drop Cliff's hand and instantly regret it. Why should I care what Becker thinks? I'm on my way out of here, and I'm no longer alone.

Cliff's car is a Ford Galaxie: red with a white hardtop, chrome trim, scabs of rust along the bottom. The hood is propped open and Bubba's grown son, Charlie, in oil-stained overalls and a baseball cap, stands bent over the engine.

When Cliff strides up, Charlie stares at the earring. Then he looks at me. I stare back at him, no longer caring what anybody thinks, and Charlie mutters to Cliff to start her up.

"Cool car," I say, sliding in next to Cliff. I run my hand along the fraying vinyl dashboard and picture us taking off down the road, the wind gusting in through the windows, whipping our hair around. He and I *are* the road. While he drives, I lean into his shoulder and wave to people as we speed past. Before today, I felt like I would never belong anywhere. Now I feel like I belong everywhere.

Cliff flicks the ignition and the engine cranks, and cranks, and...cranks. The motor won't turn over. Charlie leans out from under the hood motioning him to cut it, and Cliff hops out to talk with him.

I glance in the side mirror, back toward the house; no sign of the sergeant.

From under the hood, Charlie says something about the carburetor. Whatever that is. Cliff nods like he understands.

Switching my gaze from the side view to the rearview mirror, I lean in, trying to see myself like Cliff does. Does he really think I have nice eyes? I wish they were blue like his. Does he like my too-wide smile? I wish I had his jawline.

In the distance behind me, I see Wanda trotting down our driveway, followed by Delia and Mom. Delia's arms are crossed—she's arguing, shaking her head at Mom. Mom looks toward me in Cliff's car, her brow furrowed in a mix of anger and worry.

I fidget with the peace ring on my finger. Will she try to stop me from getting away? What if she calls the cops? What if they charge Cliff with kidnapping? I'll say the whole thing was my idea. I put him up to it. Except what if they lock us both up?

Next to Mom and Delia a blue Chevy wagon pulls into the driveway. I slink down in the seat. It's the sergeant major. Dad.

"Say a prayer," Cliff tells me, climbing in again. He turns the key. The engine cranks…and catches. We have liftoff. Cliff lets the motor keep running and hops back out to talk with Charlie.

I slide up in the seat and look in the rearview. Dad is joining Mom and Delia. Mom explains to him about me, shaking her head and motioning toward the car. Her face is full of resignation. Dad adjusts his glasses and rubs his chin, once more trying to figure me out.

Delia unfolds her arms and from below her waist she gives Cliff's car a secret invisible push: hurry up, *go*!

A pang hits my stomach; I don't want to leave her behind, this girl who's seen me through taunts and tears, heartache and anger. If it weren't for her, I'm not sure how I would've made it this far. The least I can do is stick around till I graduate.

Everybody's watching me, waiting to see what I do. They're leaving it up to me. Tears rise in my throat. I don't want to leave them. Not like this. How can I expect them to understand me when I haven't let them know who I am? It's me who's made myself a prisoner. And only I hold the key to my release.

Charlie lets the hood slam, Cliff doles out his payment and I smear the tears from my cheeks.

"Ready to roll?" Cliff says, bouncing into the seat. Then he sees my expression. "Whoa, man, what's going on?"

"I can't go with you," I say, trying to keep my voice steady.

He glances back at the crowd on my driveway. "If you want me to go talk with them—"

"No, it's not that. I want to go with you. I really, really do. It's just…"

He shoves his bangs out of his eyes, staring hard at me, trying to understand. "You want to go say goodbye?"

"No, that's just it—I don't think I can. Not yet. I'm sorry. I'm just a dopey kid."

He leans back, staring at the road ahead. Then he lets out a big puff of air and returns to me. His hand brushes across my head, patting my hair. His blue eyes are watery as he cracks a lopsided smile. "It's okay. You'll know when you're ready."

I thought he'd get angry; the fact that he's not makes me wish more than ever that I could go with him. I lean across the seat. He lets his eyelids close. I keep mine open.

I know I shouldn't do this in front of everybody, but I'm doing it. I'm letting the whole world know.

I take it slow, feeling his lips, inhaling his breath, taking in his scent, letting one sensation pour into the next, lingering in the heat of the moment. I want to remember this for the rest of my life. I'll remember him forever.

When he drives away he toots his horn and I keep watching till his car becomes a red speck on the horizon. Then I wipe my cheeks and turn toward the driveway, eager to show Delia the ring Cliff gave me and ready to tell Mom and Dad the thing they already know.

★★★★★

WALKING AFTER MIDNIGHT

BY
KODY KEPLINGER

Upstate New York, 1952

"Sorry, sweetheart. The next train to New York doesn't leave till morning."

I hurried down the platform, chasing after the conductor as fast as I could in my heels. "But I was told I'd be able to transfer here."

"You would've if we'd been running on time. But we got here late, which means you missed the train you wanna transfer to. It's halfway to the city by now. Sorry. There'll be another train at six a.m."

"And what am I supposed to do until then? It's the middle of the night. I don't have anywhere to go."

He stopped and turned to look at me. He was more than twice my age, with gray and brown hair poking out from under his hat. He looked me in the face for a minute, and I thought there was a good chance he might recognize me. I stood straighter, tried to look more regal and refined. But it was all wishful thinking. Because a second later his eyes slid lower.

"Well, sweetheart, you could always come home with me."

I took a step back and folded my arms over my chest. "Train leaves at six, you said?"

He nodded before turning and walking away.

I sighed and picked up my suitcase, trying to think of what to do. It was close to midnight, and I was stuck in some no-name town in upstate New York, still a couple hours outside of the city. I headed toward the end of the platform, hoping I might be able to find a hotel.

But when I reached the sidewalk outside the train station, all I could see were sweet little houses, their windows already dark. I walked beneath the streetlamps, unnerved by how quiet this town seemed on a Saturday night. Back in Hollywood, I knew Wally and his friends would just be getting the night started.

And I should've been there.

I shook my head and kept walking. I turned on the next block and saw a diner on the corner, empty inside but with the lights still on. I hurried toward the door, and bells jingled as I pulled it open. The place was bright and clean, with a checkered floor and a silent jukebox in the corner. It wasn't glamorous by any means, but sitting here for a few hours was certainly better than a park bench. Maybe I'd even get a milk shake. It'd been years since I'd had one.

I was about to slide into one of the booths when I heard a voice call, "Sorry, but we're about to close."

I turned to look toward the kitchen just as a waitress in a light pink uniform came through the doors. She looked like she was about my age—eighteen or nineteen—with big brown eyes and golden blond hair tied back with a white ribbon. She moved toward one of the tables, wielding a wet washcloth, but stopped dead in her tracks when she saw me.

"Oh."

"Sorry," I said, backing toward the door. "I know. You said you were closing. I'll just—"

"You're Betsey Burns."

I smiled, trying not to worry whether or not there was red lipstick on my teeth. People didn't recognize me quite as often as they used to. Over the past couple years I'd stopped looking like that little girl who got famous in all the pictures. But every once in a while, some stranger would know my name, and I had to admit, it always felt good.

"That's me," I said. "And what's your name, sugar?"

"I, um… I… Hi. I'm Laura." She cast an eyeball around the joint, like she was expecting to see the rest of Hollywood walk in behind me. "But what… Miss Burns, what are you doing here?"

"Betsey," I corrected. "I was supposed to be on a train to Manhattan, but the next one isn't until morning. And you're closing up, so I'd better get out of your hair and find somewhere else to—"

"I can walk you to the hotel," Laura offered.

"This town has hotels?"

"*One* hotel," she clarified. "And it's just a few blocks from here. I can walk you. That is, if you want me to. Just let me close up."

"That'd be peachy. Thanks."

I sat down and waited while Laura wiped off a few tables. Once she was done, she untied her apron, tossed it over the counter and retrieved a set of keys from a drawer by the cash register.

"You're the only one here?" I asked.

"Normally my boss helps close up, but he had to leave early to go out of town with his wife, so it's just me."

I stood and followed her to the door as she shut off the diner's lights. Once we were out on the sidewalk, Laura spent a minute fidgeting with the keys.

"So this hotel. It's not far? I can't walk too far in these shoes."

Laura finished with the door and dropped the keys into the pocket of her dress. "Really? I guess I always see actresses wearing heels like those in the magazines. I figured you were practically born in them."

"Born in them or not, they sure hurt after a long day."

"Well, don't worry. The hotel is close. It's right downtown."

I glanced around at the quiet street. Besides the diner, all I could see were houses. "Downtown? Where exactly might that be?"

Laura laughed. It was one of those musical laughs. The kind you heard and couldn't help smiling yourself. "Come on," she said, leading the way. "Oh my gosh. I still can't believe you're here. Betsey Burns! What is a star like you doing taking the train anyway? Don't you all have private planes and limousines and such?"

"Maybe when you're making the big pictures, but I'm not exactly a star these days."

"Of course you are. You're Betsey Burns!"

"You don't have to keep saying my name."

"Sorry. I can't help it. I just can't believe you're here, in my town, talking to me. What *are* you doing in New York?"

"I'm starring in a play in the city. Costarring. It's more of a supporting role, but it's a great show and I'm honored to be a part of it." I sighed, realizing this was the same line I gave to reporters when the news broke a few weeks ago.

"That sounds great," Laura said, and I think she meant it. "But I'll miss seeing you in the movies."

"Yeah. But it's fine. Swell, even. Hollywood's kind of a mess right now anyway. Everyone's talking about communism and a blacklist. Being in New York for a few months will be nice."

"Still doesn't explain what you're doing here."

"Oh, I was visiting my grandparents. They live a few hours from here. I flew into Manhattan last week to get settled in before taking the train up to see them." I could see more lights now, though it still didn't look like much of a downtown to me.

"That's so nice," Laura said, rounding the corner at the end of another block. "Your parents must be excited for the change of scenery. I read in the magazines that they go everywhere with you. Are they in the city? Getting your apartment set up for you?"

"Not exactly." I cleared my throat and pointed to the building straight ahead. "Say, sugar, is this the hotel?"

"Sure is."

It was a cute but small building. Bigger than the rest around it, but still only half the size of some of my friends' houses back home. Still, it seemed like a cozy place where I could rest for the next few hours.

Except that wasn't going to happen.

"I'm so sorry, Miss Burns," the concierge said. He hadn't recognized me at first, but he'd definitely perked up once I'd given my name. "But we're all booked up. There's a wedding in town and the guests have taken over pretty much every room."

"There's nothing available?" I asked.

He shook his head. "I really am sorry."

"So what will you do now?" Laura asked once we were outside again.

"Is there anything else open? Restaurants? Anywhere I could just sit?"

"It's after midnight," Laura said. "The diner stays open later than anything else around here."

"Well, then, I guess I'll just have to sleep on a park bench."

"Really? By yourself? All night?"

"Got any better ideas?" I asked.

Laura thought for a moment, tapping her finger against her chin. "Hmm. You could come to my house."

"Oh, no. I couldn't impose."

"You wouldn't be. Honest. It'd be an honor to have Betsey Bur—um, you in my home."

"Sure your parents would feel that way?"

"Remember my boss? The one that's out of town? He's also my father. I've got the house to myself. You won't be bothering anybody. My house isn't fancy or anything, but it sure beats walking around until dawn. What do you say?"

I grinned and shook my head. This girl was just so genuine. It wasn't something I was used to. But I liked it.

"All right," I said. "Thank you, Laura. Really."

"Anytime," she said. "Well, probably not anytime. Stuff like this doesn't happen to me real often, as you might imagine. But I'm glad to help… Betsey."

I smiled so hard my cheeks hurt. I didn't know why, but it felt good to have her call me by my first name. Not Betsey Burns, the name of a washed-up movie star. Not Miss Burns, the name of a stranger. Just Betsey.

"So," I said once we started walking again. "You've asked a bunch of questions about me. Now it's your turn. What's your story?"

"Oh. I don't have one."

"I find that hard to believe. Everyone's got a story."

"Not me," Laura said. "I just graduated from high school a few months ago, and now I'm a waitress at my family's diner. That's about it."

"Do you have any plans? Anything you wanna do or places you wanna go?"

She just shrugged. "Not really. I don't think I'll ever have a life quite as exciting as yours."

I stopped walking. We were passing by a tiny movie theater. The lights were out, but under the glow of the streetlamps, you could still see the posters behind the glass. My eyes caught on one of them, an ad for a Western. A good-looking young man in a cowboy hat was positioned front and center.

Laura walked over and stood next to me. "Wally Landon," she said, staring up at the poster. "I always liked the pictures you two made together. My folks would take my brother and I to the cinema every time you had a new movie out."

"Which was your favorite?"

"Oh, definitely *Timmy and Judy*. My brother and I used to reenact all the scenes in our backyard as kids."

"The tree-climbing scene?"

"Of course."

"Wally nearly broke his neck that day. Boy was a damn show-off. Still is, actually."

"All my friends at school thought he was so dreamy. Is he nice in real life?"

"Usually."

"Is he a good kisser?" Even in the low light, I could tell she was blushing. "Not that it matters to me, really, but I know all my girlfriends will be curious."

"Well, they'll have to ask another girl, because I wouldn't know."

Laura looked confused. "I don't understand. Weren't you two going together for a while? That's what all the magazines said."

"That's what the studio wanted everyone to think." I turned away from Wally and pressed my back against the brick wall of the movie theater, sliding down to sit on the sidewalk. My feet were killing me. "I love Wally, I do, but truth is, we've never been anything more than friends."

Laura sat down next to me, carefully arranging her skirt as she did so. "So Wally was never your boyfriend?"

"No," I said. "I've never had a boyfriend."

"Why not?" Laura asked. "I mean, it just seems crazy. I know I've only known you for a bit, but you seem so nice and you're really pretty…" She looked down at her lap, cheeks red again. I loved how easily she blushed. It was just so honest.

"Thank you," I said. "But that's not the problem. I've just never been interested in anyone. Not like that. Everyone is bed-hopping out there. Costars, studio execs, producers—sex is a big deal in Hollywood. And I'm just not interested in it. For me, I can't imagine sharing something more intimate than a kiss, and I've never even met someone I wanted to do that with."

"Is that why you and Wally broke up?" Laura asked. "I saw Hedda Hopper wrote that he's now going with… Oh, what's her name?"

"Charlotte *DuMont*," I said, sure to give her name the same exaggerated French pronunciation Wally always did. "My replacement." I sighed. "We never broke up because we were never together. That was all the studio's doing. We were supposed to be childhood sweethearts. But then childhood was over and Wally was still a viable star, and I became—what was the phrase they used? Oh, right. Box-office poison."

"That's ridiculous," Laura insisted. "People love you."

"People loved me as a cute little girl," I told her. "But I'm not a kid anymore, and I'm also not the bombshell they hoped for. The studio was hoping I'd be another Elizabeth Taylor, and I'm far from that. So they found another girl, one that fit the image they wanted. And I'm off to New York to do a play no one will see."

"You don't know that," she said. "And I'm not too familiar with this Charlotte DuMont, but I'm sure of one thing. She's no Betsey Burns."

"You're right about that," I said. "Because Charlotte DuMont has a bright future, and I—"

"Have lived more of a life than some of us could ever hope to."

I looked over at her, but Laura was getting to her feet. She straightened out her dress then held out a hand to me.

"Come on," she said. "We've still got a few blocks before we get to my house. And we've got to walk through the graveyard." Her voice was tight as she said this last part.

I let her pull me to my feet. I dusted off the back of my capri pants before following her down the sidewalk once more.

"We have to go through a graveyard?"

"Unfortunately, yes," she said. "I mean, we could go the long way. I do, sometimes, but I'm sure you're tired."

But I wasn't. Not as tired as I should have been at this hour. My feet were killing me, though. And my suitcase, despite only having a couple of changes of clothes inside, was starting to feel heavy.

Apparently this showed and I was moving slower than before, because Laura stopped and glanced at my shoes.

"Why are you still wearing those?" she asked. "You don't have to prove anything to me. Why don't you just take them off?"

"Here? Outside?"

"What could it hurt?"

I took a quick look around. It was dark, but from what I could see, this town did seem pretty clean. And there wasn't anyone around who might see. Slowly, I reached down and pulled off my shoes. The minute I did, a sigh of relief whooshed past my lips.

Laura laughed. "Do you feel better?"

"A bit." I straightened and shuffled my bare feet for a second. The cool, smooth concrete felt strange—but soothing—against my skin. "All right," I said. "Your turn."

"Me? But I'm not wearing heels," she said, extending a foot to show me her espadrilles. "My feet don't hurt."

I gave her a skeptical look. She'd just spent a whole shift on her feet at the diner, after all.

"Well, they don't hurt *that* bad."

"Come on," I said. "Don't let me be barefoot alone out here."

Laura sighed, but smiled, and leaned down to pull off her own shoes. A second later we were both standing barefoot and giggling on the sidewalk.

"Is it odd that I kind of want to dance right now?" Laura asked.

"Dance?" I repeated.

"Yes!" She did a twirl, the skirt of her waitress uniform flaring out around her. Then she began skipping along and waving her arms to a beat only she could hear.

"Don't you need music to dance?" I asked.

"Then sing!"

"I don't sing. If I did, I might be more successful."

"Then I'll sing." She thought for a moment, then did another twirl as she did her best impression of Debbie Reynolds singing "Good Morning" from *Singin' in the Rain.*

I laughed and, even though I'd just told her I didn't sing, couldn't help but join in. The film had only come to theaters early that year, but it was already one of my favorites. At first we sang in unison, then eventually split off into the duet.

I grabbed her hand, dropping my shoes and suitcase on the

ground, and we started twirling down the street together, laughing as we sang about the joys of talking all night. This wasn't the sort of clean, choreographed dancing you saw in the movies. It was loose and unplanned and silly. It'd been a long time since I'd been able to just be silly.

Our feet kept moving until we'd finished the song, then I gave Laura one last twirl before she came to a stop in front of me. We were both breathless and laughing, clutching each other's hands. I was so overwhelmed by it all that, at first, I didn't even notice how close we were standing to each other. Only a few inches between us.

I'd been this close to someone before, of course. But only as a character. In real life, this was new.

It may have been new for Laura, too, because I noticed her hesitate before slowly opening her mouth. "I…uh…"

"Who the hell is making all that racket?" a voice yelled from down the street.

Laura and I jumped apart. Honestly, I'd forgotten anyone in this town even existed besides the two of us.

"It's the middle of the damn night!" the man screamed. "I have half a mind to call the police!"

"Run!" Laura whispered, half a giggle still on her breath.

We grabbed our things off the ground and took off down the street, the angry man still shouting from his front porch. "Hooligans! Rotten kids!" We ran as hard as we could until we reached the end of the block. We swerved around the corner onto a nearly pitch-black street and skidded to a stop next to each other. I'm not sure if we were out of breath from running or laughing, but we were both gasping.

"Whoops," I said.

"I hope he didn't recognize me," Laura said, clutching her chest. "My father would be so mad if he heard." But she was giggling so hard that she snorted. Then she looked down and covered her mouth. "Oh, no. Betsey, your shoes."

I looked down. I was still barefoot, and so was she, only Laura was holding her shoes in hand. And I was only holding a suitcase. "I must've left them."

"I'll go back and get them."

"Leave them. Tomorrow some lucky woman will walk outside and find a pair of expensive heels right outside her door. Hopefully they'll make her happier than they made me." I looped my arm through hers and began leading us down the dark street. "So where's this graveyard we have to walk through?"

"Just up ahead," Laura said, with that same tightness in her voice.

"You don't like graveyards, do you?" I asked.

"Just this one."

We walked for a few more minutes before reaching the cemetery. It was smaller than I'd expected, with dozens of gravestones speckled across a grassy hill. Two lanterns glowed at each side, lighting it just enough to navigate through the headstones, but still dark enough to be a bit eerie.

"Okay," she said, sighing as she stepped off the sidewalk. "My house is just over this hill."

I followed her in silence for a minute, watching her shaking silhouette weave between the graves as she stared straight ahead.

But I couldn't find much to be scared of here. Now that I was seeing it up close, I thought there was something kind of calming about the place. There were fresh flowers and stuffed animals placed on many of the graves, and the headstones all seemed to be engraved with kind, warm sentiments. "Beloved Mother and Wife," "Dearest Grandfather" and so on. It was clear the people here were loved.

"Laura," I said, stopping near the top of the hill.

"Yeah?"

"You said you don't like this graveyard. Is there a reason why?"

She stopped then, too, and turned to face me. "It's just… Nothing. It's nothing. Let's just keep going."

"Come on," I said, reaching out and clasping her hand. "Tell me. Are you scared of dying?"

"No," she said. "Not exactly. No more than anyone else is, I suppose. It's just… I'm scared of dying here."

"In this cemetery?"

"In this town."

"What do you mean?"

She sighed and tugged on my hand. "Follow me." We began walking back down the hill, the way we'd come before, but then veered off to the left, where several dusty headstones sat in a neat row.

"See that one right there?" she said, pointing to the one farthest from us. "That's my grandmother. And the one next to it—that's my grandfather. And there's my great-grandmother and my great-grandfather and my great-great-aunt and, really, every member of my family for the past hundred and twenty years."

"Laura," I breathed, kneeling down to look more closely at the series of family stones. "That's amazing."

"It's terrifying."

I looked up at her. "What do you mean?"

"I'm gonna be just like them." Her voice had become so small. This beautiful girl who'd been singing in the streets at the top of her lungs, waking up the neighbors, was speaking at barely above a whisper now. That unsettled me more than the graveyard did. "I'm gonna work at the diner, eventually get married and have kids because that's what I'm supposed to do, and live in this town forever. I'm never gonna see the world or do anything people will remember."

"Oh, sugar." I stood up and took both of her hands in mine. "You're being ridiculous."

She scowled and tried to pull her hands away, but I kept my grip.

"Listen to me," I said. "Your life hasn't even begun yet. You've got time to do whatever you want."

"But that's just it," Laura said. "I don't *know* what I want. How can I ever leave if I don't know what to chase after?"

"You got time to figure that out," I told her. "Travel. Go to Paris or Rome. Or, gosh, just come visit me in the city. Just because you don't know what you want now doesn't mean you have to be stuck here forever. You're still a kid. You can go anywhere from here."

"You really think so?"

I squeezed her hands. "Trust me. Take it from a broad who's already peaked. I'd much rather be in your shoes."

"That's the silliest thing anyone has ever said to me."

"I mean it," I assured her. "Do you know how scary it is to be eighteen and know there's no going up from here?" I dropped her hands and sat down on my suitcase, facing the graves of Laura's family. "I was in a dozen pictures before I turned fourteen. My parents were proud. The studio was happy. And I thought I'd only get better. I thought I'd win an Academy Award someday."

"You still could."

"Not likely," I said. "The only work I can get now is on the stage. That's respectable, sure, but to most people it just... looks like I've failed. Even my parents didn't want to move to New York with me. They said that when they signed up for me to be an actress it was supposed to be for pictures, not plays. Hollywood, not Manhattan."

"That's awful," Laura said.

"My family doesn't have a place like this." I gestured to the row of headstones. "We're scattered all around. The only grandparents I even keep in touch with are the ones who live upstate, and this visit was the first time I'd seen them in in years."

Laura sat down next to me and gently placed her hand on my arm.

"You've got time to figure out what you want to do, do it and still come back here to this place where people love you if you need to," I told her. "You're only at the beginning, Laura."

"So are you, Betsey."

I laughed. "Weren't you listening?"

"At the beginning of something new," she said, giving me a playful nudge. "New York could be a new adventure for you. Maybe you'll love theater even more than movies. Maybe you'll be the greatest actress the stage has ever seen." She slid her hand down my arm and wrapped her fingers around mine again. "You've got so much more to offer the world, Betsey Burns. I may have only known you a few hours, but I know that much."

I leaned over to rest my head on her shoulder. "Thank you."

"Thank *you*," she said, tipping her head against mine.

I don't know how long we sat there, our hands locked, our heads nestled together as we stared out at the dark cemetery. It didn't feel eerie now. It felt safe. Like a home you could always come back to. I never thought I'd say it, but I wished I had a place like this tiny town. A place that felt like it would always be home, no matter how far away I got.

Hollywood had never felt that way to me. And I wasn't sure if Manhattan would, either.

Laura let out a muffled yawn and I laughed, disentangling

myself from her. "Come on. Weren't we headed back to your house? You've gotta be tired."

She stood and stretched her arms over her head. "Only a little. But it's not that late, I don't think."

We both looked up at the sky. The first beams of sunlight were peeking over the horizon, and the stars were vanishing one by one.

"You're right," I said. "It's not late. Seems like it's pretty early."

"Wow," she said. "It must be about five in the morning."

"We stayed up all night. Just like we sang about." I hummed a few notes of "Good Morning," unable to keep from smiling to myself.

"Your train leaves at six, doesn't it?" She sounded sad now.

I nodded. "Yeah. That can't be more than…an hour away?"

"I can't believe you're leaving so soon," she said. "I can't believe Betsey Burns was in my town for a few hours and I'm the only one who saw her."

"You and the old man we woke up." I grinned. "It was the best few hours I could've asked for. Even if I did lose my shoes." I thought for a moment. "Do you have a pen?"

"Uh, sure." She reached into the pocket of her diner uniform and pulled one out, handing it over to me.

I grabbed her hand and scribbled as best I could in the dim light. When I gave the pen back to her, she had an address scrawled in blue ink across the back of her hand. "The theater where I'll be working," I said. "I meant it what I said about you having time to figure out what you want to do. And if Manhattan is one of the stops on your adventure, come find me."

She blinked, and for a second I worried she was crying. She stared at me, still and quiet, for a long moment, before lunging forward and wrapping her arms around my shoulders. I was so startled that I stumbled backward, but after a second, I returned the embrace.

"Thank you," she said. Slowly, she stepped backward. "And since your family is all scattered around, if you ever need…if you need a family to come home to, our little town will be glad to oblige."

I smiled. "You'll be my family?"

"I'll be your anything," she said.

My heart fluttered in a way it hadn't before. And I was overcome with the urge to do something I'd never wanted to in my life. Something that had always felt too intimate for anyone else. But slowly, nervously, I stepped forward, placed my hands on her cheeks…

And I kissed the beautiful waitress.

It was just a quick peck on the lips. I wasn't ready for anything more and I wasn't sure I'd ever be. But I hoped Laura knew how huge even that small gesture was for me. How much it meant.

How much *she* meant.

I think she understood, because when I pulled back, her face became warm beneath my fingers, and her cheeks swelled into a smile. I lowered my hands and slid them down her arms until I was able to lace my fingers through hers.

She rested her forehand against mine. "Your train leaves soon," she said.

"I know," I whispered. "But there's still time to watch the sunrise."

Together, we turned and made our way up the hill at the center of the graveyard.

And we watched a new day begin.

★ ★ ★ ★ ★

THE END OF THE WORLD AS WE KNOW IT

BY
SARA FARIZAN

Massachusetts, 1999

It's kind of shitty to think that on the eve of the apocalypse, I'm wasting my last hours watching Carson Daly in Times Square awkwardly ask burgeoning pop star Mandy Moore the most banal of questions. The news has everyone in hysterics, wondering if all computer systems will freak out and civilized society will be done for. The stock market will free-fall, people will riot, people's tomatoes wouldn't make it from California to their local supermarkets, some speculated aliens would find us. Chaos was to take place at midnight, but Carson was asking Mandy if she could kiss any guy at midnight who would it be? 1) How is that any of your business, Carson? She's a teenage girl and you're a grown man. 2) She answered Ryan Philippe instead of telling him that maybe she'd like to be asked more pressing questions like "Do you think all major computer systems will shut down at midnight?" and "Is there potential for a more utopian future in the new millennium?" I guess that's not really the vibe they're going for on MTV. Being a girl is stupid. People only want to know whom you want to kiss and nothing else.

So what kind of girl am I if I have no one to kiss on the brink of the world's demise? Does that make one…useless? Well, at least after midnight, I will be rid of the patriarchy forever should the computers freak out, or whatever calamity is supposed to happen. My parents didn't seem too worried about Y2K, but my mom did stock up on an awful lot of canned soup on our last shopping trip. My dad took out a bunch of cash from the bank before Christmas. Just in case, I guess.

My folks asked me if I was going out, which was a very generous assumption on their end. There was a party at John Findlay's house, but I didn't see the point. It was senior year, and the rules of cliques no longer applied so it wouldn't be weird for me to go to a cool-kid party, but I couldn't stand the idea of spending what could be the beginning of the end around people who didn't really know me. Most of the people there still couldn't pronounce my name after four years at Milton High School. Ezgi Olmez does not always roll off the tongue in the outer suburbs of Boston, but my Turkish parents obviously didn't give much thought to that. I do love that about them though. They are unapologetically foreign.

"Askim," I hear my mother yell from downstairs. "Do you want to come join us downstairs? Or do you want to be by yourself and have a sad, lonely year?" Mom has never been a fan of beating around the bush. I pad downstairs and find my parents both wearing paper top hats with Happy New Year written on them and an assortment of snacks with a bottle of sparkling cider on the table.

"Ezgi! You made it to our party!" my dad said enthusiastically as he stands up to give me a big hug. I saw him just two hours ago, but he's always been a big fan of New Year's Eve. He's really into new beginnings and renewal, which is maybe the reason why he came to the States twenty-five years ago. Dad squeezes my face so that I have chipmunk cheeks. "Remember when she was a little baby and she had the roundest face? It's a shame time goes by so fast." He kisses my cheek before he releases me. "I suppose I like you now, too."

Mom pats the sofa cushion for me to sit down between her and Dad. They have it on *Dick Clark's New Year's Rockin' Eve* in lieu of the MTV version of practically the same program I was watching upstairs.

"I would never go to Times Square on New Year's Eve. Aren't they freezing?" Mom wonders aloud as I pop a chip in my mouth.

"Let's go next year! We can visit Ezgi at school and she can show us around," Dad said eagerly. His confidence in my acceptance to NYU made me a little uneasy. If the computers do freak out, I won't have to worry about my future anymore.

"You go by yourself! I'm staying indoors where it is warm and I don't have to worry about where to use the restroom," Mom said. "Besides, Ezgi will be busy with all her new friends."

This is very wishful thinking on Mom's part. I have friends, maybe five or so that I hang with, but we're kind of friends out of necessity. Everybody's nice, but we don't have a whole lot in common except for the fact that we don't have anyone else to chill with. We are discards of other social circles. I used to be part of a duo, but she dropped me last year. It was weird, being best friends with someone since kindergarten and then she blew me by avoiding me at every turn.

My parents loved Katie, but they learned to stop asking about why they hadn't seen her around. I think it made my folks sadder than it made me. Mostly I was confused, a little angry and then too proud to wonder why she dropped me like a 1-800-COLLECT call on a city payphone by a bus terminal.

"You can come visit me on New Year's Eve, Dad. But I will drop you off at Times Square and come get you when all the confetti is being cleaned up," I said. Times Square and the electronic spectacle of advertisements didn't really look like my scene. I saw myself more in the West Village, though I didn't feel ready to let my parents know that yet, if ever. Another thing I won't have to worry about post Y2K. Thanks, binary code gone awry!

"Do you have any resolutions for the New Year, canim?" Dad asked me.

To figure out who I am and what I want my life to be like.

"No. Can't think of anything," I said.

"Can't think of anything? At all?" Mom asks in a disappointed tone of voice.

"That makes sense," Dad said. "Ezgi's perfect! She doesn't need to change anything in the next year." He's mushy. I love his guts.

"This is the year I stop smoking," Mom declared. My dad and I just looked at each other before we laughed. "I will! It's a special year and I am determined. Starting tomorrow."

The doorbell rings, which startles all of us.

"Did you invite anyone over?" Dad asks me as I get up to answer the front door.

"Check the window before you open the door. It might be Y2K looters," Mom said kind of seriously. If she's this paranoid as a smoker, I can't imagine how nervous she'll be when she tries to quit.

I open the door and find a rosy-cheeked Katie Brewer, her long red hair tucked behind her ears, a crop-top shirt showing off her midriff underneath her puffy unzipped Tommy Hilfiger coat.

"Hi," I utter as though it's totally normal for her to be here even though she hasn't been in my life for over a year.

"Hi, Ez." Her eyes are heavy and she's swaying a little. She's been drinking and should be shivering in the snow, but seems to be warm enough from the buzz she's got going.

"What are you doing here?" I ask, not maliciously, but out of genuine curiosity.

"We made a promise. Remember?"

Did we? I don't remember. Then she does the Macarena. I remembered Zach Bratman's birthday party and his parents insisting on supervising the whole night. His parents tried to get us all to do the Macarena, but Katie and I weren't going for it. She asked me then if I'd ever do the Macarena, and I said only if the fate of the planet depended upon it and the world was going to end.

"Right," I said, amazed that so much time had passed since then.

"Are you going to let me in?" Katie asked with a small laugh, but it didn't quite mask the tremor in her voice. I moved aside and opened the door wider for her.

"Wouldn't you rather be at your boyfriend's party?" I asked her.

"It was kind of a letdown. Besides, I've always preferred your parents to the people at John's shindigs." She shrugged off her coat, hanging it on our coat rack.

"You've been drinking," I said, matter of fact.

"What? I have? No!" She's grinning at me.

"My parents are going to know," I hiss.

"I'll keep a respectful distance," she said, holding up her hands. Has she met my parents? They never did respectful distance with Katie. They hugged her like they hugged me. I lead her into the living room, and as soon as my parents see her, they rush her like she's a quarterback about to be sacked.

"Katie! Happy New Year!" my dad said while hugging her. When he finished, Mom tags in and holds Katie close.

"Katie, where have you been? We've missed you. How did

you get so tall?" Mom says before she backs away from Katie, and her happy expression turns to a concerned one. I can tell Mom was close enough to smell the booze on her.

"It's nice to see you, Mr. and Mrs. Olmez. Really nice," Katie said a little sadly.

"Would you like to join our party?" Dad put his paper hat on Katie's head.

"I think Katie and I are going to hang out upstairs for a while," I said, hoping I could sober Katie up a little more as I took her hand and lead her upstairs.

"Okay! Let us know if you need anything," Dad said while Mom looked at us in concern. As I lead Katie up, I overheard my mom say to my dad in Turkish that she was worried about how skinny Katie was.

I locked my bedroom door as Katie plopped herself onto the edge of my bed and turned on my dinky TV.

"I feel like she can totally do better," Katie said pointing at Jennifer Love Hewitt and Carson Daly as they exchanged niceties.

"Are you okay?" I ask, because it is really weird to have her back in my room again.

"Why does everyone keep asking me that lately?" she said, exasperated, as she took off her paper hat. "Are you going to stand and judge me all night or are you going to sit and watch TV with me?"

I compromise and sit on the floor cross-legged instead of sitting next to her on my bed. She can't just show up at my door and pretend like everything is cool and she didn't ditch me to hang out with jocks.

"Just don't ask me to do the Macarena," I said coldly.

"Fair enough," she said, leaning on her side and acting like it was her bed. "Anybody good performing tonight?"

"That depends on one's definition of good." Katie and I always had major differences of opinion when it came to everything, but especially music. "I'm just waiting to see Aaliyah. She's not performing, but the commercial said she'd be on," I said.

"You have such a crush on her," Katie said.

"I do not!"

"No?" Katie said as she pointed to my Aaliyah poster by my vanity mirror.

"I just think she's really cool. Besides, I have posters of dudes up," I said, looking around my room for evidence.

"You mean that tiny cutout of Leo from *Romeo + Juliet*?"

"Whatever. Shut up."

We're quiet for a few moments and there is suddenly discomfort in our familiarity with one another.

"Do you think the Y2K thing is going to mess everything up?" Katie asked.

"I don't know. I think everything's already messed up after Columbine. Like, what kind of world do we live in if you can get shot up in your high school?"

"That was horrible. But I think it's a one-time thing. People won't stand for that kind of tragedy to keep happening."

"I hope so. I was freaked out all week." I wanted to add, "but you wouldn't know that because we don't talk anymore" but thought that would be petty.

"Matthew Shepard. That messed me up," Katie whispered. I took her in and how she was picking at my comforter. Matthew Shepard's murder made me throw up when I saw it on the news.

The way they killed him.

The reason they killed him.

It terrified me.

Come to think of it, that was around the time Katie started avoiding me.

I couldn't look at her anymore and I didn't understand why so I focused on the TV.

★★★

“I hope Everlast got paid a lot to rap with that guy,” I said, recapping the horrible junk music from Limp Bizkit.

“I kind of like their songs,” Katie said with a shrug. We were now sitting next to each other on the carpet.

“You would. Let me guess what you’re listening to these days… Orgy, Placebo, Korn and maybe some Britney Spears. How’d I do?”

By Katie’s annoyed expression, I assumed I had some spot-on guesses.

“I bet you’re listening to Whitney Houston, Mariah Carey and TLC. Just stuck on old favorites,” Katie said, nudging my shoulder with hers.

“I think *you’re* the one stuck on old favorites,” I said. “What are you doing here, Katie?”

She cleared her throat and didn’t make eye contact with me.

“At the party, everyone was talking about the end of the world,” Katie said as the crowd on the screen counted down from ten. “I thought, if it is true, if the world is going to get screwed up beyond measure…you’re really the only person I’d want to say goodbye to.”

This time she didn’t avert her eyes to the television. Neither did I.

Three.

She leaned in.

Two.

She took a breath.

One.

Her lips touched mine.

I didn’t pull myself away.

After she lightly tugged my hair, after I brushed her lower lip with mine, after she nibbled my ear and we got lost in each other, she backed away from me.

"Interesting," Katie said, looking around my room.

"What?" I asked, worried that maybe she was just drunk and didn't mean to kiss me. I was confused, and a little scared by how turned on I was by my former best friend. What the hell was happening? Who did she think she was just lunging in like that…and, wow, could she kiss! I suddenly felt a little jealous that her kissing prowess was being wasted on John.

"The world didn't end," she said, nodding to the TV as No Doubt kept playing. She turned back to me and smiled before she leaned in again. This time, I backed away.

"Hang on, hang on a sec," I said putting my hands on her shoulders. "What are we doing?"

"I believe it is called making out," Katie said.

"No, I mean, I like it. I just didn't think I'd like it," I said, trying to process what had happened.

"Because I'm a girl?"

"Because you're…you. I never thought of you in that way."

"Gee, you sure do know how to make a lady feel special," Katie said, crossing her arms over her chest.

"No! God, I mean, you were my best friend, and then you ignored me completely and now we're kissing," I said, rubbing my temples with my fingers. "What does it mean? What about John? Why did you treat me like a leper but then decide your version of an apology is to stick your tongue down my throat?"

"You always do this. You always try and make magical things logical." Katie rolled her eyes.

"What the hell does that mean?"

"You were at my house, eating chicken nuggets as many seven year olds are prone to when you lost your first tooth. You were crying, worried you were never going to have a front tooth again. My mom tried to calm you down and explained the tooth fairy. You weren't buying it. You kept asking all these questions about how it would be possible for her to make it around the world to every lost tooth. You asked so many questions, that I started to not buy the tooth fairy thing either and, damn it, I really wanted to! It sounded fun."

"Was I wrong? I mean, the tooth fairy isn't real," I said, feeling a little guilty that I ruined a bit of Katie's childhood frivolity.

"Yeah, but couldn't we have just enjoyed the tooth fairy for a moment before you rationalized the joy away?"

She had a point. The jerk.

"You're not going to wake up tomorrow and pretend like it didn't happen, are you?"

She placed her hand on top of mine.

"I'm not making any plans to take you to prom," she said and I don't think I'd be ready for that, either. She continued, "But I'm sorry about ignoring you. I thought it'd be easier than dealing with uh—you know. Feelings."

"Ugh. Feelings are gross," I said softly. "Don't shut me out again. I get why you did, but don't."

"Never. I just couldn't deal then. I still sort of can't deal now. But you know, the world only ends so often." She rubbed her thumb over my knuckles.

"Now that I've officially killed the mood, do you want to sleep over? No funny business; I'll take the couch downstairs."

"No funny business indeed," she said with a smirk. "But don't be stupid. We can share the bed. I'll keep my hands to myself."

On New Year's Day, I woke up alone. The T-shirt and sweatpants I had given Katie the night before to wear as pajamas were folded neatly at the edge of my bed. No funny business had taken place, but I thought she'd at least stick around to talk. I shifted in bed and heard a paper crinkle. I tried to figure out where it was coming from and smiled when I found the note under my pillow. Tooth fairy style.

It read: "Happy New Year, Ez. The world has not ended. We're going to be okay. Tell your mom I couldn't stay for breakfast. I have to go break up with John. Talk soon."

I read the note another twenty times on the first day of the New Year. I felt warm and thrilled, but a little uneasy as to why. Katie Brewer. Huh. Who knew? Maybe we both did. Maybe it was a long time coming or maybe it wasn't. But I knew I wouldn't be able to find a better New Year's kiss for many New Years to come.

I had a whole slew of questions about what the future would hold now.

★ ★ ★ ★ ★

THREE WITCHES

BY
TESSA GRATTON

Kingdom of Castile, 1519

I.

I'm not a witch, she says to herself as the bolt slides back on the door to her cell. *I am Violante Donoso, and I am not a witch.*

Weakness forces her slowly to the straw mattress, one shoulder pressed to the plain stone wall. She breathes carefully around pangs of hunger. Beneath her, the mattress ropes creak in the bed's simple wooden frame; she imagines her bones just as brittle holding her together—holding her alive.

Thin sunlight spears through the single high window just over her bed. At midmorning, light shines across the cell to the crucifix hanging opposite, carved of very fine black wood. That, the bed, a single chair, soft pillow and a rosary are all she's been allowed these weeks.

Two at least, though hunger and boredom—and growing terror—lost her the edge of passing time. She'd not thought, when she'd first stumbled in here, loosed from the tight grip of the Sister to fall hard on her knees, that she should scratch the floor or foot of the bed to mark the days.

"Good morning," a voice murmurs, soft as unused silk. These Sisters rarely speak, she's been told. Cloistered here, they offer their voices only to the Holy Mother.

Violante opens her eyes. Two women, both in white tunics and scapulars bound at the waist with plain leather belts: the elder wears a black mantle and black veil and holds a heavy wooden rosary in her folded hands as she positions herself in the corner, unspeaking. Her clear gray eyes watch Violante with an eerie hunger.

The younger girl, Violante's age, wears no mantle, and her black veil fits against her head exactly as luscious long black hair might. Her skin is as warm a gold as burning sunlight, and those magnificent deep brown eyes console Violante's starvation.

Morisco, Violante thinks before she can stop herself. If this girl is from a Morisco family, how did she end up a Sister of Our Lady? *A beautiful, dangerous sister.*

"Good...morning," Violante says, mouth tacky.

The young Sister kneels at Violante's bedside to place a small tray with water and a clay bowl of broth against the packed-dirt floor. She remains kneeling, hands folded in her lap. "I would like for you to eat, Violante Donoso."

"I am not hungry." Violante raises her chin, though her lips quiver at the smell of simple broth.

"If you starved yourself for our Mother, or to free yourself of the world, I would admire your force of will, but you do not, little sister, and it does not punish *us*. Eat, that we may help you."

"Tell me your name."

"And you will eat?"

Violante hesitates, glancing at the elder Sister, silent in the corner. That one stares intently; she could never persuade Violante to eat.

"Violante?" murmurs the young Morisco Sister.

The ease with which a beautiful girl can seduce Violante has been the core of her troubles all her life. A beautiful girl destroyed her once. But Violante is so hungry, and so lonely, and she did nothing truly wrong! She says, "I will eat, if you stay."

The brown-eyed Sister smiles, and after these weeks of lethargy and spiked fury, Violante is comforted.

"I am Gracia Magdalena." The Sister lifts the clay bowl of broth and brings it to Violante's lips.

Every day Gracia Magdalena comes with the silent elder Sister.

"I'm not a witch," Violante says aloud to Gracia Magdalena on the third day. She's graduated to bread with her broth, and her stomach no longer twists and knots so badly as before.

"Who said that you were?" Gracia blinks those large brown eyes.

Violante glances at the silent Sister, who leans in the corner where the sunlight never shows. Watching. "My brother, Lucas, who brought me here."

"He fears for you."

"He's wrong."

"To fear? Something put that fear inside him."

"I did nothing but love."

Gracia frowns, and it is as beautiful as her smile. "Tell me."

This is how Gracia converses with Violante: small nudges, open doors. She says nothing about herself, but offers brief contemplative words for Violante to expand upon.

Violante touches Gracia's hand; her own fingers are pink and raw from making fists and scratching at her scalp, pulling her hair. Gracia's wrist is soft, the gentlest brown, and warm. "My friend Inés. I love her, and so my brother brought me here."

"Love would not frighten a good man."

"Love alone is my sin. There is nothing else it could be."

"Love is no sin. Love alone does not harm us, or turn us from the Virgin. Acting on love, though, can lead us away from her. If the act is a sin."

"This is no confession," Violante says darkly. "I do not confess."

"You are not on trial, my sister, and I have no authority to hear confession."

Violante pulls back her hands. "Then why are you here? Why do you come again and again? Why am I prisoner? When can I go home?"

"You are ill with temptation. You need to be freed from the voices of demons. You must pray and be absolved. What... what tempted you, Violante?"

"I am not ill!" Violante stands up, swaying. She glares at the Sister standing in the corner, then at Gracia Magdalena. "Get out!"

Violante huddles in the dark corner of her cell. Through the window she hears singing: not the Sisters, but birds flitting about in the early morning, before the sun itself rises.

I am not a witch.

She thinks of the fire in her hips, the beat of her heart and how transported she'd been by only Inés's soft mouth. Better than prayer, better than wine. Better than wind in her hair when she rides on the back of Lucas's horse, or the thrill of ghostly danger when the rafters in their house moan. *Ah, Inés! Ah, your palms and flick of your eyelashes against my skin. Was that witchcraft?* The heat of the hearth their only light, their urgent breath a music more sacred than any monastic song. Joyous life, like those birds outside the tiny window. Singing for each other.

The first time Gracia Magdalena offers Violante fruit, it is a dried fig along with her bread. Violante lets the wrinkled, soft skin touch her bottom lip, enjoying the tension as her teeth press down, not quite breaking through; then the skin splits and the sticky, sweet mass fills her mouth.

Gracia's lips part, as if she, too, would eat a fig. Violante smiles.

The elder Sister never speaks, but brings with her a basket of sewing and kneels in her corner. As a guard, an honor, a chaperone. Gracia Magdalena never even glances her way. It puzzles Violante, but she determines to also ignore the woman with her strange colorless eyes.

Gracia leads Violante in praying the Holy Rosary every day, soft and gentle, and Violante does not mind, for she's never begrudged the Virgin a moment of time. The prayers are soothing, and Gracia traces the beads with an adoration that puts shivers along Violante's spine. Would that the bones of her back were beads of the rosary, and Gracia skimmed her fingers against them so ardently.

That, Violante realizes, is a thought Gracia Magdalena and Lucas and all the world would find to be heresy. But this feeling must be the same as the one Gracia feels for the Holy Mother: love. Adoration. A longing to share. For Gracia's fingers do linger at each bead, seeming reluctant to move on to the next, as if the simple knots of carved wood were the Virgin's own knuckles, fingers, wrists.

"Violante," Gracia murmurs at the end of the second decade of beads. The girls contemplate the Glorious Mysteries as they pray, for Gracia hopes meditation upon the Virgin's grace and the hope of resurrection will lead Violante away from earthly temptation. Each ten-bead decade holds space for considering a single Mystery.

"Hmm?" Violante does not take her gaze off Gracia's fingers, which hold a smooth red bead like a drop of holy blood.

"You stopped praying."

Violante lifts her eyes. Gracia sits beside her on the creaking straw mattress, their shoulders near enough the slightest breath could lean them together.

"Are you well?" Concern melts in Gracia's brown eyes.

"Yes. Please don't stop."

Gracia touches the back of Violante's hand, and it's a struggle to remain still. Violante begins the next prayer, and halfway through Gracia joins her.

In the corner, the elder Sister watches both girls, following their prayers along her own rosary beads but never speaking the words aloud.

Violante wonders, at night, if they send Gracia Magdalena to her as temptation. They know why Lucas brought her here, and had they sent a less lovely girl, or an old Sister as wrinkled as a grandmother, how could they know if prayer and isolation had cured her yet?

She dares not ask, for if Gracia stops visiting, Violante will be alone.

They bring her out beyond the cloister wall to meet her brother. It has been a month since he dragged her here.

Violante wears a clean linen shift and plain kirtle, sandals, and nothing else. She was allowed to wash with soap and water, given a cord to tie the end of her braid, and a simple veil to cover her head. Lucas will never have seen her so plain, nor anyone in her life since she was a babe. Inés would disdain such common garments after the layers of velvet and vermilion linens she'd regularly laced and pulled around Violante's body.

Her brother sits on a short stone bench beside a flare of pink roses that climb the outer cloister wall. His red hat tilts left to shade his eyes from the sun, and his doublet is rich brown, deep and magnificent and slashed to show creamy linen beneath. Its full-striped skirt covers him to his knees; his pink hose are at least two shades darker than the roses. He is so handsome and glorious that Violante pauses, afraid and desperate.

More a father to her since their own had died in the Americas eight years ago, since Lucas brought back almost immeasurable riches, he should be taking care of her, not hiding her away.

Violante pretends heavy velvet skirts hang off her hips, and a bodice with some elaborate, stiff embroidery presses her together like armor. She imagines half her hair in a crown of braids, a lace veil of perfect snowy white trailing down over her hanging curls.

"Violante!" Lucas says eagerly when he hears her footfalls. He clasps her hands and inspects her. "You're thin. They tell me you ate nothing for days, darling. Do you feel better?"

Hands limp in his, Violante says nothing. His skin is dry and stained with ink at the fingertips, which their mother would hate. She turns them over to the whiter, softer skin of his palms. "Take me home," she finally whispers. It is not strong. She does not feel strong.

"Are you…well?"

"I always have been." She jerks her chin up to glare at him.

But Lucas's loving eyes narrow at the edges as he frowns. He shakes his head. "No, you—you long for unnatural things. You must stay, if you do not see so!"

"Lucas!" Violante pulls free of him, stumbling away. She

hugs her stomach, clawing her nails into her own elbows. *I am not a witch.*

Behind her, Lucas touches her shoulders. "Try to understand, little sun, I beg you. I want you to come home, but... I won't have it in my house. I need you good and pure and ready to do your duty, whether that be to our family or to a husband."

"I am!"

"Your soul, little sun. I worry on it."

Violante bites her lip. Her brother sleeps poorly in the summer, when the days are longest and hottest, and cries out with nightmares he never had before he went to conquer across the sea. Only Violante soothes him, only she cheers the haunting woe from his voice, the tears from his eyes. He is excellent at covering it, but it soon will be Easter, and then the nightmares will come again. He means to say, *"My soul. I am afraid for my soul, little sister."*

"I am well, Lucas," she whispers, leaning back against him.

"Another month here." He squeezes her shoulders. "Find peace, and righteousness, and the Holy Mother's blessings."

Grief and fear sink down through her, dragging at her heart, heavy in her guts, like a hot stone in her womb. She covers her belly with both hands and feels the sinking sensation that presages her bleeding. "Lucas, don't leave me here," she begs.

"Violante, give up your sins and come home."

They aren't sins.

But she isn't certain.

Blood stains the hem of her shift, and Violante huddles in the very corner of the cell that silent elder Sister prefers. All night she weeps, bleeding trickles of life out of herself because she refuses to call for help. She whispers the Holy Rosary, wondering if Mary, the Mother of God, bled. She had to, did she not? To bear a child.

The Holy Mother was a virgin who never knew any man, and so is Violante. She prays, she knows the ecstasy of love and longing, desire, and the pure, perfect happiness of hands on hands, lips on lips, the breeze of fluttered lashes. Yet she has never known any man.

Is that not perfect love?

"Why is desire not holy?" she asks Gracia the moment the girl enters in the morning.

But Gracia Magdalena screams and drops her tray of food and water. "Violante! Violante!" She scrambles to Violante, who startles back in shock.

"What have you done? What is..." Slowly Gracia regains herself, leans back on her heels.

"It is only my menses, Gracia Magdalena," Violante says calmly, a bit breathless at the fear that had played in Gracia's raised voice. Fear for her!

In silence, Gracia begins to clean the spilled food, gather the broken clay bowl that had held a simple stew of vegetables. Salty, sweet broth and the uncomfortably similar scent of blood mingle in the cell. Violante stands, wiping the floor with the hem of her shift.

Another Sister, one Violante has never seen, and formidable in the black veil and mantle, comes with a clean shift and wrappings for Violante. To prevent such an inappropriate mess. A third Sister brings fresh food and drink. There is no sight of the silent Sister and her basket of sewing.

Violante washes and changes, then eats in the presence of all. When she finishes, Gracia is left alone with her, but only briefly. She gathers the bowl and water onto her new tray and watches Violante for a long, resonant moment.

"Desire can be holy if it is desire for God," she says, and before Violante may reply, leaves.

Violante sinks to her knees and whispers, *"Hail, Holy Queen,"* but it is not the Virgin's bright cheeks and warm heart to whom she prays.

II.

Oh, Holy Mother!
Blessed Queen of Heaven!
To you do I cry in my moment of desperate need.
To you.

I don't know what to do.

Hail, Holy Queen. Mother of mercy, of life, of sweetness and hope, hail. To you do I cry, a poor banished daughter of Eve, to you do I send up my sighs, my mourning and weeping from this, the vale of tears. Turn to me, most gracious Advocate, your eyes of mercy, and after my exile, show unto me the blessed fruit of your womb, Jesus Christ. Oh, clement, oh, loving, oh, sweet Virgin Mary. Pray for me, that I may be worthy of the promises of Christ.

Salve, Regina, Mater misericordiae,
Vita, dulcedo, et spes nostra, salve.

Salve.

Salve!

I want to let her kiss me.

The blood frightened me, and also gave to my mind's eye the thought of His sacrifice—the poor seeping wounds of Christ. That is wrong, wrong! I know it, but her eyes blaze with such ferocity of purpose, Holy Mother. To disregard her is like disregarding my own heart. I do not know how to turn away.

I should refuse to visit her, deny the will of the prioress, on behalf of my soul.

Yet I know they wait for such weakness in me, weakness as they profess did haunt my mother's soul. My poor mother.

I returned to her this morning with the prayers of a full night bolstering me. Her eyes remained bright, her pale cheeks hollow but pink with passion. She holds her lips parted always, as if she tastes the very world, oh, Holy Mother.

It stirs me, though I would it did not. It stirs me, for I never have seen anything outside this cloister, in sixteen long years of life. These walls are my only world, and I know it so well there was never new taste, until her.

Oh, Holy Mother! Salve, Regina, forgive me. This place is a refuge, my home. I know it as I know my heart, and so I need not long for anything other than your perfect self and the Beloved Heart of Your Son.

I said to her, to Violante, "You must give up this desire, if you would be holy."

"Unless my desire is for God?" she asked, glancing to the empty north corner. She does this sometimes, as if she fears some other might overhear us, though we are always alone.

I pursed my lips, knowing not how to respond, and held out the food for her. She accepted, and ate. I said, "Your brother upset you."

"He needs me. Who did you leave behind?" she asked. "When you made your profession of faith."

"None."

"No family? You are an orphan?"

"Yes. Born in the Church."

"They give you to such danger, here with me, if they think I am near to the demons of Hell."

"Say no such thing," I warned, flattening my palm toward her.

She caught my hand in both of hers and glanced to the empty corner again. She stepped closer to me, to ask in confidence, "Why do they risk a girl like you?"

"It is no risk," I promised, eyes lowered to our joined hands. I could not confess to Violante that my mother died in the Inquisition's prison, awaiting her trial for reversion. They told me once my mother had screamed an infidel name as they took me from her, barely born, dripping her womb blood off my skin.

Thus I began my life promised to heresy, and baptism saved me. Gracia Magdalena they called me in God, for thanks and for my lack of innocence.

Violante leaned toward me. "Are you certain I am no risk?"

"A risk to yourself," I whispered to her. "Please pray with me, Violante, for absolution."

"I cannot ask to be absolved of love. I won't. I love."

I shivered then, and had a vision of my mother, whom I never met: she knelt and leaned forward against the earthen floor, murmuring a prayer. "I love," she said as she sat and looked directly at me. "I will not give in."

A martyr's words.

"I will not give in," I said to Violante.

"I will not give in," she returned to me, and took my hand. She curled her fingers around my wrist, tugging gently at me. "I feel it in my heart, my very soul, Gracia Magdalena."

She said my name slowly, tasting the flavor of it.

"Help me," she whispered.

"I don't know how, except..."

I meant to say, "except to pray, to lead you to absolution."

But Violante touched my cheek to kiss me, and I fled.

★★★

Hail, Holy Queen.
Mother of mercy.
Of life.
Of sweetness.
Of hope.

Have mercy on me.
I can't stay away.

It is my duty to face this. I must face this temptation. Which is the true way? What is the temptation? To give my love to her or to abandon her? Which is your will? Which is the path of love?
I must love. Oh, Holy Mother, Regina, have mercy.

III.

She crouches unseen in the corner, waiting.
This is the moment.

One girl has seen her before, because it pleased her to be seen.

The other girl never has. She had not been ready.

Now.
Now.
One girl kneels beside the narrow bed. The other sits on the mattress edge with her knees together. One touches shaking brown hands to the other's pale, unhappy fingertips.
One whispers.
The other shakes her head.
They pray.

But this one crouches, unseen.

She hopes. She thinks of sweet things while she watches the two girls:

Of mercy.

Sunset.

Bonfires under the full moon.

Dancing and screaming!

Figs.

Choice.

She stands, her body forming from the shadows, eyes gray as twilight, a smile on her plain face.

They are choosing her world.

Choosing love.

This is the moment.

When they kiss, she laughs and throws out her hands. Both shall fly with her!

Salve, maleficia!

*****

THE INFERNO & THE BUTTERFLY

BY
SHAUN DAVID HUTCHINSON

London, 1839

Wilhelm appeared. Not in a cloud of smoke or a flash of light, but in the moment where the heart skips a beat.

He exhaled, his eyes closed, and I watched him smile and gracefully bow as the audience applauded and cheered, even though he couldn't see them nor they him. Wilhelm was the one who truly deserved their love and adoration, though they were, and would remain, ignorant of that fact.

When he opened his eyes and saw me, his smile faded and he said, "Alfie, you shouldn't be here."

I stepped forward, determined, and said, "I'm asking, Wilhelm. I'm asking now."

The Mystic Mycroft, better known to me as Thierry Dubois, had rescued me from a life of crime and misery after I foolishly attempted to pick his pockets on the streets of London.

I might have succeeded had I been paying better attention and seen the carriage bearing down on us. Its passing splashed water on Mr. Dubois, causing him to turn his head toward me while my thieving fingers were in his pockets. Rather than shout for a constable to haul me away, he backhanded me hard enough to send me sprawling into the street wall and then offered me a bed and a hot meal, neither of which I'd had in as long as I could remember.

My intention in accepting his offer had been to stay with Mr. Dubois long enough to earn his trust and then relieve him of whatever belongings he possessed, but he introduced me to the world of magic and I gladly left behind my life of occasional housebreaking and perpetual hunger. Well, the hunger part anyway.

Mr. Dubois's persona, the Mystic Mycroft, had purportedly traveled the entire world—the Americas, Africa and the peaks of the Himalayas—seeking the wisdom of ancient practitioners of mystic arts with which he could amaze and awe willing (and unwilling) spectators, but the truth was that Mr. Dubois's early life shared many parallels with my own: he'd grown up poor and been forced to steal to survive. He'd traveled from France when he was fifteen and, after sneaking into a third-rate prestidigitator's show, had endeavored to become the greatest stage magician in living memory.

Under the less-than-patient tutelage of Mr. Dubois, I flourished, and the crowds clamoring for more Mystic Mycroft swelled as a result. Mr. Dubois's skillful legerdemain was unparalleled throughout London, but he'd lacked a certain necessary theatricality, which I'd been more than happy to provide.

When it comes to the art of illusion, nearly every member of the audience walks into the show suspecting deception. They believe themselves intelligent enough to discern the nature of the trick—that if they watch closely and pay unwavering attention, they can detect the misdirection and unravel the secret—but the Mystic Mycroft was too good. His performance too perfect. Before meeting me, he'd more often left his audiences feeling duped and foolish rather than dazzled by his wondrous feats of magic.

Even with my nimble fingers, I could never hope to attain the Mystic Mycroft's level of dexterous mastery, but I possessed an intuitive sense of drama that he did not. I taught him how to lure the audience in, show them something they shouldn't believe while giving them just enough to convince themselves that if they paid the admission and returned frequently they might one day learn the secret.

By the time I was sixteen, Mr. Dubois and I were selling out the Gramary Theatre five nights a week.

Though Mr. Dubois was often difficult and prone to violent outbursts, I'd never expected to live or die anywhere other than the gutters, in a workhouse, or in gaol, and I'd never entirely forgive myself for betraying him.

The illusion was called the Butterfly, and both it and the magician performing it had been bleeding away our audience for weeks.

The Butterfly served as the climax of the show during which the Virtuoso, whose real name was Percy Beevers, brought out a young man about my age whose hands remained shackled throughout, and made him vanish.

Before doing so, the Virtuoso invited audience members onstage to test the floor for trapdoors and his assistant for wires. When they were satisfied neither existed and had returned to their seats, the Virtuoso began a ludicrous dance while chanting gibberish we were supposed to mistake for an ancient language. As seconds passed, he moved faster, his long arms and legs flapping and stomping, his chanting growing louder and more deranged, so much so that when I first witnessed it I suspected him of having a fit.

And then, in a puff of smoke, the young man would disappear and be replaced with a beautiful young woman in a flowing, brightly colored kimono, who would raise her hands and drop the manacles to the stage with a dramatic thud.

The audience loved it. Mr. Dubois was less enthusiastic.

Over the years, I'd proven adept at perceiving the nature of other magicians' tricks, and Mr. Dubois frequently sent me to spy upon his rivals, but no matter how often I watched the Butterfly, I couldn't discern its secrets.

I'd suspected at first that it was a cleverly hidden trapdoor that allowed the manacled young man and the beautiful woman to quickly trade places, but I'd managed to get myself onto the stage more than once and could find no seams in the floor. It was either ingeniously concealed or something else entirely.

"We're ruined, Alfred," Mr. Dubois said as I helped him undress for the evening. "That old fool Bostwick has warned that if we can't fill the Gramary, he'll replace us with a touring ballet company or some such rubbish."

Mr. Dubois had been the Mystic Mycroft for so long that he rarely broke character anymore. Whatever French accent he might have once had no longer existed. I poured him a glass of wine and handed it to him as he flopped heavily into the chair by the fireplace.

"Good lad," he said. "But I fear our days together may be at an end if I can't expose the Virtuoso for a fraud."

"I've seen him perform it a dozen times," I said. "And I still have no idea how he does it."

"Then you have failed," he said, and the indictment stung more than I was willing to admit. "I believe it's time we unveil the Inferno."

"Sir, please no. It's too dangerous. I can learn the Virtuoso's secret."

I'd first learned of the Inferno from Mr. Dubois during one of his drunken soliloquies in the midst of which he'd lamented the possibility of dying without creating a trick the world would remember him for. He believed the Inferno would be his legacy.

His idea was to place his assistant—me—in a box similar to the type used during our underwater escape act. The difference was that the box would be filled not with water, but with fire. The Mystic Mycroft would drop me, my hands bound, into the box, close the lid—which would extinguish the fire as it consumed the oxygen—and then I would escape and appear to walk out of the smoke and through the box unharmed.

I'm afraid I can't divulge the secret of the trick without further betraying my mentor, but it would prove to the world that the Mystic Mycroft was the greatest magician to ever live. It was also extremely dangerous. Our success to that point had allowed me to delay Mr. Dubois from incorporating the Inferno into the show, but with the Virtuoso's steady theft of our audience and income, however, I feared I could no longer prevent my inevitable conflagration.

Mr. Dubois glared at me coldly through heavy-lidded eyes. "I love you like a son, Alfred, but I would sooner see you dead than allow Percy Beevers to ruin me."

"I know, sir," I said. "I'll learn the secret of the Butterfly. I swear."

And as I promised, I knew my life depended on my ability to keep that oath.

Which was how I met Wilhelm Gessler.

During previous viewings of the Virtuoso's show, I'd spent the majority of my time focused on the stage, on the Virtuoso himself, but little on the young man in shackles.

A magician relies on misdirection—a flash of light or smoke

or a pretty girl, anything that keeps the audience from seeing what they ought not. A prestidigitator says, "Look over here," while the actual magic is happening elsewhere.

I'd noticed that the Virtuoso practically begged the audience to focus their attention on the manacled boy, so I assumed it was because we were meant to pay attention to him so that the mechanics of the trick could play out unnoticed. Which was the beauty of the Virtuoso's act. That we believed we were being deceived *was* the deception.

One afternoon, while in attendance, I decided to pay special attention to the young man. He was tall with broad shoulders, curly blond hair and clear blue eyes so bright I could see them shining from five rows back. As the moment of his transformation approached, I determined not to blink so I wouldn't miss it, whatever *it* was.

The Virtuoso began his absurd dance and Wilhelm closed his eyes. While the others were watching the magician, I watched Wilhelm. He dropped what I assumed was a smoke bomb—a commonly employed distraction—that exploded in a thick grey haze, and then he vanished.

If there'd been a trapdoor I would have expected to see movement created by the suction generated by Wilhelm's downward movement, but the smoke remained still. And almost simultaneously the woman appeared where Wilhelm had stood not one second before.

I wasn't certain *how*, but I understood in that moment that Wilhelm was the trick. *He* was the key to the Butterfly.

A magician guards his secrets more fiercely than any other thing he possesses. Without his secrets, a magician is naught but a pauper. Mr. Dubois kept a workshop filled with devices and schematics that did absolutely nothing except act as a ruse to tempt and thwart would-be thieves. Not even I knew all of

Mr. Dubois's secrets, and he trusted me more than any other. If I was right about Wilhelm, the Virtuoso would guard his young assistant with his life.

I spent two weeks following the Virtuoso until I knew his schedule better than my own. Meanwhile, the Mystic Mycroft's audience continued to decline, and our patron, Sir Charles Bostwick, had grown tired of excuses and declared his intention to replace us if we couldn't reverse our fortunes.

Each Thursday afternoon at exactly 11:30, Mr. Beevers left his workshop to attend lunch with a young woman who was not his wife, and stayed with her well into the late afternoon. If the scandal of an extramarital affair would have been enough to destroy either Beevers's or the Virtuoso's reputation I might have sought out some way to expose him, but there were few men of means in London who would not have sympathized with the Virtuoso, and instead of ruining him, such knowledge might have increased his popularity.

Since coming to live with Mr. Dubois, I'd had numerous opportunities to keep my thieving skills sharply honed, and in some circumstances—such as with picking locks—I'd even learned some new ones. I'd expected to find the Virtuoso's workshop guarded, but the lock was easily dispatched and the studio empty.

The workshop seemed as wondrous as Mr. Dubois's, but these were no mere decoys. Percy Beevers was either careless with his secrets or confident none could unravel them. I stopped to examine a box fitted with gears and mirrors that changed its internal structure and gave it the illusion of being empty, and I flipped through a notebook, written in plain text rather than in cipher, detailing numerous ideas for tricks the Virtuoso hoped to incorporate into his act. All of these I committed to memory so that I could report back to Mr.

Dubois, though nothing I found revealed the answer to the puzzle that might keep me from the Inferno.

I felt a rush of excitement at being in the Virtuoso's inner sanctum that reminded me of my early life of thieving. The difference was that I was no longer merely skulking about to keep myself fed. I knew that Mr. Beevers wouldn't return for some hours, but the thrill that he *could* return at any moment was exhilarating.

After I'd thoroughly searched the workshop, I turned my attention to the stairs leading to the cellar from the ground floor. I crept down them, testing each step for creaks before resting my full weight on it and keeping my feet to the far sides of each step.

In all my observations of the Virtuoso, I'd never seen him with his young assistant anywhere other than inside the theater. In fact, I'd never seen the boy other than when he was onstage, which only made me more certain that *he* was the real key to the mystery of the Butterfly.

The cellar was relatively clean if a bit dark, and it took my eyes a moment to adjust to the lack of light. I searched around for a lamp but found nothing. There were crates stacked along the walls and I was about to give up when a voice called to me from the far end of the room.

"You shouldn't be here."

I froze, unsure whether to run or attempt to hide, which was foolish because clearly I'd already been caught. I searched the darkness for the source of the voice and noticed a heavy shadow where before I'd seen none.

"Hello?"

"Mr. Beevers will return soon." I noted a slight German accent in the voice.

"No, he won't," I said. "I imagine his mistress will keep him occupied for some time still."

Emboldened, I moved toward the back of the cellar. A lamp flared to life and drove back the darkness. I felt exposed and a little foolish that I'd been caught so easily. At the far end of the room stood a cage roughly half the size of my own room in Mr. Dubois's house, which was to say quite small.

"What is this?" I asked. "Why are you in this cage? Does Percy Beevers keep you prisoner?" Anger bubbled up from within me that a charlatan such as the Virtuoso could treat anyone so cruelly. Mr. Dubois might have beaten and cursed at me, but he never would have imprisoned me in such a manner.

I crossed the rest of the distance to the cage and shook the bars. I searched for a door or hinge or lock but found none, which only added to the mystery and further stoked my rage. "Tell me how to open this cage!"

"He'll be angry if he finds you here."

"This is inexcusable," I said. "I should fetch the constable."

"Please don't."

"Why shouldn't I?"

The young man stood and pressed his face to the bars of his cage. He was dressed not in the fine suit he wore each night on stage, but rather in plain clothes, ragged and filthy. His hands were manacled and his hair unruly. Though not consciously, I committed every curve and angle and detail of his face to memory. The scar under his left eye, the constellation of freckles across his nose, the one slightly crooked tooth in his smile. He was beautiful.

"This is where I belong."

"I refuse to leave you here like this," I said.

"You must."

"I won't."

"I know who you are," he said, which startled me. "You're the Mystic Mycroft's assistant."

"Alfred," I said.

"Wilhelm Gessler."

We stared at each other for some time, neither speaking. I was at a loss for what to do. I'd come to steal another magician's secrets and had found something I couldn't explain. Why would the Virtuoso keep Wilhelm locked in a cage that seemingly had no door? I was baffled and angry and uncertain what to do.

"You've come to learn the true nature of the Butterfly, yes?" Wilhelm said finally.

"Yes," I said, almost ashamed to admit it.

"Then return the day after tomorrow. Mr. Beevers will be otherwise engaged and I'll tell you what you wish to know."

"Why then?" I asked. "Let me free you now and you can explain everything when you're safe."

"You must trust me," Wilhelm said.

"Trust you? I barely know you!" But part of me *did* trust this young man, though I couldn't explain why. There was an honesty in his face I didn't believe he was faking.

"The day after next," Wilhelm said again. "Return then."

I didn't want to leave Wilhelm alone in the cellar, but I had few options. I couldn't see a way to open the cage, and unless I was willing to fetch the constable and explain why I was in Percy Beevers's workshop to begin with, I had no choice but to do as Wilhelm had asked. Despite my lingering questions and against my better judgment, I nodded and left.

Two days later I waited for the Virtuoso to leave his shop. He usually spent Saturday entertaining acquaintances and wouldn't return until the following day.

More boldly than before, I picked the lock to the workshop and made my way to the cellar. I'd brought my own lantern this time and lighted it before descending the stairs. Wilhelm was standing in his cage, holding the bars, as if he'd anticipated the hour of my arrival.

"I brought you something to eat." I unslung a bag from my shoulder and pulled out a corner of fresh bread, an apple and a wedge of cheese I'd stolen from the kitchen.

"Mr. Beevers feeds me well," Wilhelm said, but he took the food regardless and set to eating.

I sat down on the ground outside of the cage. "Why are you locked in this cage?" I asked.

Wilhelm sat as well. Only the bars separated us.

"The answer is also part of the answer to what you really wish to know."

"What is the secret of the Butterfly?" I said, though I'd only meant to say it to myself.

"Yes."

"Tell me."

"The secret is me."

"I don't understand."

Wilhelm sighed heavily. "I was born in Wernigerode, the son of a butcher. My life was dull until, when I was fourteen, I was trapped in a burning building. I was certain I was going to die, and I wished only to hug my mother one last time. Suddenly, I found myself standing beside her in our kitchen. With nothing more than a thought, I had transported myself from the building."

I listened intently to Wilhelm's story. Of how his parents, rather than being glad he was still alive, were horrified by what he'd done and had beaten him, believing he was possessed by demons. He was rescued by Percy Beevers, who had been passing through on his way to Munich and heard about the demon boy who could vanish and reappear at will. He'd paid the Gesslers a fortune for Wilhelm and had incorporated him into his act.

Such a thing could not have been possible, and I struggled to believe him. Had anyone else spun such a fantastical story, I would have called them a liar, but if Wilhelm could do what he said, it would have explained why I hadn't been able to detect the trick behind the Butterfly.

"Can you…?" I asked.

Wilhelm nodded once and without preamble vanished from where he was sitting and instantaneously reappeared outside of his cage beside me. Then, before I could register my astonishment, the world dimmed and I found myself on the other side of the cage.

I patted my own body to make certain I was whole. Panic gripped me; I grabbed the bars and shook them, my brain unwilling to believe what my eyes were showing me. My hands trembled and my voice broke as the thought of him leaving me there forever became a real possibility in my mind.

"It wasn't until Mr. Beevers purchased me that I discovered I could also transport others," Wilhelm said, smiling.

"Let me out of here immediately!"

And then Wilhelm once again reversed our positions, returning me to the outside of the cage. I steadied myself against the floor, feeling disoriented.

"Don't ever do that again!" I said.

Wilhelm bowed his head and turned his eyes from me.

"I apologize," he said. "I only meant to show you how it worked."

"I was startled is all." I held my hands up to my face and looked at them—first the fronts and then the backs—to verify that everything was as it ought to be. Once the shock wore off, I felt exhilarated. I'd been transported through the air! If I hadn't experienced it for myself I scarcely would have believed it. Mr. Dubois was going to be inconsolable when he discovered that we could never hope to reproduce the Butterfly. "This thing you can do is magnificent. It's *real* magic, not simply the sleight of hand performed by the rest of us."

"It's a curse," Wilhelm said.

"How can it be a curse? How can *anything* you do be a curse?"

"You cannot understand."

I thought not only of the ways in which Wilhelm's ability could be used in a stage act, but of what I might have done with it before I'd been found by Mr. Beevers. With such a power, I could have become the greatest thief London had ever known. I could have traveled the world, vanishing in one city and reappearing in the other, my life limited by only my imagination.

"How far can you travel?" I asked. "Can you only move other people to switch places with them?"

Wilhelm shook his head. "I can travel as far as my eye can see," he said. "Or to places I have previously traveled, no matter their distance. I've only used my ability to carry Mr. Beevers with me, but I believe it would be possible to carry more than one person. And I can move another without needing to take their place."

The possibilities were endless. But one question burned within my mind, demanding an answer above all others. "If you can do these things, then why do you remain the Virtuoso's prisoner?"

I was not sure what answer I expected. It seemed possible that Mr. Beevers might be holding Wilhelm's family hostage in exchange for his good behavior, but I doubted Wilhelm held much love for the parents who sold him in the first place. I was not, however, expecting the answer Wilhelm finally gave.

"The cage was my idea."

"What?"

"I owe Mr. Beevers my life. He took me in when my parents would have killed me, believing me to be possessed by a demon. Mr. Beevers has assured me such is not the case, though I'm not sure I believe him. I *am* cursed. There are those who would use me for more nefarious purposes than my master, so I stay in this cage to make certain no one may take me against my will and force me to do things that might cause harm to others."

Though I had only known Wilhelm Gessler for a few scant hours, I didn't believe him capable of ever hurting another living soul. That he voluntarily spent his days in a cage said more about him than anything else.

"Come with me," I said. "Allow me to introduce you to Mr. Dubois. You'll have the finest rooms and we'll tour the world. You do not have to stay caged. You could be free. You *deserve* to be free."

Wilhelm shook his head. "You should leave now."

"Please—" I began and then I found myself standing outside the Virtuoso's workshop, staring at the door. Wilhelm had transported me out of the cellar and into the street in the space of a single breath.

Mr. Dubois would never think of me as a son or even care for me more than he cared for the pigeons he'd used in the first show I'd seen him perform in, but he had given me a better life than I might have had otherwise, and for that I owed him a debt.

Yet however strong my allegiance to Mr. Dubois, I found myself unwilling to tell him about Wilhelm's strange abilities. No good would have come from revealing Wilhelm's secret without the means to replicate it, and I didn't believe it possible without convincing him to betray Mr. Beevers.

My guilt over withholding vital information from Mr. Dubois caused me to finally agree to perform in the Inferno despite my serious misgivings that it might result in my death.

Despite Wilhelm having ejected me from the cellar during my previous visit, I returned the following night after the Virtuoso had left for the evening, and I did so each night thereafter. Wary of again offending Wilhelm, I didn't speak of escape.

Instead we spoke of our lives before we each met our equally ignoble magicians. I shared stories of thieving on the streets of London. Of the days spent in hiding, of the nights spent hungry and cold. Of my favorite memory of my mother—I remember that she sang to me but couldn't remember the song, only her voice.

Wilhelm told me of his own life in Wernigerode. Before he discovered his abilities, his home had been filled with warmth and love the likes of which I'd never experienced. That Wilhelm's parents had loved him so dearly and yet still rejected him must have caused him pain I could scarcely begin to comprehend.

Nearly two weeks after first discovering Wilhelm, I returned to the cellar in a foul state.

"You've injured yourself," Wilhelm said, glancing at my hand. Since the first time he'd used his gift to reverse our places, he had not left his cage, and I had not asked him to, fearing he would send me away again.

I looked at the back of my right hand, where a watery blister, about the size of a shilling, had risen angry and red.

"It's nothing," I said, but Wilhelm reached through the bars of his cage and took my hand.

"How did you do this?"

"During rehearsals for our newest act," I said. "The Inferno."

When Wilhelm didn't speak, I explained how the Butterfly and the Virtuoso's success were ruining Mr. Dubois, and that we had less than two weeks to reclaim our audiences or face eviction from the theater.

In fact, I'd sneaked a look at Mr. Dubois's personal ledger and learned that the situation was far more dire than he'd been willing to admit. Our debts were outrageous, and if we could not perform, Mr. Dubois's debtors would surely see him imprisoned, where he would work until he could pay what he owed or he died. I couldn't imagine him surviving long in the lice-and-rat-infested conditions, and I knew he would do anything to avoid such a fate, including risking my life to save his own.

"I'm not certain I can escape the Inferno without grave injury, but Mr. Dubois is desperate and won't see reason."

While I spoke, Wilhelm continued to hold my hand, and I did not pull it away. I felt a tingle of fear and excitement in his touch, and I wasn't certain what it meant.

"You can't do this," he said. "Your life is worth at least as much as his. More, in my opinion."

"I don't see that I have any other choice."

"What if you die?"

"I owe Mr. Dubois my life," I said. "If he requires I give it, I can't refuse him."

Between breaths, Wilhelm vanished from his cage and appeared at my side. He was so close I didn't even need the light of my lantern to see the curves of his angelic face. "Alfie," he said. "Please."

"What would you have me do?" I asked. "You keep yourself locked in this cage and yet beg me not to save the only person in this life who has ever cared for me."

"Your master isn't the only person who cares for you."

Wilhelm's bold statement struck me dumb, and I could only stare at him as he took my injured hand again and pressed his lips to it.

"Wilhelm…"

"Ask me to leave with you," he said. "Ask me and I will go."

"But Mr. Dubois," I said. "If I leave him now it will surely ruin him."

"Ask me, Alfie."

"I owe Mr. Dubois everything."

Wilhelm leaned forward, closing the scant distance between us, and kissed me. He pressed his lips to my lips and eased me gently back, the weight of his body against mine too powerful to resist. I lost track of time in Wilhelm's embrace. In his kiss and the feel of his hands on my skin. We shed our worries as easily as we shed our clothing, and everything was forgotten until we lay together on the cellar floor, our bodies slick with sweat, the afterglow of what we'd done still surrounding us.

And it was in that moment that I understood what it meant to be loved. Not simply appreciated and cared for as Mr. Dubois had done my entire life, but to be truly and perfectly loved.

"Ask me," Wilhelm said in the darkness.

I wanted to. I wanted to ask Wilhelm to run away with me where no one would find us. I wanted to see the world with him, to stand in the sun with him and explore what lay inside every shadow. But that would mean abandoning the man who'd raised me out of my wretched life and leaving him at the mercy of his creditors.

"I can't."

Mr. Dubois peered from behind the curtain into the audience. He'd been more excitable than usual in anticipation of the unveiling of the Inferno.

"The theater is full for the first time in weeks!" he said, giddy with glee.

"I'm not certain I can do this," I said. Mr. Dubois believed we'd perfected the Inferno—I was to wear gloves to protect my hands, my suit would be soaked with water to keep from catching fire, and we'd even worked out the timing so that the flames extinguished within a second of my being dropped into the box—but I was still afraid.

My escape depended upon my ability to unlock and escape the false backside of the airless, smoke-filled box. I'd successfully performed the trick eight times in ten, but if I couldn't escape and forced the Mystic Mycroft to release me in front of an audience—or worse, if I suffocated before escaping—I might sentence us both to death. In the flames and smoke, I might suffocate quickly, but my master would suffer long before his inevitable end. Maybe if I hadn't met Wilhelm, I might have been more willing to risk my life, but now I had something to lose and all I could think about was holding on to the thing I'd found.

Mr. Dubois gripped my shoulders and stared into my eyes with a frightening intensity. "You *must* do this, Alfred."

"But, sir—"

He cuffed me across my cheek, sending me sprawling to the ground. He stood over me, a fierce, towering giant. "You were nothing but a worthless wretch before me," he said. "And if you refuse to perform, then you may return to the streets from which I dragged you."

His words stung more than his fist. "I could die, sir."

"Then you shall die and consider yourself lucky to have lived at all." Without another word, he stormed off, leaving me alone.

I hung hoisted by the ropes bound about my wrists over the raging inferno inside the box. The flames licked the inside and the heat radiated up and out, causing sweat to soak my suit and drip into my eyes as the Mystic Mycroft strutted about the stage. I scarcely heard his carefully prepared speech, as I was too preoccupied with my own potential demise.

I hadn't seen Wilhelm since we'd lain together in the cellar but, other than the Inferno, I'd thought of nothing else. All I had to do was close my eyes and I could feel his hands caressing my chest and his lips brushing my ear. Neither of us had family to return to, but in Wilhelm I saw the possibility of more than the life I'd been leading. Of a future spent with someone who viewed me as a person rather than property to be discarded when it had outlived its usefulness. I vowed, if I survived the night's performance, to go to Wilhelm and tell him the truth—that my heart beat for him alone.

"And now," said Mr. Dubois, "prepare to witness…*the Inferno*!"

The hoist released its hold and I plummeted into the box. The lid slammed shut over my head, snuffing out the flames. The heat was unbearable and the smoke burned my eyes. In my chest, my heart became a cornered beast, terrified and erratic. My lungs shriveled as the if the air and moisture had been drawn from them. All our careful preparation fled my mind, and I began to panic. I became disoriented in the thick clouds of smoke and sucked in a breath that contained no air, only death. I slipped the ropes easily, even in my confused state, and felt around the box for the back, but couldn't find it.

I grew light-headed and faint. My movements sluggish. As if cursed with a premonition, I felt with certainty that I was not going to escape the box. This was where I was going to die.

My last memory of my mother flashed through my mind. She lay dying in the single room we'd called home. The vomiting and diarrhea had ceased but she refused all water and food, and was so weak she could barely move. I was barely five but I'd remained by her side for days, ignoring my own hunger. She loved me, she'd said before she'd taken her final breath, and that was the last time I'd believed anyone could truly care for me. It was the last time I'd believed myself truly worthy of care. Until Wilhelm.

And I was going to die without him knowing I felt the same for him.

The growing shouts from the audience as they realized something was wrong were distant in my ears as my consciousness began to flee. I imagined Mr. Dubois struggling to decide whether to free me and risk his career and life or wait until the last possible moment to see if I could escape. My life meant nothing to him if it did not serve his purpose.

As I closed my eyes, believing it to be for the last time, I felt a familiar tug in the center of my chest and then the chill of air. Real air. I involuntarily breathed, filling my lungs with life as the audience cheered and applauded.

"The Inferno!" shouted the Mystic Mycroft beside me.

The audience roared their approval, believing I had escaped on my own, though I knew I had not. My eyes watered, and I blinked to see clearly, searching the back of the auditorium until I found the face I sought. Wilhelm, in the suit he wore for the Butterfly, stood near the back. When I caught his eye, he bowed his head slightly before he vanished.

I ran from the stage—the Mystic Mycroft was too busy drinking in the adoration of his audience to notice—and fled out the back exit into the street. I made my way to the theater where the Virtuoso was, even then, performing, and sneaked inside. No one stopped me as I made my way to the stage and down the stairs that led under it. I waited in the dark while above the Virtuoso danced madly and chanted gibberish, the audience enthralled.

And then Wilhelm appeared. Not in a cloud of smoke or a flash of light, but in the moment where the heart skips a beat. Not there and then there.

He exhaled, his eyes closed, and I watched him smile and gracefully bow as the audience applauded and cheered, even though he couldn't see them nor they him. Wilhelm was the one who truly deserved their love and adoration, though they were, and would remain, ignorant of that fact.

When he opened his eyes and saw me, his smile faded and he said, "Alfie, you shouldn't be here."

I stepped forward, determined, and said, "I'm asking, Wilhelm. I'm asking now."

"It's too late," he said.

"You saved me. I would have died, but you saved me."

Wilhelm's lips parted in a smile, and I might have tried to memorize it, but I planned to never live a day without seeing them again.

"And I would save you every night if necessary."

"But it's not," I said. "It won't be. I'm leaving. We're leaving together."

"I'm cursed," Wilhelm said.

"Then we'll be cursed together."

Wilhelm's hands trembled. "I'll only bring you misery."

"I'll take a lifetime of misery with you over a day of love from Mr. Dubois."

"Without their greatest acts, both our masters will be ruined."

"Then let's ruin them," I said. "Will you come with me, Wilhelm? I'm asking."

Wilhelm crossed the space between us and kissed me. He kissed me as easily as breathing. I wrapped my arms around his waist and we vanished, leaving only his chains behind.

★ ★ ★ ★ ★

HEALING ROSA

BY
TEHLOR KAY MEJIA

Luna County, New Mexico, 1933

Rosa was a summer girl, and I was a winter girl, but that fall we made magic.

It was the year we put my abuela's whisper of a body into the ground. The year my mama told me to take her candles and feathers, her bound herbs and bones, and bury them at the edge of our land.

I'd been a child the first time I watched my grandmother heal, and the memory came back so clearly as I gathered her things. The boy on the floor of her room, candles burning all around him. The room itself, hot even through the glass of the window where my forehead was pressed. Her voice, low as she chanted into smoke sometimes too thick to see through.

Mostly the unbearable brightness inside, as I stood alone in the dark.

But into that brightness, something dark had been born. A shape, rising up from the boy's chest as he thrashed and sweated beneath Abuela's hands. It had chilled me to my bones just to look at it, the fear that had been haunting his bones made suddenly visible under her curandera's eye.

She'd shouted, at the end, just once, and preoccupied by the darkness I hadn't been prepared for the shock. I didn't step away in time. She chased the dark shape out the window with her herb broom wrapped in string, and for a half second it brushed against my cheek.

Abuela's face was pale when she saw me, mouth hanging open like I'd been marked.

I was sick for a week afterward. I woke up sweating from dreams that weren't mine. I couldn't eat, could barely force down sips of milk steeped with herbs.

"It'll pass," my abuela had said. "She needs quiet, and rest. Her spirit needs to find its way back home."

And it had. One night I drank a mug of hot water with a cinnamon stick and slept without dreaming. Then came the broth, and the tortillas still warm from the stove, and one day when my abuela cracked the egg into her tall glass she closed her eyes and smiled.

"You're strong," she'd said, and for the first time in my life, I felt it.

But now, in her empty room with nothing but sticks and stones to remind me of all she'd taught me, I felt anything but strong. "Mama, let me keep them," I begged, wrapping my grandmother's things in a large embroidered handkerchief. "What if you get sick? Or papa? What if..."

"No," my mother interrupted, her voice sharp as the knife she used to take the heads off chickens in the yard. "Whatever she was mixed up in, it's done. She's your father's mother and I won't disrespect her memory, but it goes. Tonight. We don't need any mal de ojo on this house, and you'll be a teacher, m'ija, not some kind of witch." She crossed herself, and went back to stirring the big pot on the stove.

Barefoot, twin braids flying behind me, I headed for the property line just as she'd asked. It never occurred to her that

I would disobey the rest. But it was the end of my sixteenth summer, my abuela was gone and I needed whatever magic she'd left behind.

When I reached the edge of our land, the line I'd been warned never to cross again, I could smell Rosa like it was last fall all over again. Rosemary like the green needles we'd used as perfume. Dry earth. Marigolds. The smell of the sun on her skin before she got sick. The smell that clung to my hair when we'd let our heads touch too long in the grass.

Rosa had been my neighbor since her father carried her over the border in his arms, a child that deserved better than perpetual war. But she was more than a neighbor.

More than even a friend.

She was with me when I cleared the shallow-rooted grass from the cracked ground, with me when I salted the earth so it would remain bare as a tabletop. I set the candles out one by one, wicks pointed skyward, and I whispered her name into the wind until the tears came. For my abuela, who was gone, and my mother who was scared, and Rosa, Rosa, Rosa, whose papa would never let her come.

When the storm of my grief had passed, I closed my eyes. I felt Abuela's papery hands on mine, heard the brush fire of her whisper as it stirred the air to combustion. It was her arranging the bones to ground me, the stones to focus me, the herbs to calm me, but when I struck a match in the still air my eyes were open, and I was alone.

"Rosa," I whispered, and the wick caught in answer. "Rosa, Rosa, Rosa."

My mama watched me with patient eyes that first week, looking for the dirt of Abuela's grave in the new lines around my eyes. I wasn't sleeping enough, she said, and made me hot water with a cinnamon stick.

I didn't tell her it wasn't the same, but maybe she could tell. She didn't make it again.

Every day when I left for the property line, I held my breath for the no I was sure would come. But every day she said: "Don't get too much sun."

And that was that.

I lit the tiny pink candles on the third day. Pink like the hearts Rosa had drawn with cactus flowers on the flat of my stomach. I burned rosemary until the oily smoke made my eyes water and sting. I sang songs to the cracks in the ground, and once I thought I felt my abuela's hands in my hair, but Rosa didn't come.

That night, as I scuffed my bare feet in the dust on my way home, I thought if she didn't come soon I'd brave her daddy's liquor breath and easy swinging fists. I thought I'd march right up to that door and tell him it was time he let me help her.

But even the thought of him kept me up all night. His bloodshot eyes when he told me never to come back. When he told me my abuela, with her beautiful curandera's magic, was nothing more than a bruja. An evil woman who would cloud the eyes of God as he looked for Rosa's suffering soul.

My abuela said the war had turned him, that there was a darkness nesting at the ends of his nerves, making him fearful and sharp edged and angry. She could help him, but only if he wanted to heal. Until then it was best to stay clear of him.

So I obeyed. I stayed clear. I sat at the edge of that property line day after day and called to Rosa in every language I knew.

It was the sixth day when a breeze kicked up. I was lying flat on my back, toes teasing the line. The red dust beneath me gave my dress clues about the woman growing inside it. The first stars had just been born in the sky, and it was like my abuela had written Rosa's name in their unearthly sparkle. It was finally time.

On my feet, my heart got so warm and so full that it spilled out of my eyes and I blinked hard until I could see her, black against the blue, coming closer.

"Rosa," I whispered, and then I was running.

Her body was too thin in my arms and her laugh was a mariposa's wing beat, but she was here and alive and I felt so fiercely in that moment that I was meant to belong to her.

"I dreamed of you," she said.

"It wasn't a dream."

I didn't kiss her then, not on those papery lips that were strangers to me. If I kissed her I'd be admitting I might never see her whole again, and I wouldn't. I couldn't. So I squeezed her hands like they were healthy, and her cheeks went pink and her eyes were the same and the candles around us danced to our heartbeats and I thought: *Forever, forever, forever.*

"Papa will be back soon," she said. "He won't like this, but… I *saw* you, and you were bright as the moon, and I couldn't stay away."

I buried my face in her hair, and for a while all we did was breathe.

"Rosa," I said when the silence broke. "My abuela is gone."

"I know." There were tears in her eyes. "He says that's why I'm getting sicker. He says she's haunting us."

Her eyes were wide and calm, her lashes long. Her mouth was turned up at one corner, lifting her cheek into a half smile that said, "What can you do?"

But I wouldn't do nothing. Not this time.

"I need you to tell me what's wrong," I said in a rush. "Everything."

The thick wings of her eyebrows disappeared into her flyaway hair. We had always pretended the sickness wasn't real when we were together. Like if we didn't mention it we could make it disappear. But Rosa had carried a darkness with her since she was a child. Since her father had taken her hand and together they'd run from the war. It had only grown as she did, that darkness, building a wall between her soul and its home until her body started to give up in pieces.

A susto, my abuela had called it in a whisper, and the memory of fear's creases beside her eyes haunted me still.

We had been kidding ourselves, to think our silence would make it all disappear. The only thing that had disappeared was Rosa.

"Please," I said again. "Tell me."

"We don't have to," she said, a hand against my cheek. "We don't have to talk about it. Not when we have so little time..."

"Rosa," I said, needing her to understand. "My abuela isn't haunting you. But I think...she can help me make you better."

Now her chin was trembling, and instead of the hope I needed to see in her eyes, her head was slowly shaking. "We've tried everything," she said, the edges of her words too careful. "My papa says there's nothing left to do. That if God wants me to live He'll take the ghost away, that He has a plan and we can't interfere..."

"Your papa's scared," I said, pleading. "He doesn't understand, but I do. Let me try."

"I can't..." She was backing away. She was backing away and I was frozen. I thought getting her across the line would be the hardest part, but how could I have forgotten?

She'd never been able to disobey him.

Not then, when it meant keeping me.

Not even now, when it meant saving herself.

"Rosa, please." I hated the smallness of my voice. My abuela would have been able to make her understand. "Don't walk away again."

The pink candles at my feet went out.

"I'm sorry," she said. "I wanted to see you. I needed to. But I can't... He'll never understand."

"What does it matter if he understands? You'll be alive! We'll be together!"

"I'm all he has," she said, and her tone told me her decision had been made.

"So you'll die? You'll die so he doesn't have to face his own prejudice?"

Her eyes filled with tears, and I hated myself for them. "He's my father. I'm sorry." She turned away. She ran. She didn't look back.

Summer seeped out of the sky, leaked into fall's still-dry ground. The cold brought no relief to the thirsty earth, or to the people walking on it.

I'd always been a winter girl, at home in the cool nights, the comfort of warm tortillas on chilly fingers, the sharp brightness of the constellations. But there was no joy in it this year, not for me. I sat at my window for long hours, watching the sky change, watching the dark come earlier. I didn't go back to the property line. There was nothing to find.

When I slept, I dreamed of Rosa, of cold spirits sucking the last of the warmth from her body. Each time she died I tried to run to her, to save her, the knowledge of how I'd do it on fire in my heaving chest. But the harder I ran the farther away she grew, and eventually I'd wake up sweating, like I'd really run miles across the desert.

Sometimes, when I woke, I'd go to the room that was still my abuela's and curl up on the floor. My tears salted her floorboards those nights, and if I turned my head just right in the days that followed, I could see the places where they paled the wood. It made me feel so close to her, and so terribly far away.

"You look sick," my mama said over the bean pot.

It had been weeks, I thought. But they could have been days, or years.

"You need rest, warm weather. Your grandmother's spirit is haunting you."

"Spring will come," I said, but my fingers felt cold.

"Winter will come first. I'm sending you to live with Tío José until you're feeling like yourself again."

Where I'd been empty, I turned to stone. "You aren't sending me anywhere."

The lines of her face went hard and flat. There was no understanding, no pity. If it had been a normal fall, I would have accepted defeat—but there would be no surrender here today. I was alive, and Rosa was dying. If I left now, her last breath would be drawn in a place I *used* to live. When she died, she'd be a girl I used to know.

The thought was unbearable. If I couldn't help her, I deserved to feel it when she went.

I stared at my mother with the eyes of a girl who had loved and lost. Eyes that had once belonged to a child, but had seen too much sadness. In the steam rising from that pot something changed between us, and she shrugged her shoulders.

"Suit yourself. But no more moping. You'll do your chores. You'll pull your weight."

Instead of answering, I went back to my window. Night fell first over Rosa's house; was it some kind of sign? I would have taken on her father, but if she didn't want to heal there was nothing I could do. My abuela had made sure I understood that the moment she sensed the healing spirit in me.

I'd kissed Rosa in every season, mapped every mountain beneath her skin. She'd made no secret of her love for me. Her father had turned a blind eye in those golden days, muttering about girls and friendship and how the world was changing before turning his boots toward the woodpile.

But now, when all I wanted was to save her, he was determined to keep us apart.

I wondered if he would know, when she died, that his stubborn grip on the past had taken her from both of us.

When lightning struck, I was elbow deep in chicken feathers out back. Pulling my weight. Staying close. One moment it was just the dull ache of the inevitable, as it had been for weeks. The next I was on the ground, panting for breath, choking on summer dust and marigolds.

There was a weight on my chest, so heavy I couldn't get up.

There were feathers in my hair.

A bucket of blood had spilled; it was seeping into the dirt.

In their enclosure, the chickens were restless.

Those were my last thoughts before the sky closed up and I drifted into darkness.

When I woke up, my abuela was leaning over my bed, silhouetted in the light from the gray sky beyond the window. I reached for her, but when I blinked again she had my mama's no-nonsense face.

My heart fell, and she saw it, and for a moment I was sorry.

"You're going to Tío José's," she said. And this time I knew: even my most grown-up sadness wasn't going to change her mind.

I wanted to hate her, to scream, to beg. But the marigold scent was gone, and my chest still ached and at that moment I wanted nothing more than to be the girl who used to live here. A girl who barely remembered Rosa going or already gone.

"Okay," I said.

"He'll come for you tomorrow. Your papa walked to the telephone to let him know."

I nodded. My head was heavy. My heart was nowhere to

be found. "Would you make me some hot water with a cinnamon stick?" I asked, and when she smiled, I smiled.

"Of course, m'ija," she said. She laid her hand briefly on my forehead, sniffing before disappearing into the hallway.

I reclined back into my pillow, closed my eyes and with everything I was, I tried to wish Rosa well, in life or in death. To forgive her father, even though it was his fault. Even though it was all his fault.

The world disappeared; the empty place throbbed. There was so much cold in the world. Maybe at Tío José's, in a country that knew me, though I had never known it, I would get to be warm again.

But first, I had to let Rosa go, and my dreams seemed to know it. As I slept I lost her in a million ways, and it hurt and hurt and hurt.

When I woke, the dark air was thick with cinnamon, and my mother was screaming.

I put my feet on the floor, expecting to feel dizzy, but everything was still and clear, and I walked to the door like someone was leading me there.

Metal and smoke and booze filled the room, and I knew him before I saw him. Rosa's father.

"Tell me where she is," he growled, advancing as my mama hit him again and again with the house shoe from her own foot.

"Get out of my house!" she screamed. "I won't let you hurt her!"

But he didn't want to hurt me. I could see grief beading up on him like the sheen of whiskey sweat. In the air between us, his heart was breaking, and it was more powerful than his hate.

"It's all right, Mama," I said, and for once she didn't argue. Maybe she could feel it, too.

The walls whispered, *Be still*, as he approached. Closer.

Closer. Until I could see every vein in his bloodshot eyes. Until I could see his heart beating.

Wait. Be still.

"She's dying." His voice was gravel on glass. "She's… I'm losing her."

Wait.

"She says you can help. Says your…grandmother…showed you how."

Just a little longer.

He sighed, realizing I wasn't going to give him an easy out. I could almost hear the clock ticking in his chest, shaking his skull until his teeth ground together. "Save my little girl," he said around a lifetime of fear. "Please."

My heart was a cage that had been unlocked, and a thousand hopeful birds took flight.

"Thank you," I said. And then I ran.

There was no time to go back for the bones and pink candles or the stones I hadn't buried, but with Abuela whispering in the wind I grabbed handfuls of sage, rosemary, desert willow and lavender. My heartbeat urged me on. My memories told me my intentions mattered more than my tools, and Rosa was alive. Alive and waiting for me.

Her house rose like its own sun on the horizon as I drew closer, the burn in my legs nothing to the desperation in every step. The texture of the walls, the rounded edges—so familiar, so bright with the joy of her being.

"Rosa!" I cried, banging through the door like I'd never been banned. "Rosa! I'm here!"

Her whisper was too quiet to be heard, but I felt it. I would have followed it anywhere.

"You brought flowers," she whispered through parched lips that cracked when she smiled. "For me?"

The skin stretched tight across her cheeks; her eyes were

swollen and red. The hair I'd once delighted in braiding with tiny bright flowers lay limp and lifeless against her pillow.

"I love you," I said, crossing the room to lay the herbs across her chest.

She closed her eyes and breathed in the scent of the desert. "I love you, too."

The words were a string from her heart to mine, and in its pull I could read what would come. When I touched her forehead with mine, when I pressed my lips to hers, it wasn't because I couldn't be sure. It was because I could.

"Tell me," I said. "Tell me what hurts."

She closed her eyes tight. "I can't," she said. "You know I can't. You're here, querida, and it's enough. Just say goodbye."

"Nobody's saying goodbye," said a gruff voice from behind me.

"Papa!" Her eyes were wide and fearful. "It's not what you think! She only..."

"Rosa," he said, his eyes clear for once and focused on her wasted face. "Tell her."

She closed her eyes, and something like peace touched their corners. "Thank you," she said, and I could feel the tears in his throat that kept him from answering. But he wasn't the one that needed healing today.

I turned back to Rosa, placing my hands on her chest, just above the place I'd always wanted to. Inside her was a darkness so thick it made my pulse pound, and it was swirling around her heart.

Her eyes were closed, and I could feel her gathering strength. The darkness hissed and spit at the light, and I let her be for the moment. We needed all the fight we could muster.

My mama came in with candles, lit them and bound the herbs I'd gathered into a broom with bright red string from an apron pocket.

"You came?" I asked.

"She would be proud of you" was her only answer. She placed the broom in my hands before taking Rosa's father's arm and leaving us alone.

"Rosa," I said, and she opened her eyes. "It's time."

She nodded, and despite the weakness of her body there was determination there.

"It started with the dreams…" she began, and I followed her inside her darkness. "I'm small, hanging over my papa's shoulder. He's running and it's hurting me, and there are gunshots and screaming and everything smells like smoke." So this was it, the war my mama had never let me hear a word of. The war that had brought Rosa and her papa desperate to our door all those years ago.

"I'm screaming, too," she said, her voice far away, fleeing a war that had stolen her family and her home half a lifetime ago. "He tells me to be quiet. The noises are too loud. The smoke is too thick. I can't breathe." She choked then, and I held her steady by her frail shoulders until the coughing subsided. The candles flickered, burning low as the darkness began to stir in the air between us.

A quiet voice in my heart told me to stay still, to let the thread unfurl, and for a moment I smelled my abuela's rose water cologne.

"I'm crying for my mama," said Rosa, sightless eyes still lost in the past. "The noise took her. The smoke. And my papa says she's coming but his eyes are too sad…" Her own eyes were sparkling with tears unshed, and her hand found mine between us, the bony fingers applying the slightest pressure. "There's blood. Blood on his jacket. Blood on my bare feet."

She was breathing too fast, starting to sob, choking like the stuffy air in her room was on fire. The candle burned brighter, and I closed my eyes into the feeling around me, trying to smell the smoke of her fear, trying to breathe it all in and hold it.

"I know she died," she whispered, a break in the tears. "I know there was a war, and we ran, and he saved us. I've never told anyone about the dreams." She took a deep breath. "Not even Papa. What right do I have? When they all died, and I got to live? But when I wake up my heart is pounding, and I feel so weak. Food tastes like dust. My head spins." She closed her eyes against the spinning, and for a moment I felt it, too. Like we were one heart living in two bodies.

"Keep going," I said, and lit incense from her bedside table that made her cough till her cheeks were pink.

"At first it only happened when I woke up," she said when she could speak again. "But now it never stops. I smell the war, the metal and the gunpowder and the burning. I see the blood everywhere, and I miss my mama, and my papa hates me for having her face and..." She was reaching the limits of what she could stand. I could feel the darkness taking shape as her words and the herbs and the candles drew it from her chest. "He saved me, but I'm dying anyway. I'm dying and I'm so sorry..."

She was sobbing in earnest, big racking sobs. The darkness ran from her in rivulets and I swept the incense over her body like I'd seen my abuela do a hundred times. Her fear was sucking at us, both of us, but I wouldn't stop. Not until she was free.

Pray, said the roses and the walls, and Rosa must have heard them, too, because she closed her eyes again, moving her lips now, beseeching. I fanned her with incense and swept her body with the broom. My heart wanted nothing but to beg for her life, and I let it, opening wide, letting all the light inside me loose as an offering to whoever would listen.

Please. Please. Please.

In that dark, smoky womb we joined our wills and waited. Until sweat poured from our skin. Until a second was an hour and a minute was a year. Until I thought my legs would have no choice but to give way.

And then—were my eyes open or closed?—the darkness that had puddled on the floor rose up, a feathery creature indistinct in the haze. When I looked into its cold, punishing eye, I wanted to run. Everything inside me quaked and shook and all the joy healing my Rosa had brought threatened to go out like a candle in the wind.

My own fear swelled in my belly, answering the call, and it was all a horrible mistake. Me, coming here. Me, believing I could heal her darkness when I couldn't even face my own.

But out of nowhere came the smell of cinnamon, the memory of my abuela's strong hand in mine as I battled to get free all those years ago. I could do this. I had done this. And she was here, in the haze. I didn't have to see her to know.

"It's time to go," I croaked, and it laughed a sinister laugh for my ears alone.

"It's time to GO!" I shouted, and it quivered in the air.

With the herb broom I beat the shadow toward the window, shouting wordless banishments, and Rosa was shouting, too. The door opened with a bang, and my mama ran to the window, throwing it open into the night.

"Be gone!" bellowed Rosa's grief-soaked father.

With a last sweep of the broom that I was sure would take my arms with it, I felt the last wing beat of the dark feathers leave the room.

My mother slammed the window shut.

All was quiet.

The flame of each candle grew to twice its size until the room was bathed in golden light. On shaking, unsure legs I crossed to Rosa's bedside.

"Are you okay?" I asked, all the hope in the world at the back of my throat.

"See for yourself," she said, and guided my hands to her chest, closer than ever to the place they'd always wanted to be.

I closed my eyes, and plain as a picture, saw my abuela smiling.

See for yourself.

In the tangle of veins and pulse and heartbeat, I looked for the darkness. But where it had been, there was nothing but light.

It's springtime now, and the cactus flowers are in full bloom. Rosa's cheeks bloom, too, as she traces one along the planes of my stomach, painting hearts until I giggle and pull her down beside me.

The days are getting longer, the darkness on its heels for another season.

In the setting sun, I kiss her, and she tastes like marigolds.

★★★★★

ABOUT THE AUTHORS

Dahlia Adler (she/her) is an associate editor of mathematics by day, a blogger for the B&N Teen Blog by night and a writer of kissing books at every spare moment in between. She's the author of *Behind the Scenes*, *Under the Lights*, *Just Visiting* and the Radleigh University series, and a contributor to the historical young adult anthology *The Radical Element*. She's also the founder of LGBTQ Reads, a resource dedicated to promoting LGBTQIAP literature for all ages. She and her overstuffed bookshelves live in New York City.

Sara Farizan (she/her) is the daughter of Iranian immigrants and grew up feeling different in her private high school, not only because of her ethnicity but also because of liking girls romantically, her lack of excitement in science and math, and her love of writing plays and short stories. So she came out of the closet in college, realized math and science weren't so bad (but not for her), and decided she wanted to be a writer. She is an MFA graduate of Lesley University and holds a BA in film and media studies from American University. Sara has been a Hollywood intern, a waitress, a comic book/record store employee, an art magazine blogger, a marketing temp, and an after-school teacher, but above all else she has always been a writer. Her first novel, *If You Could Be Mine*, was the 2014 Lambda Literary Award winner for youth fiction, and both the Debut Fiction and LGBT Fiction Triangle Award winner. Her second novel, *Tell Me Again How a Crush Should Feel*, was named one of the 2015 Capitol Choices: Noteworthy Books for Children, and was a finalist for Young Adult Fiction in the 2015 Indies Choice Book Awards.

Tessa Gratton (she/her) has wanted to be a paleontologist or a wizard since she was seven. After traveling the world with her military family, she acquired a BA (and the important parts of an MA) in gender studies, then settled down in Kansas to tell stories about monsters, magic and kissing. She's the author of The Blood Journals series and the Gods of New Asgard series, coauthor of YA writing guides *The Curiosities* and *The Anatomy of Curiosity*, as well as dozens of short stories available in anthologies and on merryfates.com. Her current projects include *Tremontaine* at Serial Box Publishing, her adult fantasy debut, *The Queens of Innis Lear*, from Tor, and YA fantasy *Slaughter Moon* from McElderry, both available in 2018. Visit her at tessagratton.com.

Shaun David Hutchinson (he/him) is the author of numerous books for young adults, including *The Five Stages of Andrew Brawley*, which won the Florida Book Awards Gold Medal in the Young Adult category and was named to the ALA's 2015 Rainbow Book List; the anthology *Violent Ends*, which received a starred review from *VOYA*; *We Are the Ants*, which received five starred reviews and was named a best book of

January 2016 by Amazon.com, Kobo.com, *Publishers Weekly*, and iBooks; and *At the Edge of the Universe*. He lives in South Florida with his adorably chubby dog, and enjoys *Doctor Who*, comic books and yelling at the TV. Visit him at shaundavid-hutchinson.com.

Kody Keplinger (she/her) is the *New York Times* bestselling author of several novels, including *The DUFF*, *Lying Out Loud* and *Run*. She is a writing teacher, a fashion and makeup lover, and a cofounder of disabilityinkidlit.com. She lives in NYC with her service dog and two black cats.

Mackenzi Lee (she/her) is a Boston bookseller with a BA in history and an MFA from Simmons College in writing for children and young adults. She is the author of the young adult historical fantasy novels *This Monstrous Thing*, which won the PEN New England Susan P. Bloom Children's Book Discovery Award, and *The Gentlemen's Guide to Vice and Virtue*. You can find her on Twitter, @themackenzilee, where she curates a weekly storytime about badass women from history you probably didn't know about but should. She loves Diet Coke, sweater weather and *Star Wars*. On a perfect day, she can be found enjoying all three.

Malinda Lo (she/her) is the author of several young adult novels, including most recently *A Line in the Dark*. Her novel *Ash*, a lesbian retelling of Cinderella, was a finalist for the William C. Morris YA Debut Award, the Andre Norton Award for YA Science Fiction and Fantasy, the Mythopoeic Fantasy Award, and was a *Kirkus* Best Book for Children and Teens. She has been a three-time finalist for the Lambda Literary Award. Malinda's nonfiction has been published by *The New York Times Book Review*, NPR, the *Huffington Post*, *The Toast*,

The Horn Book, and *AfterEllen*. She lives in Massachusetts with her partner and their dog. Her website is www.malindalo.com.

Nilah Magruder (she/her) is a writer and artist based in Los Angeles. From her beginnings in the woods of Maryland she developed an eternal love for three things: nature, books and animation. She is the author of *How to Find a Fox*, a picture book. Her young adult webcomic, *M.F.K.*, won the inaugural Dwayne McDuffie Award for Diversity in 2015 and was published in print by Insight Comics in fall 2017. She has also drawn for Disney and DreamWorks, and written for Marvel. When she is not drawing or writing, Nilah is reading fantasy novels, watching movies, roller-skating and fighting her cat for control of her desk chair.

Tehlor Kay Mejia (she/her) is a YA author and poet at home in the wild woods and alpine meadows of southern Oregon. When she's not writing, you can find her plucking at her guitar, stealing rosemary sprigs from overgrown gardens or trying to make the perfect vegan tamale. Her debut novel, *We Set the Dark on Fire*, is available from Katherine Tegan/ HarperCollins.

Anna-Marie McLemore (they/them) was born in the foothills of the San Gabriel mountains, raised in the same town as the world's largest wisteria vine, and taught by their family to hear la llorona in the Santa Ana winds. They are the author of *The Weight of Feathers*, a finalist for the 2016 William C. Morris Debut award, and 2017 Stonewall Honor Book *When the Moon Was Ours*, which was longlisted for the National Book Award in Young People's Literature. Their latest is *Dark and Deepest Red*.

Natalie C. Parker (she/her) is the author of Southern Gothic duology *Beware the Wild*, a 2014 Junior Library Guild Selection, and *Behold the Bones* (HarperTeen), as well as the editor of the forthcoming YA anthology *Three Sides of a Heart: Stories About Love Triangles* (HarperTeen). She is the founder of Madcap Retreats, an organization offering a yearly calendar of writing retreats and workshops to aspiring and established writers. In her not-so-spare time, she works at her local university coordinating programs on climate science and Indigenous communities. She holds a BA in English literature and an MA in women's studies. Though the roots of her family tree are buried deep in southern Mississippi, she lives on the Kansas prairie with her partner and requisite number of beasts.

Alex Sanchez (he/him) is the author of the Rainbow Boys trilogy of teen novels, along with *The God Box*, *Getting It*, *Boyfriends With Girlfriends* and the Lambda Award–winning middle-grade novel *So Hard to Say.* His novel *Bait* won the 2009 Florida Book Award Gold Medal for YA fiction. His works have been recognized as an American Library Association's Best Book for Young Adults, International Reading Association's Young Adults' Choice, New York Public Library Book for the Teen Age, and *The Bulletin of the Center for Children's Books* Blue Ribbon Winner, and have been multiple Lambda Award finalists. Alex received his master's degree in guidance and counseling from Old Dominion University and for many years worked as a youth and family counselor. Visit him online at alexsanchez.com.

Kate Scelsa (she/her) is a playwright and the author of *Fans of the Impossible Life* (HarperCollins/Balzer+Bray), a 2015 Indies Introduce Debut and Indie Next pick. Her new YA novel is forthcoming from Balzer+Bray. Since 2002 she has performed in New York and on tour around the world with experimental theater company Elevator Repair Service in their trilogy of works based on great American literature, including an eight-hour-long performance that uses the entire text of *The Great Gatsby*. Kate grew up in New Jersey and now lives in Brooklyn with her wife and two black cats. Find her at katescelsa.com

Born in a backwoods cabin to a pair of punk rockers, **Tess Sharpe** (she/her) grew up in rural Northern California. Following an internship with the Oregon Shakespeare Festival, she studied theater at SOU before abandoning the stage for the professional kitchen. Now a full-time author, she lives, writes—and still bakes—near the Oregon border. Her debut novel, *Far From You*, was one of *Kirkus Reviews*' Best Teen Books of 2014, the May 2014 pick for the *Guardian*'s Teen Book Club and a Carnegie Medal nominee.

Robin Talley (she/her) is the *New York Times* bestselling author of six novels for teen readers: *Our Own Private Universe*, *As I Descended*, *What We Left Behind*, *Lies We Tell Ourselves*, *Pulp* and *Music from Another World*, all of which focus on LGBTQ characters. Her first book, *Lies We Tell Ourselves*, was the winner of the inaugural Amnesty CILIP Honour and the Concorde Book Award. Her short stories have also appeared in the young adult anthologies *A Tyranny of Petticoats: 15 Stories of Belles, Bank Robbers and Other Badass Girls* and *Feral Youth*. Robin lives in Washington, DC, with her wife, their daughter and an antisocial cat. You can find her at robintalley.com.

Scott Tracey (he/him) aspired to be a writer from a young age. He is the author of the Witch Eyes and Moonset series. His debut novel, *Witch Eyes*, was named to the 2012 Popular

Paperbacks for Young Readers list in the forbidden-romance category, named a 2014 YALSA Popular Paperbacks list and, ranked among the top ten gay and lesbian Kindle books of 2011 at Amazon.com. He lives near Cleveland, Ohio.

Elliot Wake (he/him), formerly known as Leah Raeder, is a transgender author of four novels: *Unteachable*, *Black Iris*, *Cam Girl* and *Bad Boy*. His work has hit the *USA TODAY* bestseller list and earned starred reviews from *Publishers Weekly*, *Kirkus Reviews* and *Booklist*. Aside from reading his brains out, Elliot enjoys video games, weight lifting and perfecting his dapper style. He lives with his partner in Chicago.

Saundra Mitchell (she/they) is the author of *Shadowed Summer*, *The Vespertine*, *The Springsweet*, *The Elementals* and *Mistwalker*. As Alex Mallory, she wrote *Wild*, and as Jessa Holbrook, she wrote *While You're Away*. In non fiction, she's the author of the They Did What!? series for middle-grade readers. She also edits YA anthologies, including this volume, and her first collection, *Defy the Dark*.

Shadowed Summer was the 2010 winner of The Society of Midland Authors Book Award for Children's Fiction and a 2010 Edgar® Award Nominee. It was chosen as a Junior Library Guild selection and an ALAN Pick in 2009.

Her short story "Ready to Wear" was nominated for a 2007 Pushcart Prize after appearing in the *Vestal Review*, issue 27. Her short fiction and nonfiction has appeared in anthologies, including *A Tyranny of Petticoats*, *Foretold*, *Grim*, *Truth & Dare* and *Dear Bully*.

For twenty years, she was the head screenwriter and an executive producer with Dreaming Tree Films on their various teen filmmaking programs, including the largest teen filmmaking program in the United States, Fresh Films. They produced more than four hundred films from her screenplays, and she earned Academy Award eligibility ten times during her tenure.

Ms. Mitchell was interviewed by the *New York Times* and the BBC for her part in exposing the Kaycee Nicole hoax, and she's been tapped by morning radio shows all over the United States as a guest expert on urban legends and folklore.

In her free time, she enjoys fandom, studying history, papermaking, and spending time with her wife and her daughters. You can visit her online at www.saundramitchell.com.

Thank you for reading All Out!

Look for the companion collection

Out Now: Queer We Go Again!

featuring seventeen stories of today's queer teens
having adventures, falling in love and shaping the world around them,
by amazing queer YA authors.

Only from editor Saundra Mitchell and Inkyard Press!